Cages

Cages

A Novel

MICHELLE YOUNG

Rock Forest Publishing

Cover Design by Michelle Young
Cover Photograph © Pixabay.com
Author Photograph © Youngs Photography

ISBN-13: 978-1-7750983-5-5

Cages / Michelle Young. – 1st ed.

Rock Forest Publishing

ALSO BY MICHELLE YOUNG

Salt & Light
Without Fear
Your Move
There She Lies
The Sleep Clinic

For K.

"Birds born in a cage think flying is an illness."

– Alejandro Jodorowsky

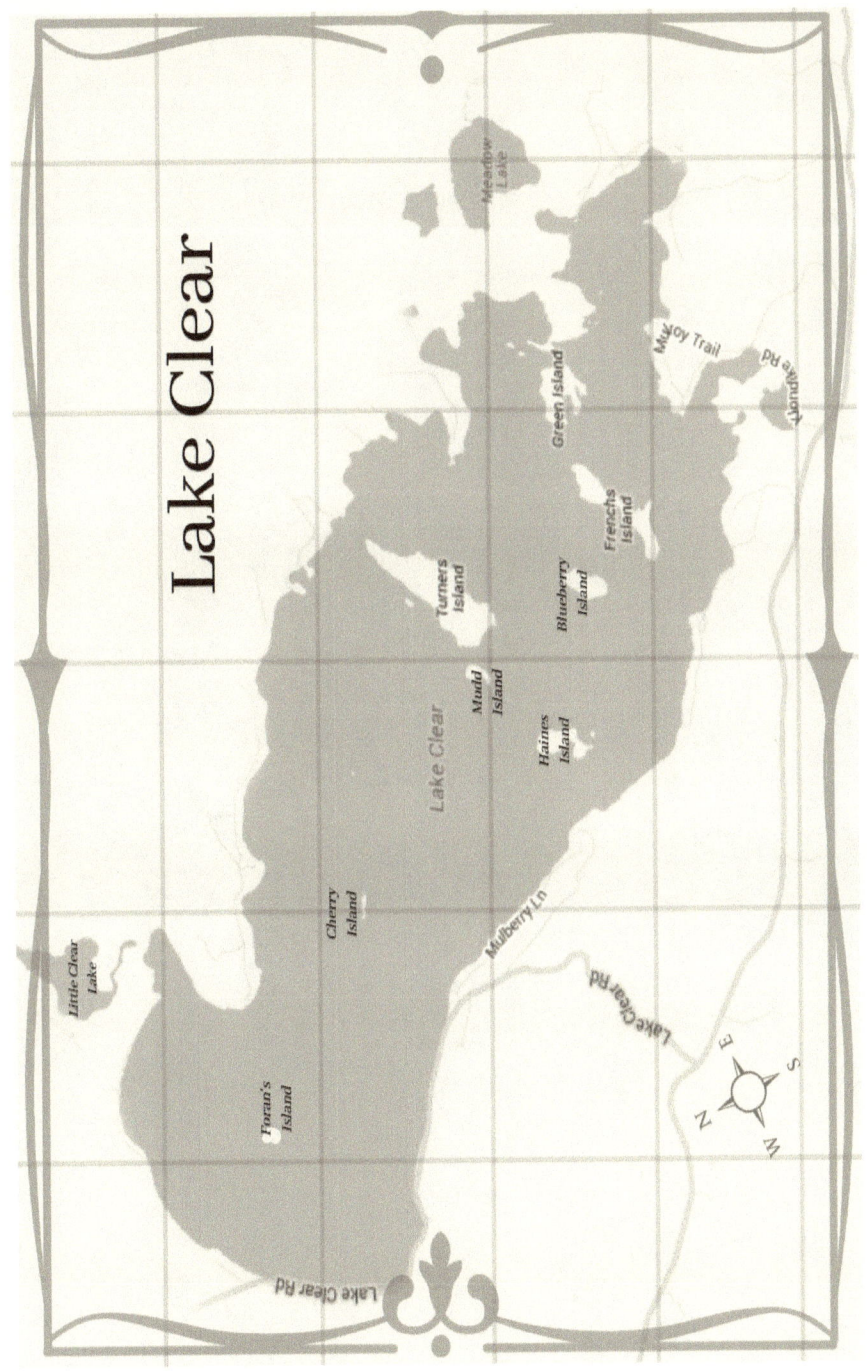

Lake Clear

Prologue

I'd never given much thought to the quality of my life, the regrets that would gut me, the memories that would haunt me in my last moments, or the way my body would physically feel when it neared the end. Not until now, that is.

They say drowning is one of the worst ways to go. It's quiet—soundless.

One moment I'm swimming above the water, splashing around, enjoying myself, cooling off on a hot summer's night. And the next, a wave covers my head, wrapping me like cling wrap, suffocating me, making me choke and cough, except there is no oxygen, only lake water.

It fills my lungs. I gasp, swallowing water by the mouthful, desperate for air. I never appreciated air as much as I do right at this moment. I'd give anything to reach the surface and take a deep breath of it, feel my lungs expand with it. But I'm a little too late.

I convulse and choke, gripping my throat and claw at it as though this helps anything. Delusional and deprived of air, I'm sinking. Can anyone see me? Does anyone know I'm dying?

Chapter 1
GEMMA

Cradling the phone between my shoulder and ear, I listen, distracted by the large and overflowing basket of dirty laundry balanced on my hip as I walk down the stairs to the main floor. One of the basket handles cracked years ago but I've yet to replace it. The hard plastic digs into my hand pinching my finger. I should stop and put the basket down—give my full attention to the caller. But I have too much to do. I can't stop.

"I'm sorry Gemma," he sighs heavily, bringing my attention back to the man on the phone. "You would have been a great addition to the team, but we've gone in a different direction."

My heart sinks. I hadn't wanted this particular job that badly, just a job. Still, the sting of rejection feels raw. I'd already started picturing what my days might look like with the new routine and how I might make some friends amongst my co-workers. In an instant, the wishful thinking is snatched away like evaporating smoke out of a kettle.

"Thank you for coming in and I hope you find something soon," he adds reassuringly and my cheeks heat up with embarrassment. Of course they'd chosen someone else. I shouldn't have gotten my hopes up in the first place.

I've barely managed to reply when I miss a step and abruptly slip down the flight of stairs.

My back collides with a step, sending my neck backwards, my head hitting another step higher as I tumble down the remainder of the staircase. With a heavy slap of flesh on the hard floor, I land on my stomach in the middle of scattered laundry. It's as though a volcano of fabric has erupted.

Panting and gasping for air. I can't breathe. Urgently, I attempt to move, but I can't. I begin to panic and my vision turns spotty. *Oh Christ, I can't move. Why can't I move? Did I break my neck?* I'm spiraling and quickly realize that I'm having a panic attack. As quickly as the thought occurs to me, a blast of sharp pain shoots through my body and the darkness overtakes.

I come to only minutes—or maybe it was hours—later. I have no real way of telling time at the moment. Based on the sun's rays still shining on the honey oak floors through the bay window, I don't think I've been out for very long. I hesitate, dreading finding out the result of my fall. Still, I force myself to move and feel a jolt of intense discomfort in my back and neck.

I wonder if I might have a concussion. I'd fallen down the stairs many times as a child but had almost always caught myself on a banister or reacted quickly enough to only slip down one step before righting myself again. This time, I hadn't been so lucky.

With a deep breath, I try to move different parts of my body. Thankfully, I'm able to wiggle my toes. Not paralyzed then. Well, that's a relief.

Gritting my teeth, I struggle to lift my body beneath me. Crouched on my floor, I swear off fuzzy socks forever as tears fall down my face. How many times had Niall warned me about wearing those damn socks? He's always said I'd break my neck wearing those damned things down the stairs one day. I shudder. He hadn't been wrong.

The only reason I wear socks in June is because Niall insists on cranking up the air conditioning to a near-arctic freezing temperature. He's always complaining about being too hot to sleep properly at night. But then he's gone to work all day, leaving me to freeze half to death, forcing me to wear fuzzy socks, sweats, and warm sweaters all summer. I should feel resentful, but deep down, I know he's not doing it on purpose. He works so hard for us, and so do I, but it's different.

Being a stay-at-home mom while the girls were younger made sense and saved us a bunch of money in daycare fees. Plus, I'd loved watching them grow up; being present for all their major milestones, teaching them their ABC's, and how to ride a bike. But now with Amber being sixteen and Beatrice turning thirteen next month, I'm left in an empty house all day pondering the meaning of life and my place in it.

Sure, there are still a lot of things I can do even now that my children are grown. I've gotten quite good at using up the day, making myself useful by keeping our lives organized, the lunches packed, the laundry folded, and the house clean. But it's not enough. I'm ready for something else. Even so, maybe my timing is off. Based on the phone call I just received, maybe the world isn't ready to hire a woman in her forties who hasn't worked outside of the home in almost two decades.

Sighing, feeling the weight of the world on my shoulders, the deception of unmet expectations adds to the realization that this might be all there is for me. I attempt to move my body weight around and mentally check for broken bones. A stab of pain radiates through my back. My breathing is ragged but the air is starting to come in finally. My wrists hurt from holding myself up. Someone walking by might simply think I'm in the middle of my morning yoga practice, perfecting cat pose. My back is sore. I reach out to touch a painful bump, certain that a bruise is already forming. The throbbing pain of an impending headache announces its presence at the back of my head where the stairs so abruptly greeted it earlier.

My gaze lingers on a neglected English ivy plant in the entrance. Its once rich green leaves are sparse, leaving mostly dry-looking, brown ones. I imagine the crunch they'd make if I reached over and plucked each leaf, one by one until its vines are completely bare. What a terrible spot for a plant to live, so far from the window and completely out of sight. No wonder it's dead. It didn't stand a chance. I'll have to take better care of the next one.

As I glance around at the mess of laundry I'll need to pick up, I'm thankful for the small mercy that it wasn't clean laundry I'd just spent an hour folding but rather the girls' dirty clothes that are going straight into the washing machine. Lifting my hand slightly off the floor, I notice a smear of dark blood on my palm. Confused for a moment, I frantically scan the floor and find a matching mark underneath me. Rubbing my index finger under my nose, it comes back clean, with only grey residue from watered-down make-up. Wiping against my lip, my finger comes away with bright red blood.

I've bitten my lip, then. Hard apparently. Running my tongue over my bottom lip, I flinch at the sting of the open wound. My lip is most definitely split and swollen. I might even need stitches. *Oh God, what if I hit my head so hard that I'm bleeding internally? I should have been paying closer attention to what I was doing. I should have been holding the banister.* I can feel the panic rising but quickly stop myself. I always do this—assume the worst. My mind automatically goes there, I can't help it.

I wasn't always like this.

When Niall and I met, I'd been a wild thing, up for anything. The adventurous, daring type of girl. I was the one encouraging *him* to try new things, pushing the boundaries, making my parents' hairs turn grey prematurely. But motherhood has changed me, altered my sense of safety. Now, I'm afraid of everything and anything. It's my life's mission to keep everyone alive and safe. With so much responsibility on my shoulders, it's practically impossible to let loose or even catch a glimmer of the woman I once was.

Motherhood hasn't always been easy. My eldest, Amber, seems to have adopted many of the same daring and dangerous traits I'd once had. She was constantly putting herself in harm's way with no regard to her own safety. She was exhausting to parent. Yet, I've always admired her carefree way of living. Amber seemed to crave experiences, never fearing the consequences.

She is my wild child, my spirited girl. My first child, the one who made me a mother.

She's the one who enlightened me as to what it truly means to be a parent, the one who pushes me to the edges of my mental health, forces me to reevaluate the deepest, darkest parts of myself as she watches on, observing my every move, copying my mannerisms, and echoing my words. Reflecting the worst parts of me, like a cracked, dirty mirror.

She taught me to be careful. To watch myself. To be more aware of my reactions. To second-guess every decision.

From the moment I had her, my world changed. My life was no longer all about myself but all about her, her well-being, her happiness, her feeding times, her naps, her clothes, and her school. And the same goes for her little sister, Beatrice. My world revolves around my girls, and I love it—I love them. I've shed the skin of the woman I used to be and given myself wholeheartedly to raising them. I've dedicated my life to being the best mother for my children. They bring me so much joy, I can practically feel my heart burst with it. But when one of them gets hurt, I feel it deeply too. Part of me feels like I'm responsible for that as well—for their happiness but also for their pain.

Isn't it my job to prepare my children for the world? For both the good and the bad? To teach them how to cross the road, how to read, how to present themselves, how to dress, and how to brush their teeth? I've spent years teaching about preventative things, but so rarely ever about pain.

I remember when Amber was born, how tiny she'd been in her cocoon of blankets, snuggled up like a taco, only her pink face poking out beneath a donated white knitted hat at the hospital. Her big eyes were like tiny jewels, the colour of dark amber with flecks of yellow gold sparkling in them, almost a warning of her spark for life—a nod to her personality. I'd inhaled her newborn scent in the deepest pockets of my lungs, hoping to savour it there forever as I'd silently cried tears of joy, promising her the world, happiness, and safety.

It hadn't taken long before the realities of motherhood came crashing down on me. Like a tsunami, wiping clean every expectation of a peaceful, cooing baby basking in the warm sun rays as birds sang in the background.

How naïve I'd been then. How unprepared! I hadn't been ready to feel heartbreak or disappointment in this new reality I was bound to. I'd tried to make the best of it, but life kept throwing punches.

Amber had suffered from colic for months, crying relentlessly for hours at a time. Her screams penetrated the heavy fog of exhaustion just enough to set my nerves on fire. I remember being scared the neighbours would call the police on us. I'd barely survived the sensory overload, one short nap at a time.

I'd been desperate for relief from her screams. I'd tried absolutely everything, researching online when I'd ought to be getting precious sleep at all hours of the night and well into the morning until my eyes burned from strain. I'd spoken to specialists until my voice was hoarse, but nothing had worked. Only time made the colic episodes lessen and finally peace returned. Until the infamous toddler years, that is.

Despite all the memories of sleepless nights, or the strain of her challenging nature on my frayed nerves, thinking of Amber brings a smile to my lips. Only today the smile cracks and disappears into a scowl. I wince. I'd forgotten about my busted lip.

On shaky legs, I push myself upright and notice my phone lying beside me. The shattered screen looks like a delicate spider web. I reach out to grab hold of it and run my thumb over the dark screen, scraping my skin on its rough surface. Hopeless—it's destroyed.

I force myself not to panic. If the school needs me but can't reach me, they will call Niall as is protocol. Staring at the useless device, I waver but quickly admit to myself that no one is likely to be needing me.

My phone is attached to my hip, at the ready, in case of an emergency. The device is practically an extension of my own body. It goes with me wherever I go, connecting me to everything and everyone, allowing me to be up to date on every social media account, tracking my girls' whereabouts and getting regular weather updates. It's a useful little thing, but it's rarely ever used for phone calls.

Nobody likes talking on the phone nowadays preferring text over voice, staring at bubbles waiting for a reply rather than dialing the number and speaking directly to the person. It's ridiculous, but I do it too. Now, if my phone rings, I feel slightly irritated by the shrill noise—an interruption to my day. The only calls I seem to get these days are either from a doctor's office with appointment reminders, from solicitors trying to sell me something or scam me into paying a large sum of money, or very rarely, from the office at school asking me to collect one of my children due to illness or misbehaviour.

Holding my broken phone in the palm of my hand, I debate even seeking out its replacement having just deduced how little I really use it. Still, I know I'll get it repaired or replaced. The sad truth is I'm ashamed by how much I depend on this device, by how many hours I cling to it like a life source, when in fact it is draining energy rather than providing it. And yet, I can't let go. I don't want to be out of touch.

It's a lonely life at times to be a stay-at-home mom with kids gone off to school, spending hours wandering through the empty halls of the house once filled with noise and toys scattered about, an abandoned coffee resting somewhere on a shelf.

Life was once full, messy, and chaotic. Now, my days are mostly predictable, stable, clean, and quiet. I hate the silence most. Once I'd craved peace more than anything in the world, but now I worry the quiet will swallow me whole. To beat the loneliness, I keep busy with household chores, running errands, or organizing and sorting out items from the closets for goodwill.

I'd be lying if I didn't admit that I enjoy receiving texts from friends or having the ability to send a quick note to Niall during his day. It helps me feel not so far from him. Sometimes I see the little ellipsis moving over the reply box, and I hold my breath waiting for his reply only to realize after much time has passed that he's started a message but gotten distracted and never finished it.

Standing up, bending slightly forward, walking with great care, I make my way to the nearby sofa and lay down on my back. Whimpering, I wipe a stray tear from my cheek, smearing my finger with residual mascara. I close my eyes feeling the throbbing of the muscles in my back and the intensifying headache pounding away. Remembering lessons from being in labor, I take deep breaths and exhale slowly through a whistle-sized O-shape between my lips. One breath at a time.

Losing all sense of time, I remain in this position unable to move a muscle. I lie there helplessly, worried my kids need me. I hate how useless I feel. Not only am I unemployable, but now I can't even be there for my children and keep up with my chores.

The last time I felt this depressed was when I lost baby "C". Sighing loudly, I force myself to stop this train of thought in its tracks before I go deeper into the darkness.

In all my years of being a mother and caring for the girls, it had never occurred to me that I might one day need them to care for me. At least, not in my forties. I can't bear the thought of them seeing me in this state, but what am I to do?

I have no way of calling for help and the computer is far out of reach in the office down the hall. Against my will, I realize I must remain in this position until my muscles stop throbbing, or someone comes to my rescue. Never in a million years could I have anticipated this turn of events for my life—that I should be in need of saving.

"Ha! Now that's rich," I scoff under my breath.

While I'd been protecting and keeping everyone else safe from all the dangers in the world, no one had been protecting me.

Chapter 2
GEMMA

With a heavy arm thrown over my eyes, I try to shield them from the bright sun's rays seeping into the room.

When a knock at the front door comes, it startles me. I swear under my breath as a new twinge of pain bursts through my body at the sudden movement. Momentarily muted by pain, I swallow, noticing how desperately dehydrated I've become from lying in this position for the better part of the day. Blinking rapidly, I realize I have no other option. Unable to move towards the door to answer it, I simply croak out a response.

"Come in!" I say as loudly as I dare push my vocal cords not wanting to aggravate my dry throat or shift my neck. It had taken me hours to find a comfortable position.

For a second, I worry that inviting a stranger to open my unlocked door was a grave mistake, possibly a fatal one. My heartbeat ramps up at my uncharacteristic lack of judgement, and I urgently attempt to sit up when I hear my sister's voice float through the space.

"Gemma? You in here?" her sing-song voice calls to me, like a beacon in a storm. I sink back into the couch, allowing relief to wash over me.

"In here!" I mumble in a timid voice, ashamed of my state but unable to fix it. *I'm saved,* I think happily.

My voice is weak and husky from having my mouth shut for hours on end. I barely recognize it in my own ears. I had stupidly thought I was in better shape than I was, just killing time as I waited for the pain to subside, but the look on Grace's face tells me otherwise.

"Oh my God, Gemma! What happened here?" her eyes scan the room in horror, undoubtedly noticing the scattered clothing at the bottom of the stairs, which is in complete contrast to my otherwise immaculately kept home.

She drops her purse on the glass entryway table making the lamp sway slightly with the quick movement. She then rushes over to my side without removing her shoes. Under normal circumstances I'd scold her for it, but considering things, it really doesn't matter. The floor is hardwood, and the weather is warm outside, so the possibility of her dragging dirt or mud inside is extremely unlikely. Plus, she's wearing some sort of fashionable wedged strappy sandals so how much dirt can they actually dredge up?

I'm ashamed of my thoughts, more concerned over the appearance of my home than of my own well-being. When did my priorities change so drastically? Why do I care so much if there's dirt on my floor or not? My kids aren't toddlers anymore, grazing the floor and stuffing their sticky fists full of dust-bunnies into their mouths. No one hardly ever comes over these days, so why worry? Control? Order? I'm the only one who cares about keeping things tidy in this house, so why do I drive myself crazy over it anyway?

Grace's eyes search mine as I lie here deep in thought. *Maybe I've hit my head harder than I'd originally thought*, I ponder. I'm squinting as I turn towards her trying to make out her face, but the sun is glaring at me obscuring her features.

"Are you alright?" she asks finally, looking over my slumped body. Her hand hovers over me seemingly afraid of touching me as though I might be plagued with the flu and contagious—as though my bad luck might rub off on her.

"Yeah, I think so," I finally manage. "I slipped down the stairs earlier and I haven't been able to move since."

"Oh my God, Gemma! That's awful!" She looks at my bruised limbs, her eyes landing on my feet. "Were you wearing those stupid socks again?" she interrogates me in her most condescending tone.

I scoff, insulted. What the hell is so wrong with my favourite socks that makes everyone hate them so much? My muscles spasm in response. I guess I see her point. They are the main reason I slipped—but still, I love them.

"I was, but I was on the phone and carrying laundry downstairs, so it wasn't entirely because of the socks," I reason, but she's already standing up, dismissing me.

I watch her effortlessly bend over, picking up the array of laundry—my family's dirty clothes—from the floor and feel ashamed. Laundry is one of the only things I get to do nowadays, and I can't even get it right. I'm so embarrassed, and Grace seems to sense it. Still, she makes no remarks about my inability to do my job and seems perfectly happy to help out. She puts every item in the laundry basket and places it away from the stairs right beside the laundry room, out of sight as though it never happened.

Grace is two years younger than me, but there may as well be ten years between us for her appearance and energy certainly surpasses mine by that much. She's tight everywhere I used to be and everything still perks up the way it should. I've long ago given up on my looks. She takes care of her appearance the way I pride myself on maintaining my home. Grace is the envy of many of her friends as well as mine.

But I chose this life. I chose to become a mother and I cherish that. Yet, my sister always points out that just because I chose to become a mother doesn't mean I don't get to choose myself from time to time. I'm extremely grateful for her love and for how she keeps me up to date with the latest trends—taking me shopping, forcing me out of my sweatpants every so often, dragging me to the local salon for a root touch-up and a pedicure, just to keep me from losing myself entirely to motherhood. I love her for trying, for keeping that part of me alive, but I'm different now. Her good intentions sometimes feel like a rejection of the life I've chosen for myself.

Keeping up with my responsibilities as a wife and mother has all but consumed every aspect of my life over the years. I usually don't even notice how much I've changed. I can go months in the same daily, mundane routine, never seeing how far from myself I've wandered. At least, not until Grace comes over and reminds me of who I used to be. Thank God I have her. If I didn't have my sister to remind me of who I once was, I might be lost forever, only to be discovered years later, lamenting of a past life, jabbering on beneath piles of dirty dishes, discarded clothes, and grocery lists. No, I'm only joking, of course.

Being a mother is so much more than that. Yet, she's not entirely wrong in stating how much having children has changed me. I hardly ever leave this house anymore. She often jokes that I'm on house arrest, and I'm quick to snap back that I'm free to leave at any time, but I choose not to, is all. It's a sore point between us. Her, free as a bird, off exploring the world, enjoying all it has to offer while I'm trapped in a cage that I've built for myself with the door wide open. I find myself unable to step out, often wondering if I still remember how to fly.

Chapter 3
NIALL

The phone rings shaking me from my calm and pensive state as I analyze the last quarter's numbers in comparison to the previous year's figures. The graph leaves little to the imagination with a red line going down in an alarmingly steep manner. The real estate market has been hit hard. People are holding on tightly to their wallets these days preferring to build new rather than to buy a slightly older home in a quaint neighbourhood with large trees. It's all about convenience now. No one has the time or the interest to flip an older home with a smaller mortgage.

Whatever happened to working hard to make something your own? Building something over time rather than overnight? Wouldn't the gratification be greater with more effort and time invested? To know that after years of working towards something you'd finally achieved it?

It seems like people are either too busy or simply too lazy these days. Almost no one sees the value in renovations or recognizes that you can make your money back if you can just be patient enough. It's all about the here and now. Having rather than acquiring. Almost everyone wants granite countertops, open-floor concept, large windows, and exquisitely unscratched floors. Rooms have doubled in size but the number of people residing in the homes has diminished considerably.

Why do people need so much space? Gemma often remarks that having so much distance between family members requires each to have their own postal code.

Yet, people are the same way about their professional lives more often than not, switching employers and even careers every couple of years. It's rare to find someone with tenure at a bank anymore. It seems every week the clerks are getting younger and younger. The manager of the place can't be much older than thirty. It astonishes me—the fast pace of things, the constant change, this need for new and now. It's completely unrealistic.

The reduced value we place on older houses is probably our own doing.

As a realtor it's my job to find the house people want, not what a house could be. People these days just don't have the same imagination as they used to. With Pinterest boards showing sparkling, white kitchens and modern decor, it's almost impossible to sell anyone on 70's shabby, pink carpet and oak cabinets.

The ringing phone brings my attention back to the office. The number is familiar, but I can't place it right away.

Taking a deep breath, stealing myself to put on my friendly, courteous voice before answering the phone, I cough several times into my fist before lifting the receiver.

"Niall Richardson here," I answer politely, struggling to steal my focus from my work, both appreciating and feeling irritated by the distraction.

"Hey, Niall, it's Grace. Sorry to bother you at work," she states.

Surprised, but pretending not to be, I do my best to focus all my attention on her, "Hi Grace! It's no problem at all. What can I do for you?"

I'm puzzled by her call; I almost never talk to her directly. For most of my marriage to Gemma, the majority of the conversations I've had with her sister have been with my wife present or in the vicinity. I'm used to hearing details about Grace's life through Gemma. Her calling me at work is very rare and unexpected.

With the greetings out of the way, Grace begins rattling on excitedly. She describes a cluttered mess of discarded clothes on the floor, something about fuzzy socks and finally, how Gemma fell down the stairs and has been reduced to lying on the sofa, unable to move. I have to strain to hear her because my co-worker Yvonne's phone has started ringing at her desk right next to mine, and I have no idea where she is at the present time.

The phone keeps ringing, six or seven times, with a shrill, high-pitched sound that has never bothered me during a client call in the past, but it's suddenly persistent and irritating now that I'm trying to hear Grace's voice on the other end.

"Oh no! That's awful!" I manage to say finally. "Shouldn't she go to the hospital or something?" I ask, wondering how Grace expects me to help in this situation.

"She says she just needs some rest, but I'm not convinced. I'll stay with her now until..." the call waiting beep interrupts her for a second.

Sighing, not bothering to hide how annoyed I am for the interruption, I cut her off, "So sorry Grace, can you hold on for a second? I've got another call. I'll be right back," I say, suddenly feeling a rush of adrenaline. Silence all morning and now calls are flooding in. I'm glad to see that with summer around the corner, people are beginning to think about moving again.

Eagerly, and feeling a little guilty for putting Grace on hold, especially with Gemma in pain, I promise myself to be quick.

"Mr. Richardson?" a soft voice asks and I press the phone receiver harder to my ear to hear better.

"Yes, this is he," I start but I am interrupted.

"This is Patti from Cornel High School. I've got your daughter, Amber, here at the Principal's office. It seems she got into a little bit of trouble today at lunch break."

My jaw tightens. Unfortunately, this is a regular occurrence for Amber.

"What happened? Is she okay?"

"She's fine, Mr. Richardson, but we'll need you to come and pick her up right away. She has received a suspension for smoking an illegal substance on school property."

Dropping my head and shutting my eyes, I exhale heavily. *Jesus, Amber.*

"We've called your wife a few times, but we can't seem to get a hold of her, so we're hoping you're able to come," she states in a way that doesn't leave 'no' as an option.

"Yes, of course, I'll be right over," I assure her and switch back to Grace to let her know I'll be stopping by the school first but that I'm on my way home.

I tidy up my desk and wait a few moments to see if Yvonne will reappear from wherever she's hiding, but I decide that she's most likely paying a visit to a client outside the office so there's no point in waiting for her.

On her desk, I see a picture of her from years ago when she still wore her blond hair down to her shoulders. Her husband hovers over her, his arms possessively wrapped around her waist, a large smile on his angular face. His stance seems to be making a statement—*she's mine.* The picture frame is facing my desk. A message for me to back off, I imagine. Only, the poor bastard is a few years too late. I've nailed his wife on this very desk more than once after hours. He's apparently some kind of hot shot pharmaceutical salesman, always traveling, leaving Yvonne all alone. I was here. That's all it took.

Biting my lip, I have to push the images of my co-worker's naked body out of my mind. We promised to stop messing around as Yvonne's husband seems to be sniffing around a little too close for comfort. He's growing suspicious and it's beginning to make her nervous. I don't blame her. I wouldn't want my wife hanging around another man, alone all day long. Yvonne asked me several months ago to remain strictly professional for as long as we can help it. It's her way of putting her husband off the trail.

I'm lucky Gemma has never suspected anything strange is going on with me. As long as I come home every evening, she's satisfied. Perhaps I should feel bad for using her unwavering loyalty to my advantage, but I really don't.

She's only a shadow of the woman I fell in love with. She barely tries anymore. She's so comfortable with the life I've built for her, she's stopped fixing herself up like she used to. She's careful and quiet—blends in. Everything is beige, black, or grey in my life now. Gemma used to be full of life and colour. She used to be exciting. Hell, she used to be hot—like fire. Now she's just lukewarm, like weak, forgotten tea.

It was her idea to have kids. In fact, she insisted on it.

I hadn't put up too much of a fight with the first one as it looked good for my image—the doting father. Becoming a dad completed the perfect family picture I'd begun to think I required in order to become more accepted in the community and more successful in my career. It made me more approachable to new clients—less of a threat. It gave me an edge. Made me relatable.

But then, she hadn't been satisfied with just the one and she'd wanted more. We'd fought so much about it; how concerned I was about what it would do to her body, leaning heavily on the mental load it would take on her, but worrying mostly about her morphing figure. After giving birth to Amber, her tight belly had turned saggy—a collection of stretched-out, loose skin that hung off her wilting frame like a wet rag on the lip of a sink.

In those early toddler years, Gemma rarely wore her regular clothes anymore, constantly worried about the spit-up they might endure or the unavoidable food-smeared fingers that would grab a handful of her nicest skirt.

So rather than just let me buy her new clothes, she began to fill her wardrobe with leggings, sweatpants, and sweatshirts, everything dark and shapeless. Loose fitting everything, trying to hide her bony body beneath layers of cheap fabric.

Yvonne was still tight everywhere, and young. Her body hadn't been altered by pregnancy, nor would it ever be. She was apparently barren, which worked out great for me. I didn't need to worry about adding another kid to the mix and risking my wife finding out about the affair that way. It would only complicate things.

Shuffling some papers on my desk, I finish tidying up. Since our receptionist had called in sick this morning, I send Yvonne a quick email, apologizing for my quick departure and relay to her that she can reach me on my cell if she needs anything. Hovering over the keys, I debate signing with an XX, but think better of it. This isn't how I play the game. Unlike Yvonne's husband, I don't need to mark my territory. Especially not when I've already claimed it as mine.

Locking up the office behind me, I rush to the elevators and press the button.

When after a minute the elevator shows no indication that it's on its way, I decide to take the stairs, treading carefully down them to avoid the same fate as Gemma. We can't both go down on the same day.

It's like an unwritten rule for parents or something. If one of us is sick or needs a break, then it's assumed the other will take over everything and vice versa. We do it for each other all the time. This accident is no different. At least, I hope Gemma won't be out of commission for too long.

She's been under quite a bit of stress recently what with applying for jobs and such. I'd even suggested she work part-time at my office as a start, but she insisted that we need our own workplaces separate from each other.

She prides herself on being professional, and I admire her for that. She wants to be treated just like anyone else.

I've been telling her to slow down and take it easy, to let the house get messy every once in a while, but my wife is stubborn. If she gets more on her plate, she makes bigger piles instead of removing other things. She wants to do it all, be everything for everyone.

Well, maybe this incident will be a lesson to her then. Maybe it will finally show her that she's been doing too much. That maybe she can depend on others to help once in a while. With me working odd hours, often evenings and sporadic weekends, having Gemma at home has given me so much peace of mind.

Perhaps she should put off looking for a job for a little while, maybe wait until Amber finishes high school at least. I'll suggest that to her tonight. But first, I have to deal with the school.

Chapter 4
Amber

Sitting in the reception area, I stretch out my legs. My butt is sore from the hardness of the chair. Do they make these chairs uncomfortable by design? Perhaps it's a tactic they use to subconsciously make you never want to sit in them again. I wouldn't put it past Principal Asher to have selected these very chairs for that exact purpose. He's intentional about everything, freakishly so. He's like a psychic, the way he always seems to catch me when I'm breaking the rules. Funny how he never notices when I'm doing the right thing.

I've been here so often lately that I can recite word for word the slogan on the anti-bullying campaign posters littering the chalky-white brick walls. The glossy images, so familiar to me, seem to blur before my eyes and yet I can easily recall the phone numbers for the mental health crisis line by heart.

I guess I should be ashamed of being in here so often, but I don't really care. My parents and the school can try to mould me into the perfect version of what they wish I was, but I've never been like everyone else. I stand out everywhere I go. Whether it's intentional or not, I can't help it. Like a wildflower amongst fields of tulips, I don't belong.

Mom refuses to homeschool me, claiming that being around other kids my age is what's best for me. As though I have so much to learn about being social and fitting in. It makes no sense to me. All this talk about fitting in when all I hear around me is how we're all unique and encouraged to be ourselves. I guess that applies to everyone else but me.

While everyone I know is busy trying to find themselves by trying out every sport, taking expressive art courses, or making friends with ease, I already know exactly who I am. I think that's probably why no one likes me.

It's funny how when you're not seeking approval from everyone else, you end up pushing everyone away. Where some might call it confidence, others view it as strange. At school, I'm a freak. At home, I'm wild. To my grandparents, I'm trouble. People have always been quick to label me.

We watched *"The Breakfast Club"* in class last week and when they listed off the labels, Tim elbowed me when they called that one actor *"The Criminal,"* as though I should relate to him or something. I guess I do kind of dress like him. Baggy jeans, ripped at the knees, plaid shirt tied around my waist, black T-shirt to match my chipped black nails.

I don't really fit into any category at school. I'm not a loner per say. I have a few select friends, only I don't hang out with them regularly. Mainly, our interactions are limited to the odd text and sporadically sitting next to each other in the cafeteria for lunch. And yet, they seem to understand me more than most others. Maybe they're not so much my friends, but rather, they are the ones who tolerate me.

As a kid I was always trying to make friends with everyone. I didn't care who. I was so desperate to be liked that I was constantly altering myself and my interests so others would want to play with me. Still, even if I clicked with a few people, my true personality would eventually come out, unwelcome and intense after being forcibly snuffed and hidden away, and they'd inevitably get scared. Those were people who liked to draw inside the lines. That just wasn't me.

After years of trying to find others like me, it got too painful to keep trying. So, I resolved that if the world viewed me as different, then I would embrace that. After all, I was. I'd been told that my whole life. I decided to stop trying to fit in and to just be myself. Only, being myself didn't quite fit in with a society of people who followed the rules and coloured between the lines. They were constantly trying to shape me into something I wasn't, and I just kept fighting back, which of course, kept getting me in trouble.

School isn't exactly a place where you have the freedom to express yourself or to stand out. For whatever reason, when it comes to school, it's easier if everyone marches to the same beat, dresses in the same plain uniforms, and talks in the same manner. Probably something to do with order and structure, but where's the fun in that?

My parents keep telling me to just get through high school. To keep my head down and to not cause trouble. That once it's over, I'll have more freedom to be who I want to be, who I really am. But they'd said that about elementary school too. I think it's a line they keep repeating in order to stamp out my personality, and they pray I don't act out. They have a reputation to uphold.

My mom thrives on routine and organization. It's like a religion to her. She relies on it heavily. It keeps her sane.

Sometimes I wonder why she's so messed up, like, why does she always has to have everything so perfect all the time? I've often wondered if her need for control is amplified by her grief at the loss of our youngest sibling. But I've also suspected for a long time that it's most likely due to me not living up to her expectations—a disappointment since birth, unlike my perfect little sister, Beatrice.

Now there's an example of the standard I'm measured up against. God love Bea, but she can be annoying with how flawless she is. With her smooth, porcelain skin, her straight, dark hair, stick-like figure and brains, that girl will have the world at her fingertips when she's older. Only, she needs to learn how to reach for it.

We're complete opposites in that way. She asks, I take. I don't wait for things to fall in my lap because they generally don't. I don't get handouts like she does. No one pities me or lets me have a free pass at anything. I'm under everyone's scrutiny. Everything I say and do is judged and recorded right next to my last offence. But Bea? She's the angel in the family. She can do no wrong. Talking about labels, she's "The Princess"—always so fucking perfect.

But she's my little sister and I love her, despite how much I want to hate her. If she's perfect, it's not her fault. Like me, she didn't choose to be this way. She just is. And I love her for it.

Chapter 5
Amber

Shifting uncomfortably in the hard chair, I check the clock on the wall. It ticks the minutes away obnoxiously, making its presence known, highlighting the wasted time I'm causing everyone.

I know Principal Asher thinks I'm an idiot, a menace to his otherwise perfect school. He hates dealing with me, but it's because he thinks he knows what I'm about. He says so all the time, which isn't really fair. He doesn't know me at all. He's never even tried to get to know me. Only on paper. And that, of course, tells him all that he apparently needs to know about me.

The records he has access to only list my offences and my mistakes. He loves to shove the thick folder in my face at any given chance, yet he has failed to get to know the person behind the meticulously recorded list of wrongs. He has no desire to get to know me either.

He thinks he's such an important man, all pompous and proud, as though he's never made a fucking mistake in his entire life. People like him mostly haven't, but not because of their own doing. They had people protecting them their entire lives, making them feel untouchable.

My mom tried to do that for me, and she succeeded for many years, but even she can't save me from myself.

She says I'm just like she was as a child, and that's helped her anticipate several of my "great" ideas before I got too far into trouble. But she doesn't know everything.

As far as appearance, I have no choice but to agree. I'm the spitting image of her. With my wild black curls, cat-like amber eyes, and perfectly straight teeth, I can't lie and say I blend in easily with my awkward and hormone-challenged peers. But despite looking similar to my mom, I struggle to pick out any resemblance between her personality and mine. She's so eager to please, trying so hard to fit in that it's breaking her. I feel bad for her sometimes. Her entire life's purpose has been to take care of Bea and me, and now that we're grown up, she doesn't know what to do with herself.

I don't want to end up like that.

I don't want to try so hard to fit into everyone else's idea of who I ought to be, that I end up losing myself. I won't do it. I'll keep pushing—keep standing tall when they ask me to sit, keep talking when they tell me to be quiet, and keep running when they tell me to stay still. Some might call it defiance, but I refuse to call it anything. It's just me. I'm not wild or troubled or wrong. The mould didn't break when I came around. I just made a new one. No one should have to try and fit into the same mould over and over again. What's the point in repeating the same pattern? Listening to the same song?

No, I'm not stupid. I'm just angry and bored. I'm actually quite smart. When I was a child, I was told I was gifted. It had baffled Dad at first, but Mom had smiled to herself as if she'd always known this about me. To her, it explained most of my difficult behaviours. My lack of focus and my curious mind.

She used to tell me that when I first learned how to speak, I wouldn't stop for hours on end. I would talk continuously, like a never-ending, run-on sentence, until she'd have to tell me to stop because her nerves couldn't stand the constant noise any longer.

Even then, she could easily see that I had a thirst for knowledge and thought about things that were well beyond my years.

She told me once that people would stare at us at the grocery store, listening to our conversation and the questions I would ask. In my preteen years, someone once referred to me as being loquacious. I remember feeling ashamed at the time, but Mom had taken me aside and somehow transformed the word meant as an insult into a positive attribute, assuring me that I had a big imagination and asked intriguing questions. That I should never let anyone tell me to stop asking the questions on my mind, and that my asking them showed how intelligent I was. But she would also tell me that there was a time and place for asking such questions and that not everyone would react well to them. That I should choose my audience wisely or forever be seen as loud and noisy to everyone around me.

It's a challenge at the best of times and goes against everything I believe in, but it's necessary to survive. Teenagers can be mean when they want to.

I might not care about fitting in, but I do need to make it through these years to make it out of here in one piece.

Staring at the clock again, I'm beginning to feel impatient. The receptionist told me my mom didn't pick-up the phone earlier, so they had to call my dad at work. I was surprised because Mom always answers on the first ring.

In the parenting duties, taking care of school matters falls under her responsibilities. I feel a little irritated with her that I now have to deal with Dad's lectures on getting suspended so close to the end of the school year. I know he and Mom have been under so much stress lately that my suspension is sure to be a sore spot for them.

Sighing heavily, some loose hair strands float up. I notice how my hair surrounds my head, like a wild lion's mane, a sort of shelter I can hide within. I never realized before, but I almost always keep my hair down, most likely to shield and protect myself from hurtful comments and stares. Funny how I never noticed I did this, not consciously anyways.

I'm peering through my curls when the front door of the school bursts open. The handle of the door collides violently with the protective wall saver on the back as Dad storms inside. There is a fury in his movements. *Oh boy*. I suck in a quick breath.

As much as I hate Principal Asher, it's not his fault I'm in trouble—again. I don't want my dad to go off on him like last time they met. He's just doing his job, after all. Dad is too proud to accept the fact that I'm a screw-up, a nuisance to the otherwise perfect balance at the school. He refuses to acknowledge my challenging behaviours and tends to take out his anger on Principal Asher instead.

A suspension, how outrageous! I can almost hear him giving him hell before the words have even left his mouth. Instead, it's me he stares at in a rage I've never had directed at me before. It makes me shrink in my spot, doing my best to make myself smaller, wishing I could disappear.

Maybe I've gone too far this time. I gulp but my throat has gone dry. I'm embarrassed for the first time ever. One disapproving look from Dad is all it takes to reign me in.

He thinks the world of me. His pride and joy. He used to say I had a bounce in my step, fire in my spirit. I was going to go far in life. But, with anger in his gaze, I wonder what he thinks of me now.

Chapter 6
Amber

Slamming his hand against the steering wheel of the car, Dad has been full-blown yelling at me for almost ten minutes now.

"You're out of control," he states, outraged, his neck veins bulging out in red, angry worms. "You've embarrassed our family." He grits his teeth, seething in his seat. "You're so selfish!" He unleashes a fresh wave of contempt, each insult like a tiny sliver cutting my skin. "You need to grow up and think about how your actions affect others." His voice booms, echoing against the walls of the car. It makes the space feel smaller, like it's shrinking around us. "You're a fucking piece of work, you know that?" His final statement hits like a punch to the gut and I immediately shut down and build up walls in my mind. Over the years, I've learned how to protect myself by going to a happy place inside of my head, refusing to absorb any more of his words.

For self-preservation, I'd long-since learned how to effectively block his words from penetrating and imprinting on me. What I don't hear can't hurt me, right? Yet I know that if he ever figures out that I've mastered the art of ignoring him it will infuriate him even further and I'll be in even more trouble. So, rather than poking the bear, I make a point of nodding every once in a while to at least give him the satisfaction of believing that I'm listening to his scolding and feeling every bit of guilt he's expecting from me.

At first, I hadn't had to pretend at all. His disappointment in me was hard to swallow. I'd barely been able to handle it. But after he lost his calm and started spitting out his words in rage, it had almost been funny. The importance of his words was lost with the slamming of his fists and spit flying out of his mouth, distracting me.

When we'd first gotten into the car, I'd apologized profusely, hoping to once again be on his good side, to not ruin the image he once had of me. But when it became obvious that he wasn't in a forgiving mood, I'd shut down, refusing to listen any longer.

I'm starting to lose faith in adults. If they can't control their emotions and their tempers, then why do they expect me to? Shouldn't they lead by example? If Dad is my role model, then what lesson is he teaching me in this moment? That if I'm disappointed, it's perfectly okay for me to act like a spoiled toddler having a tantrum when I'm older? His behaviour is shocking and bordering on embarrassing. He's not in control and it's completely out of character.

After his speech, we sit in silence, me comfortably, him stewing most likely.

Maybe his over-the-top reaction was his attempt to provoke me—to lash out with terrible words just to get a reaction from me. But as I hadn't given him the satisfaction, he's been forced to view his own actions as foolish and immature. He's not getting through my armour. All my guards are up.

It's not long into the ride before he reaches out a shaking hand, placing it over mine and saying pathetically, "Amber, sweetheart, I'm so sorry for my outburst." His voice is barely above a whisper, as though he needs to force the words out through the tight gaps between his teeth. Every instinct he's ever had is telling him that admitting fault is a weakness and that it somehow makes him less of a man. His face twists—it's like it physically hurts him to apologize.

I don't try to make the moment easier for him. I refuse to do him any favours or come to his rescue. Let him drown in his own guilt. Be plagued by the ugliness he exposed when he lost it on me. He can smooth-talk all he wants but he's exposed his true character and there's no going back now.

He steals a glance in my direction, but I stare straight ahead, letting his hand squeeze mine without reacting. I don't give him the time of day.

"I was wrong to speak to you like that. I'm disappointed by your actions today, but it's no reason for me to act this way. I'm so terribly sorry. I lost my cool. Will you forgive me?" He looks my way, desperation and tears brimming in his eyes.

Well, well. What a change in events this is turning out to be. Lashing out and immediately feeling regretful, begging for forgiveness? I have to admit I didn't see this coming.

Dad must be really messed up right now. What a roller-coaster of emotions he's just displayed. His unpredictability should frighten me, but instead I see how it could have its advantages. Dad is already on the edge, letting me see his unhinged self seeping through the usual calm façade he puts up for the rest of the world. I doubt many others have seen it before me.

Getting this tiny glimpse into my father's character is enlightening and, suddenly, I feel powerful, like I hold all the cards. I've never hidden who I am or what I want. But he does every day. He plays this game, wears a mask for everyone, yet I now understand what he's hiding beneath. And it's ugly. Certainly, he wouldn't want anyone else to know about this little crack in his otherwise perfect exterior.

With one tiny nod in his direction, I tell myself that I agree with him that his reaction was wrong and refuse to accept his apology after that pathetic olive branch.

The tension in the car releases slowly like air leaking out of a tire. He must think that his apology is enough to guarantee my silence. But he's wrong to feel reassured. Knowledge is power and I have yet to figure out just how I'll use this newfound information to my advantage.

Reaching the house, we park and sit in silence a moment longer.

Dad seems to realize who holds the cards now and squirms in his seat. Still, the news of my suspension can't be kept a secret from my mother.

Even though I'm old enough to stay home without an adult present, her not having a job outside the home makes it practically impossible to avoid her. She'll be disappointed, no doubt, but I don't think she'll be that angry with me. At least, not for very long.

She used to be just like me—used to get in trouble at school as a teen, so she can hardly lecture me about this. And yet, I feel sweat oozing from my armpits before noticing my aunt's car sitting in the driveway next to Mom's SUV.

Considering for the first time why it was Dad who came to pick me up and not Mom, I wonder if my aunt's visit has something to do with it. Following my gaze, Dad sighs loudly next to me and shares what Grace told him on the phone earlier.

"Oh my God! Is she okay? Why didn't you tell me sooner?" I demand, releasing my seatbelt with urgency.

"We had other things to discuss," he snaps and stops himself almost immediately. I know I'm testing his patience, so I wait for him to continue. "Let's not bring any of this up until we know how she's doing, alright? She doesn't need the added stress," he adds unnecessarily.

"Fine with me." I grit my teeth and reach into the backseat to collect my backpack.

We climb the steps to the front door at the same time. My hand is on the knob when the door swings open startling me. Aunt Grace's face greets us with a large smile. It seems out of place considering Mom is hurt. After the tension in the car and hearing of my mom's condition, I'm left wondering how Grace can appear so cheery. But maybe she's putting on a show just for our benefit. Does every grown-up do this? What's the point?

If everyone just acted and spoke as they felt, there would be so much less confusion and misunderstanding. In a way, I feel that I would respect people more if they just laid it all out on the table like Dad had moments ago. But being that vulnerable can also be dangerous. Allowing the wrong person to see cracks in your armour is as good as showing them, like an X on a map, exactly where to plant the knife that could destroy you.

Chapter 7
GEMMA

I watch silently from my place on the sofa as my husband and daughter step into the room. Amber has a ridiculous smile on her face as though she's making up for something or trying to cover something up, only it seems to draw more attention to her making me wonder what she's up to.

I've managed to get myself propped up in a seated position by pressing a few decorative pillows up against the armrest to keep my posture somewhat tolerable. To say I'm comfortable is a stretch, but I'm surprised to be feeling better so quickly. The extra-strength ibuprofen capsules I swallowed earlier must finally be working.

Niall approaches me timidly and hesitantly, kneeling before me as he did years ago before asking for my hand in marriage.

The memory of that cherished moment is made fresh by his repeating similar movements, holding my hand up to his lips and kissing my knuckles softly while never averting his eyes from mine. The simple gesture brings tears to my eyes. Niall interprets my sudden emotion as pain and begins to fret over me by adjusting the pillows at my back and covering my legs with a throw blanket from a nearby wicker basket.

"Oh, honey, you poor thing. Can I do anything for you?" he asks, his eyes full of kindness and love.

"Thanks, love. I'm fine for now. I finally found a somewhat comfortable position." I wince as I shimmy in my spot, noticing I've sunk lower into the sofa cushion.

With everyone surrounding me and looking down at me in this manner, I feel child-like. I don't like it one bit. I know a small part of me had wanted to be taken care of, but this is simply ridiculous. I'm a grown woman, for God's sake. I don't need anyone waiting on me, treating me like an invalid. I've had a bad fall. I'm not dying.

I'm about to protest all this attention when I catch Amber's eyes. There's a glimmer in them. Something deep, almost unnoticeable, buried beneath her irises. Only I would notice it which is why she turns away from my stare now. She knows I've seen it. I decide to let it go for now as everyone's attention is on me. I'll spare her the questioning, but I make a mental note to talk to her later on.

I worry about Amber.

She's a blaze that makes her own way in the world, not bothering to look back at all she has burned in her path. She's incredibly perceptive and strong, but I hope she remembers that she's still a child and that she can talk to me about anything. I hope she doesn't feel like she has to do all the hard things on her own. I know I'm guilty of allowing her to figure things out by herself. But just because she's capable doesn't mean she should always hold on to her feelings so tightly that they eventually explode out of her.

I see her abilities and how smart and resourceful she is, and I sometimes forget that she's only those things because she's had to be. I remember being her age and wishing for a free pass every once in a while. To be allowed to be a kid. To make mistakes and not worry so much.

Whenever Niall and I had been too hard on her when she was younger, Amber would quietly go up to her room and change into cozy pyjamas, reminding us that she was small and needed love and care, that we should treat her more gently. It would break my heart. I'm sure that instinct to seek out comfort is still there, but over time, it's become more restrained, buried deep beneath the surface.

I've been so busy with my own stuff lately, looking for a new career, that I've almost forgotten the fundamental truth that my teenage daughter still needs me. God knows that I still need my mom. I call her almost every single day. Sometimes it's with the excuse of needing help with a recipe, advice with the girls, or tips on the best products to use to effectively remove a stain from the couch. But most times, I call just to hear her voice.

The truth is, once you become a mother, I don't think you ever stop being one even once your children grow up.

53

I worked so hard to help Amber and Beatrice grow up into independent young ladies—taught them how to care for themselves and how to resolve their own problems, but I hope they don't feel that I've pushed them away and want nothing to do with them. Perhaps applying for jobs was a little premature after all. I'd be lying if I said I wasn't a little bit disappointed that I didn't get the job but there will always be time for a career later on. My girls still need me now.

I realize with a start that I've neglected to let Niall know about the results of my interview. As I open my mouth to speak, he interrupts me gently.

"You know, I was thinking that maybe this job thing should wait a little while. I'm concerned for you. You've been so stressed lately. Maybe it's just not the right time." His lips stretch thin with a small smile as though he's worried how I'll take his suggestion.

His comment doesn't surprise me at all. Getting a job outside the house had mostly been my idea. I'd needed more for myself, wanting to learn new things, to contribute differently to our society. I'd been hoping to form an identity outside the home and away from the school. To not only be known as the mother of so and so, or someone's wife, but to be recognized for my skills, my charm, or my capabilities. But maybe my timing was wrong. Or maybe I just wasn't made to stand out all alone in a field, rising high above them, getting sunshine for myself. Maybe I was meant to blend in, to keep my head down, to appreciate what I had and stop longing for more.

Being home has many perks, but most of the time I spend my days alone with little to no gratification from my family.

I've been home for so long I often feel as though I'm part of the furniture, just something, always there to be relied on. A listening ear for each member of my family, making everyone's favourite meals, packing lunches, washing and folding laundry, sweeping counters and floors, but usually no one notices.

I know I shouldn't be upset about it, but I can't help it. This has been my life's work, what I've dedicated all my time to, and sometimes I feel as though everyone takes it for granted. The steadfast assurance that I will always be there, never one to miss a call, dependable and predictable. These expectations they have of me have been built over time and are partly my own doing. But sometimes it makes me feel bitter.

I've often dreamed about leaving it all behind for even just a weekend—a silly fantasy. The dirty dishes stewing in the sink, the laundry piling up, the vacuum leaning against the wall, unused. No meals prepared ahead of time and no one to talk to upon arriving at home. I wonder if anyone would notice my absence then. Would it simply take me not doing my 'job' for my presence to be missed? Or would they miss me, the woman, too?

Hearing Niall mention that maybe I should wait to get a job stings a little. But he's right, of course. Just look at me. The basic application process had been enough to stress me out. I've never done well handling rejections.

In my twenties, I'd been an esteemed employee as a recruiter. My numbers had broken records in our industry, I'd landed key accounts and won bids for large companies across the country. I'd dined with the president of our company and been flown out of the country to present to shareholders—all expenses paid.

I'd even trained others. I'd been great at my job, and I'd loved it. I often missed those days. But that was over twenty years ago. My resume and experience are completely obsolete now.

I'm still me deep inside, but not where it matters, not on paper. These days, it seems that paper is more important than drive or transferrable skills. On paper, I've been a stay-at-home mom for over sixteen years. Most people are unlikely to recognize this for the achievement that it is, let alone as qualifiable work experience.

Still, that doubt being echoed by my husband's insensitive comment is the biggest "I told you so" he's ever said. A slap in the face so sharp that it takes my breath away. He'd called it months ago. Somehow, he'd known all along that the whole process of job searching would be too much for me to handle after being away from it for so long.

Or maybe there'd been a part of him that couldn't stand the idea of me working outside the house, a sort of repressed jealousy. He would have loved nothing more than to keep me all to himself, caged in this castle of plaster and granite. Distracting me with meaningless tasks—iron this, pick up that. Throwing fancy jewelry and designer clothes my way to keep me satiated. All in an effort to keep me busy and limit my wandering mind from looking out into the real world. An attempt to keep me quiet and stop me from spreading my wings to explore anything else.

He'd approached the conversation objectively stating his position from the start, declaring his hesitation, the ridiculousness of what I was proposing. He'd questioned me and made me feel small and inferior for wanting more for myself.

Why should I make my own money when he bought me everything my heart desired? Why else should I make money if not to purchase things? He'd let me have full range of decision making when it came to home décor and furniture. I was also in charge of anything regarding the girls, the school, and planning our meals.

But what he hadn't brought up was that he wanted to maintain the control he had with our money, something that we'd never openly discussed but that had become blatantly obvious to me recently. Niall managed the money that came in and out of our household and thought of it as his. He managed the funds—always had and always would.

When we'd first gotten together it had made logical sense. I hadn't even questioned it. He'd owned the house and knew more about mortgage rates and payments, property taxes and other financial matters. When we wrote up our wills, he took care of that too. He set me up with a cell phone and arranged for internet and satellite to be accessible to the house. He'd taken care of me in every way. At the time, I'd viewed it as chivalry, loved him even more for it, in fact. But recently when I'd persisted in my pursuit of finding a job, he hadn't been all that enthused at the idea. Maybe, to him, it had felt like a betrayal of some kind.

I'd seen something flash across his face the first time I'd mentioned it, so fleeting I'd almost missed it. I'd convinced myself that I'd had to have seen wrong. Niall would never intentionally stop me from achieving something that was important to me. I knew that to my core. His concerns were mere reservations. He'd simply asked questions to make sure this was the right move for our family. He'd even suggested I work for him, but I'd swiftly rejected that as a viable option.

If I was to start building up my experience, I wanted to do it on my own terms, without his help. But after getting all those rejections, it was starting to be too much to take. Either I was too experienced or not experienced enough, or I'd had too much of a 'break' since my last 'real job'. All different reasons, but all the same answer. None were easy to accept.

So, there it was. My pursuit of finding work had been nothing more than my latest venture—a pipe dream no one seemed to truly believe in but me. I'd been a fool. Yet, it would have been nice of Niall to at-least pretend to support me. I guess he entertained it for a few weeks, but perhaps he'd expected me to fail this entire time. It's almost as if he'd planned it this way. Counted on it, in fact. So, that I'd have no other choice but to run back to him as a more deflated version of myself.

He knows me so well, almost better than I know myself. Knows how stubborn I can be and how I wouldn't have let this idea go until I'd given it a fair chance. *Like a dog with a bone*, he'd referred to my persistence once. And now that I've tried, put myself out there and failed, he'll be able to bring it up any time I mention it again. *"Remember last time?"* he'll say, and he won't be completely wrong. And I'll have no choice but to agree with him, cowering from embarrassment. I've fallen flat on my face, quite literally. Hit the bottom of bottoms. I almost wish that I'd never even tried to find work in the first place. Then maybe I could have saved myself the heartache, saved myself from the humiliation and held onto whatever dignity I had left.

But, no, I'd had something to prove. To myself as much as to everyone else. And now I've gone and shot myself in the foot—ruined my one and only chance. There's nothing left to do but to admit defeat and face reality. If being a mother is going to be my life's work, then I might as well make the most of it.

"I think you're probably right, honey," I manage, swallowing what feels like a large ball down my throat. Immediately, his shoulders relax as he exhales, visibly relieved by my response.

"Okay, great. I really think that's for the best." Reaching out his hand, he strokes my chin with his thumb like he used to do to the girls whenever they'd been having a hard time, to cheer them up. For some reason, I find the gesture demeaning. It offers no comfort at all. If anything, it confirms how pleased he is with himself and how well he's played this, as though this was all part of his great master plan. He comes off as the supportive husband in this narrative, when in fact, he's been nothing of the sort.

"Ah, and here's your phone. Wow, it's completely toast!" Grabbing my phone from the coffee table, he flips it in his palm. "I might be able to save the SIM card. Let me see. I think I've got a spare phone in the office you can use for now," he adds triumphantly. As though this solves everything, like a peace offering—something tangible he can fix, unlike my disappointment.

"That's great, thank you," I manage, though the words feel bitter on my tongue.

If I'd had my own job, I would have been in a position to buy myself a new phone. Instead, I'm left, once again to graciously accept my husband's help, his generous hand-me-downs—in this case, one of his older, long-ago discarded phones.

I don't know what bothers me more: the fact that he thought I should be appreciative of this "gift," or the smugness and pride oozing off him, thinking this was a wonderful solution to all my problems. Either way, what choice do I have but to take his *generous* offer and accept his old phone? I know I sound incredibly spoiled and unappreciative, but it's just one more thing I don't get to choose. One more part of my life that he gets to control. I don't like it. I want to say something, but I bite my tongue.

He doesn't see what's wrong with his proposition. He thinks he's saved the day, offered me freedom by giving me his old phone to use. He's too proud of himself to notice how his gift makes me feel inferior, like a dependent. How every time he gives me something, it feels like he's buying me—taming me, confining, controlling, and making my decisions for me.

My old spark of youthful rebellion is burning hot, deep in my belly. I must suppress it. I need to believe he's doing this from the goodness of his heart, but I can't help feeling that this gift, like all the others proceeding it, is just another way to add more weight to my shackles. A sure way to tie me to this house, tethering me to him beyond our marriage and our life together. Forcing me to stay, keeping me bound to this life, locked inside this cage to ensure that I'll never be able to fly away.

Chapter 8
Niall

When I'm certain that Gemma is comfortable, I excuse myself and head upstairs to our room. Changing into sweatpants and a plain T-shirt, I sit on the bed, attempting to collect my thoughts while I wait for my breathing to return to normal.

I'm so angry with myself for how I acted with Amber in the car. I'm not even sure if any of what I said to her resonated at all or if it went in one ear and straight out the other. Her eerie calm had completely freaked me out. The level of control she exerted was like none I'd ever seen before. Almost like she wasn't affected by anything I said, which, of course had made me even angrier. I'm so ashamed of how I reacted. It was a force beyond me, an internal, deep need to keep probing, to keep hurting her with my words.

I knew better. Of course, I did. But I hadn't stopped even when I knew I'd gone too far.

I'd pushed until I'd worked myself up enough to raise my body temperature. I'd looked like a red version of the Hulk. I had totally lost my composure—my cool edge. I'd struggled to reign in my anger, realizing it had stemmed more from guilt and embarrassment than from Amber's suspension.

As a child, I'd learned in school how the tongue could be the deadliest weapon, above any gun or knife. The tongue had all the power to heal or to destroy. With one word, a person could alter the trajectory of a person's life. I remember my father reading from the Bible to me before bed, about how if you sin with your hand, you should cut it off to stop from sinning again. That's how this feels right now. Like I should cut off my tongue for it seemed only capable of spewing hatred, bitterness, and other equally horrible things. I can't believe I'd talked to my baby girl that way.

I'm supposed to be a good dad, an example to others. I have a reputation to uphold. People tell me all the time what a great father I am. But that's only because I choose which stories I share. I paint the picture I want them to see. Making sure I share the highlights and keeping the shadows where they belong. Most of those well-meaning people have never actually seen me in action. They might not be so quick to offer compliments if they had.

My chest aches, as though a dark hole is forming in my heart, silent and corrosive, slowly deteriorating all the good left inside of me, reaching deep within my soul until it's turned everything black. I thought I had pushed away that side of me long ago. Gemma had only ever seen it once and, thankfully, I'd been quick to apologize, to claim it was a lapse in judgement that would never happen again. She'd believed me. Unfortunately, and unknowingly to her, my entire life is a lie—a scheme.

I should be wearing a top hat and singing through every act as though my life is a musical production. I've fooled everybody. I've played the part perfectly, so well in fact that I've almost begun to forget who I really am deep down.

There's no changing that, no matter how hard I've tried. My core is rotten, and nothing can heal it. So instead, I've focused my time and energy on perfecting the outward elements, the things others can see.

I've spent years perfecting how I speak, walk, eat, shave, dress, make love, drink and work, playing the part of the attentive husband, father, and friend. Things I can control and manipulate however it suits me. But I can't change who I am in the deepest sense.

If only I could control everything else as easily, manage my urges, my perverseness, and my darkness better. However, they must all remain hidden, suppressed in the deepest parts of my being. Squashed so no one ever finds out. I can't allow another slip up like today with Amber.

She saw what was behind the mask. I can tell she sensed something. The dynamic between us has changed. I don't like it, but I screwed up. It's my own damn fault. And it's up to me to fix it.

I learned long ago that if I want to shift attention away from something I don't want exposed, I need to force the focus elsewhere. An act of diversion of some sort. A redirection very similar to a magic show. Throw smoke over here, while you pull the bunny from your hat with the other hand.

I have to think of something quick.

I need to distract Amber and give her something else to think about so she forgets what happened in the car. I have to wipe her mind clear of how I acted and replace those memories with better ones.

Do five good things for every bad thing. That's what my mother taught me. I have a lot of work to do, and I have a feeling I won't enjoy any of it.

With my head hung low, still sitting on the edge of my bed, I come up with an idea that might work.

Tensions have been high for everyone. Gemma had reluctantly admitted her latest job rejection, how it had preceded her fall down the stairs. I'd been harping on about how perhaps it wasn't the right time for her to work outside the home when I saw her face crumble. She'd been distraught at the news of another job passing by. To me, her fall was concrete evidence of her not being quite herself lately. It was proof of her inattention and why, perhaps, this wasn't the right time for her to seek employment. How could she keep up with the laundry, meal preparation, and running errands if she was out working for most of the day?

The option of me or the girls picking up some of her chores was daunting to say the least. I don't know where half of the dishes go and forget folding laundry as neatly as Gemma. That was a laughable suggestion. The house would fall apart without her. She has such a way of keeping it in order.

She knows everyone's favourite food to buy, keeps track of all the schedules, keeps us up to date on everything happening in town, and makes this space peaceful and warm to come home to.

Decidedly, I slap my knees and stand. Somehow, I have to persuade Gemma that staying home is what's best. Not only for her but for our family. It might take some convincing, but I have no doubt that in time, she'll start to see it too.

Removing my phone from my work pants, I quickly swipe through my emails to see if Yvonne has sent me anything pressing requiring my immediate attention. There are several new prospective client emails but nothing flagged as urgent. I send off a few replies, answering basic questions—list prices, square footage, number of bathrooms, etc. I swear I spend half of my time repeating information that could easily be found in the listing description available on our website, but still, I can't afford to be a jerk about it. The competition is high around here and there aren't that many listings to begin with, so if someone approaches me with a silly, redundant question that wastes my time, I'll happily respond in a timely manner. Beggars can't be choosers.

After checking off a few standard messages, I begin to clear off previously read emails, deleting them as I make sure I've attended to them. One email remains at the bottom and gives me pause. I don't recognize it straightaway. It looks like junk mail, but just before trashing it, my curiosity gets the better of me and I take the bait. Deciding my phone spam filter will alert me if there's anything off about it, I figure the risk is probably small.

The email turns out to be from an old realtor friend living in a rural town nearby. I do a quick pass over the email and smile widely. Suddenly, I know just what to do.

Chapter 9
Beatrice

The rumours of my sister's suspension had flooded through the school hallways like a tsunami. There was no way to stop gossip from reaching every single person, student and teacher alike. Not in high school anyway.

In elementary school, teachers would have protected my sensitive ears, sheltered me, maybe even sat me down and calmly explained the situation, offered to call my parents and have me sent home early to avoid any confusion or embarrassment. But not in Junior high. Here, I was alone to deal with the impacts of my sister's actions.

I can spot teachers huddled together, speaking in hushed tones, looking my way from time to time. They're judging me and are no better than the hundreds of students staring at me.

Until now, I'd been able to make my own way, build my own reputation at this school. But now, I can't help but wonder if the teachers had expected this day to come. Had they been able to sense something else below the surface? I wonder if they'd had bets about how long it would take before I turned out to be just like Amber. Were there signs they were on the look-out for? Maybe they were making assumptions, or reading into the way I sat down at my desk or how I spoke to my superiors. Did they compare notes and try and gauge just how far down the rabbit hole I'd fall? Maybe they believed that our shared DNA was stronger than any willpower I might have left in me to be different from my sister.

It isn't easy, living in Amber's shadow.

"There goes that *other* Richardson girl," kids teased behind my back as though I couldn't hear them.

Unfortunately, I don't miss much around here. I'm not an idiot. I know what they say about me and about my family. While Amber's been an open book—exposing everything, keeping nothing hidden—I've managed to keep mostly to myself. I don't think Amber means to spill everything, but everyone knows by now that if you corner her, she'll do just about anything to get out alive. It's always been about survival for her, not who she might hurt in the process.

I sincerely doubt that she cares how any of her actions affect me or my experience at school. It's a hard time for most people, but when you've got an older sibling, people expect things from you. Good or bad. They expect *something*.

It's not fair. We're so completely different. We wouldn't even be friends if it wasn't for the fact that we're sisters. We have nothing in common except where we come from and where we spend our days.

It makes no difference how hard I work to get good grades, or how pleasing and flexible I am.

People only see what they want to see.

I guess everyone has an unwritten role in a family dynamic. Some are meant to create, while others destroy. Some wreak havoc, others keep the peace. Some spend money, while others cling to it. Some work hard for what they get, and others get everything easily.

It's a constant teeter-totter and I'm usually the one trying to keep the balance. It reminds me of being on the playground with Amber. A rule-follower by design, or perhaps by necessity, I'd played on the teeter-totter like everyone else did. Stretched my legs to make Amber crouch, stood on my tip-toes, my legs not quite long enough to reach the ground. Before I knew it, I'd be up in the air, in a precarious position and completely in her control.

Oh, how I'd hated that. How vulnerable she'd made me feel.

There would always be a second or two of me begging silently, watching her face for any hint of trouble, wondering if she would let me fall hard and hit my butt against the playground dirt or gently lower me down. Sometimes, Amber would start lowering me slowly, making me believe I was safe, only to suddenly jump up and let me crash to the ground. No matter what she chose to do, it always left me feeling stupid for believing she's being nice about it, as though I should have anticipated this result.

I'd get mad at myself for hours after, trying to figure out how I could have read her so wrong. But Amber was unpredictable. I never knew what to expect from her.

It drove me crazy. I've never been one for uncertainty, fearing suspense. I prefer to know exactly where I'm going and plan accordingly.

With Amber, you might think you know what goes on in her mind, but you can never really know. I'm not even sure if she knows what she's about to do half the time. There's a storm brewing behind those fiery eyes, like a resting volcano with the constant threat of eruption as a possibility. I just pray I'm not the one who ends up setting it off and that whenever it does, I'll be far off its path.

Stepping off the bus and walking up the driveway, I notice that both Dad and Mom's cars are home, as well as Aunt Grace's. My first instinct is surprise. Mom never told me Aunt Grace was visiting today. But just as quickly as the excitement builds, I feel dread creep in. My heart sinks at the possibility that my aunt's visit might indicate something terrible has happened. I swallow hard. The stillness of our house worries me. Suddenly, I have no doubt that something happened.

I race the last few steps and climb the stairs, taking them two at a time, ripping the front door open. My heart thumps hard as I step inside. The sun had been so bright outside that it takes my eyes a minute to adjust to the darkness of the house.

I don't know what I expected—to be greeted with exclaimed relief at my arrival, to be pulled into hugs, tears staining my shirt, as my world crashed before me with horrifying news—but the sight before me is nothing quite as exciting.

Mom is sitting at a strange angle on the sofa, cradling a cup of tea or coffee—I can't be sure which. Stepping further into the room, I notice my aunt sitting in the high back chair by the window facing my mother.

They are deep in conversation, undisturbed by my hasty entrance. Did they really not notice me come in?

Dad is carefully stepping down the stairs, gripping the handrail with one hand, holding a phone in the other. I watch him hand the phone to Mom, as if this is all unfolding on television and not a mere ten feet from me. She inspects it before offering a reserved nod in his direction as he reaches for a second phone I hadn't noticed on the coffee table. I'm confused and step closer, letting the light from the window shine over me like a theater beam projector.

"Oh, Beatrice, my dear! I didn't see you there!" Mom exclaims.

I half expect her to rise and greet me with one of her usual warm hugs, but to my surprise, she doesn't move. I'm stunned to realize how empty and rejected this makes me feel. I hadn't realized until this very moment just how much I longed for her hugs and reassurances at the end of the day. Her attention and kindness have always been my favourite part of arriving home, somehow erasing any and all discomfort I'd experienced in the last six hours. Just being near her feels like starting fresh, like letting go of all the tension of the day.

In her eyes, I can do no wrong. She sees me for me, not who everyone else wants me to be. So when she doesn't stand to greet me, I feel panic rising, as though I've exhausted all of my chances at making her believe I was different.

She seems to catch my despair—always noticing my micro expressions and feelings. I feel tears threatening to fall but I quickly blink them away feeling ashamed.

Looking at her more closely, through my blurry eyes, I notice she's struggling with this too. I can tell she wants nothing more than for me to bridge the gap between us. But for some reason, something is preventing her from reaching me and giving me a hug. I breathe out, feeling slightly better knowing whatever is going on has nothing to do with me. There has to be an explanation for this.

Dad turns towards me and gives me a quick hug and a pat on the back.

"Hey Bea, how's it going?" he smiles warmly, and I can't help but return it. "Mom had a bad fall down the stairs, so she's going to be taking it easy for a little while, alright?" He motions over to Mom, talking as though she isn't sitting in the same room. Like now that she's hurt, she's also lost her voice.

Worried, I turn to her trying to read her expression. "Oh Mom, are you okay?" I feel bad for needing her to hug me earlier. How selfish of me. She needs *me* now. I can be there for her.

"I'm fine hon, just a little sore," she grimaces slightly as she adjusts her position on the couch. "It'll probably take me a couple of days before I'm up and running again."

"Well, whatever you need, I'm here. You can ask me for anything," I reassure her.

It'll be nice for a change to be the one taking care of her. She does such a good job of caring for everyone else. I have big shoes to fill, but I'm up for the challenge.

I head to the kitchen and begin to put some cheese and crackers on a plate, adding a few grapes to the mix for some colour, and bring the snack to the living room. On my way, I spot an old decorative bell on a dusty shelf in the hallway and pick it up in my spare hand.

"Here you go, Mom. I made you a little snack. I also brought you this bell, so if you need anything and nobody's around, you can just ring it." I'm proud of myself for thinking of it. I lay the plate on the table, close enough for her to pick items off as she chooses.

"That's so thoughtful of you, sweetheart. Thank you." Her voice is thick with emotion. I'm glad to know that I've touched her with my actions. It feels so good to help out. I can now see why Mom enjoys it so much.

Grabbing my backpack from the entryway, I bring it upstairs to empty and get started on my homework. I spot Amber sitting on her bed, texting on her phone. I should be angry with her for the trouble she caused for me at school today, but I'm surprised to feel nothing. I'm completely void of emotions towards her.

Maybe today was the last straw. I've used up all my compassion for her. I've given her so many chances to change, to be good and to care for anyone but herself, but she's thrown it all away.

I can't really blame her; this isn't something new. She's always been like this. But something occurred to me today—a universal truth that seemed to tip the scales. I don't have to tiptoe around her. I don't have to live my life responding to her actions. I'm my own person. I refuse to go on reacting to whatever scheme she's up to next. I want to make my own way, use my own voice, and let my words be heard.

Normally, I'd force myself to step into her room, sit on the edge of her bed and let her unload on me, listen for hours as she complains about how brutal the world treats her, all while pretending to care. But not today. Instead, I simply walk on towards my room, ignoring her. I don't know if she looks up as I pass, but I no longer care.

72

I'm surprised at how nice it feels to make this small change. It's a silent victory for me. I'm taking charge of my own life, learning how to set boundaries. It's time for Amber to grow up and take responsibility for her own actions. I'm not going to clean up her messes anymore. I have my own life to worry about.

Chapter 10
Amber

My aunt left a few moments ago and now my parents are talking downstairs. The low timbre of their hushed voices floats up the staircase and resonates slightly through my open bedroom door. I can barely make out any words, but I hear my name as clear as crystal. I've never had trouble hearing my name, whether it's shouted, hissed, whispered, or mouthed. It's like a sixth sense I have. I know when people are talking about me, and all my attention goes towards the sound.

I find it slightly disrespectful that my parents are discussing my mistakes one floor below me, trying to be subtle, but knowing I'm well within earshot of their conversation. If they truly didn't want me to hear, or cared about my feelings at all, they wouldn't be talking about me while I'm in the house. They should know better.

If my door was closed, the furnace vent would transport the sound up to my room. Like a tunnel, it makes it as easy to hear as if I were sitting in the same room. I discovered this specific register and its benefits when I was little. It's actually the reason why I chose this smaller room rather than the larger, more obvious choice my sister got.

They go easier on her—that's for sure. But then they made all their mistakes with me as their first born. *I* made them into what they are today.

I pushed and tested the boundaries, frayed the edges of their perfect ideals of what daughters ought to be like, pulled the rug from beneath them, made them throw out everything they thought they knew about raising children, and forced them to learn on the fly. Caused them to jump in with both feet.

They didn't have a choice. I was a constant reminder of the independence they'd lost. I often feel the disappointment steaming from my mom. It's in every exasperated sigh every time I don't meet her expectations. I know she'd hoped to return to work after I was born, but something changed, and she ended up staying home instead—because of me. I'm not sure if it was truly a choice or more out of necessity. I know deep down that she blames me. She'd never admit it and would rather die before I found out that a big part of her misses who she used to be before I came into this world.

I can't stand it. I've been in my room for hours and no one has stopped in to check on me.

Beatrice walked right by after getting home from school, practically ignoring my existence when she stormed by my room earlier and once again just a moment ago as she headed back downstairs. She was wearing her pyjama bottoms and a hoodie that used to belong to me. It had been my favourite one, soft and grey, the sleeves frayed at the ends from nervous chewing in my pre-teens. But since Mom put me on birth control pills, my boobs have almost doubled in size and the sweater got too small for me.

The pill was a necessity. Mom keeps track of my comings and goings and even checks my phone periodically. I don't mind the intrusion; I've got nothing to hide. She already knows everything. It doesn't mean she agrees with it all, but I've been very open about what I'm up to when I'm not home. Plus, she keeps assuring me that there's nothing I could do or say that would shock her, of all people. Whatever that means. My mom is practically a saint, although she denies that whenever I mention it to her.

"We all have a past." She'd laugh it off while never actually going into details about her own.

I've tried to piece together parts of her wild years from the few stories she's shared with me over the years. As a toddler, I'd beg for one more bedtime story and more recently, while asking her advice about a boy I'd liked in grade five and about safe sex, I'd hoped I could get her to talk. Once, I tried to pry it out of Aunt Grace, only to come out even more confused.

My mom's a good listener, I have to give her that. It's safe to say that she could have easily made a career out of it. She's always saying that if you wait long enough and let the silence stretch out, that's when you get to the root of what someone is actually trying to say.

Then, when you know what you're working with, it's easier to start putting the pieces of the puzzle back together. Over time, everything that person told you, everything they've ever done, will become clear, because you took the time to truly know them, one piece at a time—forming a picture. Not just what they like or don't like, but who they are at their core.

Mom is my best friend, even if she can be a pain in the ass sometimes. She never lets anything slip. She keeps me accountable, makes me cringe under her knowing stare until I have no other choice but to be honest with her. There's no point in lying. She made me. She knows all about me. *Trust your gut*, she says. She repeats it all the time, so much so that it's become my mantra. I repeat it in my head every time I begin to doubt myself.

She told me once that because I feel everything so strongly, I'm in tune with my emotions and therefore have good instincts. I don't always listen to them. That's the problem. Mom has been telling me to follow my gut my entire life. But what if my gut is encouraging me to do the wrong thing? I asked her once about it and she said that wasn't my gut talking but something more primal and more sinister. She warned me to squash it down until I really needed it if I ever found myself in a desperate situation.

When I was younger, she'd spent days trying to teach me to listen to my own conscience. She tried to train me to hear the lies and to separate them from the truths.

I still struggle with lying on a daily basis. It's like a heavy weight of guilt covers me whenever I go against my gut instincts, a presence I simply can't ignore.

She used to tell me 'Lies are like tiny invisible threads that get tangled up ending up in a big mess. The truth isn't always pretty by comparison, but at least you don't get as mixed up in the retelling. It's far easier to stick to the facts. Don't assume you know, don't make up reasons for other people's actions, and don't spew lies. Just like a spider web, lies can be enticing and capture your attention, especially when the silvery threads shine in the sunshine. But to get caught in a lie, just like in a spider's web, could be the worst mistake you ever make. It can be very hard, if not impossible, to free yourself from it.'

She was right, of course. People love to repeat gossip. The more damaging the better. But she also would warn me that 'If your friends are always telling you intimate things about other people, what are they saying about you behind your back?'

I want no part of that—too much drama.

There's only one circumstance where I might consider lying as a suitable alternative to speaking the truth and that is to spare someone's feelings from getting hurt.

The sun has set outside of my bedroom window when I remember Bea's pyjama pants. I begin to wonder if I've missed dinner altogether. Obviously Mom is in no shape to cook tonight, and I highly doubt Dad will whip up his famous lasagna this late in the evening, but my stomach is growling.

Unfortunately, I don't know how to make much in terms of dinner. Baking is more up my alley. I love the precise measuring, the aromas of cinnamon, melted butter, dark chocolate, and coconut flakes all mixed together creating a new flavour. Chocolate chip cookies are my specialty. I don't make them often because we need variety around here, but they're my favourite.

Mom loves my carrot muffins with a cream cheese filling and pecan topping. Bea's favourite dessert is my Nutella brownies with a sprinkle of sea salt, and Dad loves my oatmeal raisin cookies. The trick to making good cookies is to chill the dough just enough that when I shape it into little balls it retains the shape and helps it cook to the perfect combination of chewy-soft texture.

If it's not baking, I'm pretty hopeless in the kitchen. I can barely cook an egg without breaking the yolk. I've burnt toast on more than one occasion. Unless everyone votes to eat cereal for dinner, they'll have to fend for themselves.

After another five minutes, my stomach groans again and I finally decide to leave my room. Mom has moved from her position on the couch and is now seated at the kitchen table with a steaming mug between her hands. I go over and give her a quick peck on the cheek ignoring the stares from Bea and Dad boring a hole into the back of my head. They're mad at me, that much is obvious by their not so very subtle huffs and sudden clanging of pots and pans. I look up, irritated, daring them to say something, but neither of them does.

It looks like they've just finished drying the dishes. The laundry basket from the bottom of the stairs is now sitting empty on top of the washing machine, the rumble of the machine turning lazily fills the silence.

Aunt Grace must have taken care of it before she left. Mom looks pleased but still in quite a bit of pain. Her movements are slow and careful. Wanting to help a little, I make my way towards the office and grab my mom's heating pad. I plug it in the nearest outlet and drape it around her shoulders.

"There, that should help. Do you need any more painkillers?" I ask, my voice tender and patient.

"Thanks dear, no. I'm alright for now." She pats my hand gently before adding, "Dad just ordered a pizza for dinner. It should be here at any moment."

It's impossible for me not to hide how excited I am about this news. Pizza is comfort food. It fits so perfectly with my craving for greasy, cheesy goodness that I could run up and kiss Dad, but I don't.

Instead, I nod and say, "Alright, that's cool," using the most indifferent tone I can muster.

Of course, my mom isn't fooled. She knows my weak spots and that, after a hard day and my suspension, I'm really craving pizza. Dad might have done the ordering, but I'm sure my mom had a hand in the decision making. I sit next to her and smile knowingly, silently thanking her with my eyes. I watch her smile back at me, acknowledging my thanks.

We do this a lot, she and I.

We have a kind of non-verbal, secret language that only we seem to know. Similar to ESP, like our minds are connected on a deeper level, it's as though we can read each other's thoughts. It gets pretty freaky at times, like on days when I'm mad at her and call her all sorts of horrible names in my head, I watch her eyes narrow, a hurt expression on her face, almost like she's heard me.

I've since been more careful about my thoughts when I'm near her, just in case. I wouldn't want her to ever hear something by accident. Something I might say in a fit of rage and regret forever. That would be heart-breaking.

Chapter 11
Niall

The pizza arrives right on time and the whole family lights up with excitement. It's funny how such a simple thing as having take-out for dinner is enough to bring out the child in all of us.

Gemma has spent the last hour checking out her new phone, seeing what contacts remain and what pictures she lost in the fall. Unfortunately, she lost everything, but she resolves that she won't need all the work contacts she's accumulated. The prospect of her finding work is minimal since her most recent hope of getting called back was squashed this morning.

Gemma has been moving more with each passing hour. Her muscles seem to be loosening slightly, providing more mobility. She claims her pride is more hurt than her back, but I'm not convinced. These types of injuries can manifest and worsen over time if they aren't looked after properly.

Despite her seemingly speedy recovery, I booked her an appointment tomorrow with my physiotherapist. I think she hit her head and bruised her spine pretty badly.

When I suggested she start some sort of treatment to help manage the pain, she didn't disagree with me. I took a quick look at her back earlier but couldn't see any outward injury, but it's difficult to know how much damage happened internally.

That's a scary thought for me. Gemma may be acting fine now, but who knows what's going on inside of her, what organs she might have crushed or stressed, what nerves were pinched, or if her memory will be impaired because of the concussion she most likely experienced? Better to get looked over, just to be safe.

Once everyone has grabbed a slice of pizza and is seated in their usual spots, I start explaining the opportunity that's fallen on our laps.

"Tim says we can stay there for a whole week!" I exclaim. "It's right on the water. There's a dock and we'd even be allowed to use his boat while we're there!" I look around, trying to gauge everyone's reaction.

"And he's just letting us use it for free?" Beatrice questions, her expression doubtful.

"Yes, well not exactly. He wants us to review it for him. You see, he's hoping that if we enjoy our stay, he'll be able to rent it out to other families throughout the year," I explain.

"And where is this house?" Gemma asks, her curiosity visibly peaking.

"It's not a house per-say," I begin, "more like a cabin or a small cottage." I see her expression fall slightly at this. It's not the grand, luxurious vacation home she was hoping for. "It's definitely rustic and we'd be the first ones to stay there since Tim's family's been there years ago."

My excitement begins to falter when I notice that all three ladies are staring at me with apprehension, but I stand my ground.

"I really think this would be a great way to start our summer holidays. There's only a week or two left of school, so it's perfect. Tim is hoping we can get there at the end of the month, from June 26th through July 3rd. Think about it," I hate how desperate I sound to my own ears. I'm practically pleading with them. Why do I feel like I need to sell this idea to them?

"It's not exactly free, but it would be a very good rate. He wants us to estimate how much he could rent it for and review it for him. If there's something amiss, he wants to know so he can fix it before putting it up on those vacation rental websites for the summer months."

"Where is this place?" Gemma repeats.

"Not too far. I think a little over an hour away from here, near Eganville."

"Where's that?" she asks, confused. "It sounds familiar, but I can't place it."

"Remember, years ago, before the kids, we went and explored the Bonnechere Caves?" I wait a beat and she nods, recognition in her eyes. "It's right around there."

"Wait, like actual caves? Cool! Mom, can we go there? Please?" Amber is the most excited I've seen her be in a long while. I smile brightly.

"Going swimming in the lake does sound really nice, too," Beatrice adds almost shyly.

I can see I'm winning them over, one by one. I look at Gemma and raise my eyebrows in question. Yay or nay? Even though I'm almost certain of her answer, I'm glad when she smiles and agrees. She can't say no to the girls.

We watch our kids in awe as they scarf down their dinner, place their dirty plates in the sink and rush upstairs to get ready for bed. This little family vacation seems to be just what we all need.

"Do you really think it's a good idea? I mean, right now?" She's hinting at her fall and her lack of job prospects.

"Yes, right now," I smile gently. "Honey, you've been so stressed with this job hunt. The girls will be done school and appreciate a place to let loose, especially Amber. But don't worry, she'll be with us the whole time. She can't exactly get in trouble where we're going—there's practically nothing to do but to enjoy the scenery. I think it will be good for all of us. A nice restful place for the family to unwind and relax."

"It does sound rather nice," she laughs, slowly allowing herself to get used to the idea. "I can't even remember the last time I swam in a lake!"

"It'll be nice to get out on that boat and enjoy the water," I add.

"Maybe I'll finally get to read a book all the way through!" she finally exclaims, and I know I've got her.

I smile and reach a hand over the table and squeeze hers, feeling her rings dig into my palm pinching the skin a little, but I don't let go.

Things may have felt out of control only a few hours ago when I'd lost my composure. But I'm proud of myself for having turned things around in just a few hours. I enjoy the sense of control it gives me. Like a puppet master, everyone jumps when I tell them to. I stand and grab our plates.

"Honey, why don't you go and lie down upstairs, and I'll bring you a book to read if you want?" I offer.

"Sure, that sounds really nice. I'm very tired suddenly." As if on cue, she yawns and stands carefully.

I watch her go, pondering if I should help her up the stairs, but afraid I might insult her by offering. I hope she knows to ask me if she needs help. I'm more than happy to provide it. But I also know she's stubborn, and I don't want to take this small independence away from her.

I finish cleaning the dishes and wiping the table, grab a book from the bookshelf, lock the doors and shut all the lights off before climbing up the stairs after her, feeling my steps lighter than they were the last time I ventured upstairs with despair and guilt weighing on my shoulder. Now, I'm grinning and optimistic with a skip in my step. We have a plan. A little family vacation will get us back into shape and help us to get out of this funk we're in. I can hardly wait.

Chapter 12
GEMMA

The next couple of weeks fly by so quickly, they're almost a blur.

The days are filled with physiotherapy appointments, list making, and packing for our trip, not to mention the girls' end of the year Spirit Week activities. Each day they need to wear different colours to honour whatever the theme is for the day. It's been a struggle to find the right shade of blue and green for Earth Day, purple for Lollipop Day, pink for Friendship Day, yellow for Honesty Day and orange for Silly Day. Beatrice went to school with dozens of braids in her hair and her clothes mis-matched. Amber decided to go dressed in what she deems 'preppy' clothes. It's her own way of rebelling against the crowd. She's being ironic or something like that.

Niall has been working long hours as the market has picked up in the last few weeks.

I worry that he'll have to work during our vacation, but he assures me Yvonne will manage the office just fine without him and that he'll check his email periodically to pacify his boss, just in case a crisis arises.

I didn't want to admit how badly we were in need of a vacation until we were getting ready for it. I'd been in denial, pretending all was fine, that the mundane routine and scenery wasn't taking its toll on my mental health, but I can't deny the appeal of going somewhere new. I feel rejuvenated.

Even though the timing isn't great with my recent injury, I'm looking forward to it—the whole family spending quality time together in the fresh air. It's just what we need right now. I'm slightly apprehensive about the cabin we're staying at, but at the same time, I keep reminding myself that we'll be spending most of our time outdoors anyway so it doesn't really matter how rustic it is. As long as we have a place to sleep and wash up, we'll be fine.

The bitterness of getting rejected for every job I'd applied for has started to fade a little. Day by day, I'm making peace with my fate. The days of breaking records and reporting to superiors, travelling to make presentations, and meeting co-workers in the lunchroom were long gone. My work is at home now.

My world is my family. There was a time when that would have made me sad. When that wouldn't have been quite enough. But this is my only option. I'm an undesirable candidate—too old to start again with no relevant skills to contribute to a company. If anyone were to hire me, they would be taking a gamble. With my references long gone or retired, most likely unreachable, to say yes to me would require a leap of faith on their part.

Of course, *I* know that I would do a good job, but I'm not quite sure how to translate this to a future employer without ever getting the opportunity to prove myself. It feels like a desperate situation. In fact, I'm tired just thinking of it. Better to stick to what I know. There are so many women that would kill to be able to stay home with their children. I'm very grateful to have the chance to do it. And for the most part, it's the best job in the world. There's a lot to be grateful for, but it's lonely.

I miss seeing other people's faces, taking coffee breaks in the lunchroom, and driving to work with the music loud. Heck, I even miss traffic. It would be a nice change to my usual routine of vacuuming floors, cleaning bathrooms, and folding laundry. If I worked outside the home, I would be alone while executing my tasks, but at least there would be other people around—other adults to converse with regularly. Here, within the constraints of home, the only people I see other than my family are the UPS guy and occasionally, my neighbour from across the road when she steps out to walk the dog.

There was a time when the girls were little that I felt like playing with them—going to the park and dressing up in silly costumes kept me young. Now, I'm only 47, but I feel like I'm going on 70. My limbs are tired, and I lack the motivation to even go upstairs during the day. The long walk up seems daunting at best. The hallways appear to stretch endlessly, swallowing me up with every step, the silence deafening.

Abruptly, I stand up and switch on the radio and let the soothing music wash over me. The piano notes and lyrics envelop my every thought and take me away from this place for just a moment.

Already, I feel better. My chest is breathing normally again. I don't feel claustrophobic any longer. I don't know what I'd do without music.

Thinking about the cabin and the silence waiting for me there, I feel the panic rising once more. I grab my phone from the kitchen counter and begin to look for an app that might help me download some music to bring along with us.

It had taken me quite some time to organize the 'new' phone in a way that suited me. I'd spent hours downloading various apps; one to help me organize my grocery coupons, a step-tracker, and a slew of redundant social media apps. At first, I'd struggled to remember all my passwords for them, but I'd eventually succeeded. The device still feels strange in my hands but I'm getting accustomed to it and making it my own. There are a few folders that contain some of Niall's old files, but there is still quite a bit of memory left, so I haven't bothered to delete them.

I'd chosen an old family photo of us from our last holiday at the beach in Bermuda to use as my background image. It's a favourite of mine. We're all wearing crisp white clothes, looking sharp against the turquoise blue water behind us. The sand is so pale that if it weren't for Amber's and my dark hair, we'd have blended in completely with it. We girls are wearing matching loose-fitting, summer dresses and strappy sandals, while Niall looks handsome in a button-down white dress shirt and khaki shorts.

Putting the phone down on the kitchen counter, I sway my hips to the upbeat song that comes on and turn up the dial. Pharrell William's *Happy* blasts through the house and changes my morose mood almost immediately.

I remember the song from a *Despicable Me* movie the girls used to watch on a loop years ago. They were obsessed with those little minions, but seemingly overnight, they outgrew the movie and anything else belonging to their childhood.

Letting the beat fade away, I head down to the basement to retrieve my old, black suitcase. After removing it from a shelf, I unzip it to reveal a slightly smaller one nestled inside it like a set of little Russian dolls.

I'll put the smaller of the two in the hallway between the girls' rooms for them to fill with their things. We've long passed the days when I used to pack up their clothes for them. Nowadays, they are understandably very picky about which outfits they want to bring on vacation as most teenage girls likely are. Unfortunately, this usually leads to them fighting over the spare space in the front zipper pocket of the suitcase, cramming each inch of it so full the zippers might burst under the pressure of holding it together.

Unlike my girls, I was never a girly-girl, squealing over dresses with frilly bows and sequins. Tight-fitting clothes and make-up have never really been my thing. Rough around the edges and uncharacteristically confident, I'd stomp everywhere I went while belting out the wrong lyrics to popular songs without a care in the world that I was most often off-key.

Amber is like me that way. She's a natural beauty and doesn't require anything to make her stand out from others. She gets noticed. Her dazzling eyes grab attention everywhere she goes, and her wild mane of curls makes it almost impossible for her not to stand out. She doesn't even have to try. People recognize her just by looking at her. You don't forget a face like that.

I used to look like her once upon a time. I remember walking into a room and every head would turn. When you're effortlessly beautiful, especially in a unique way, people either hate you or love you for it. There's absolutely nothing you can do to influence it. It's not logical but simply a natural reaction.

People either want to protect it, to capture it for themselves, admire, and get near it, perhaps even become more like it, or they want to squash it, kill the threat, and resume their rightful place as superior beings. In my experience, most people can't handle the shine and try to scratch at it until it dulls—unfortunately for me and Amber.

I see her struggling and acting tough, like none of the comments and stares bother her. She tries so hard to pretend that she's completely unaffected by the negative attention she gets, but I know how she feels. That used to be me. Amber deals with it by attempting to make herself smaller and less obvious, but a girl like Amber will never easily blend in with a crowd—she can't. The best thing for her to do is to embrace her differences. She's a strong girl. She's had to be. I know she'll be okay. She just needs to survive high school first.

Niall told me about the suspension she received on the same day as my fall. I was disappointed but not entirely surprised. Amber had been winding up to something—her stress had been building up in the few days leading up to her suspension. It had shown in her increased irritation and rash movements—a bottle fizzy with bubbles, expanding beyond capacity. She has the tendency to act out rather than break down when things are bothering her. The trick is to give her the space to feel what she needs to feel and not get in the way.

I've often tried talking to her about how to express her emotions in a more positive way, but it usually backfires. That's just not who she is.

She can't help it—she's a sensitive child, even though she would be quick to refute that. Amber tends to feel things very deeply but doesn't know how to process those feelings. She's quick to get angry and lets her emotions build up to the point of explosion. You'll almost never see her cry. While Beatrice will cry into her pillow like a Disney princess, Amber would rather break things, slash a sword around, and scream into the empty void. For better or worse, my eldest is more prone to try and change her situation, take charge of it, grab it by the horns, tempt it to mess with her again, or else. She'd rather fight her pain—kick it, and scratch at it until her fingers bleed—than wallow in it. Refusing to be a victim of her circumstances, she'd rather die fighting.

We all have our own way of dealing with stress. We feel what we feel, but some methods used to regulate our moods are seen as more acceptable, less destructive, and quieter than others. Regrettably for Amber, her emotional release usually comes with destruction. Like a forest fire, it's not easily contained and destroys much in its path. And yet, sometimes, that's exactly what's necessary to start over again.

When I'd broached the subject of her most recent suspension, Amber wouldn't tell me who'd given her the *Salvia* hallucinogenic drug that she'd snuck out of third period to smoke behind the portables. She'd claimed she alone was responsible and that no one had been with her, forcing her to do it. She had no reason to lie, especially not to me.

I believed her, but it didn't mean I agreed with her choices. It also didn't explain how she obtained the drug in the first place—something to revisit later.

Still, I knew well enough now that grounding her would only wind her up once more and I needed Amber to be on her best behaviour until school was over. If not for her own sake, then for Beatrice's.

The poor girl deals with the fallout from Amber's outbursts. Her quiet demeanour is often overshadowed by her sister's regularly angry disposition. Bea often gets forgotten, not because we don't love her the same, but because she usually does what she's told and doesn't seek trouble. We trust her to be on her best behaviour even when no one is looking. I can't say the same for Amber, however. Experience has taught me never to leave her to her own devices.

Instead of punishing Amber for getting suspended, once again, I decided to try a tactic that used to work with her when she was younger—something called *heavy work*. Apparently, the act of lifting and pushing heavy things can help people feel calmer. Anything causing a certain resistance could work.

I remember a mother mentioning the tactic to me at a playgroup when Amber was just a toddler. I'd rushed home to try it right away, so excited to have something constructive to try to help Amber release her excess energy. Nothing else I'd tried before seemed to work with her. Scolding her only brought out a vicious determination in her spirit, as though I'd just provoked her, providing the perfect challenge—a dare she just had to prove she could do.

Everything in my mind had to switch gears. My instincts were wrong for her. My discipline methods were ancient. I had to start from scratch.

I spent many evenings staying up late, scouring the internet for blogs and advice, reading up on spirited children and discipline tactics. I remember being utterly surprised to learn of this new one. I'd been so desperate and grateful when, at last, it had seemed to work.

I'd kept using it even as Amber grew older. Every time I noticed her getting too worked up or needing some sort of release, I'd remind her of her breathing exercises and physical activity, but also provide something more hands-on with heavy work in mind.

Instead of punishing Amber, tightening the noose in response to her actions, forcing her to acknowledge that her mistakes had to her suspension, I'd asked Amber to help me plant some flowers in the front garden. Shovelling heaps of dirt and stabbing the ground—the repetition and physical effort, bending, digging, and planting under the hot sun—had turned out to be the perfect activity to help her release the tension of the suspension.

It had offered her uninterrupted time to think and process. The task had kept her mind busy and focused on a goal. Whereas most kids, like Beatrice, would have benefitted from some time alone in their room to regroup, to perhaps read a book or play a quiet game, the silence would have simply had the opposite effect and pushed Amber to the edge of an already crumbling cliff.

Amber craves noise. She needs to keep her hands busy, or they might find more trouble to grab onto. Leaving her alone in her room would have been a very bad idea indeed.

Amber acted on impulse, never taking the time to consider the implications of her actions, only feeling the emotions as they charged through her body.

Since there aren't many varieties of heavy work around here, I'd had to improvise, resorting to asking her to bring the laundry basket upstairs for me or periodically getting her to rotate her mattress as a last resort. If she suspected my method, she hadn't yet mentioned it. It's not a secret or anything, but it's a trick I plan on keeping under my belt for as long as I possibly can.

Tomorrow, we will make our way to the cabin.

There is a lot left to do, but there is a vibrant energy in the house. Like the building has its own heartbeat, as though it's a living thing. The music seems to get everyone excited and out of their rooms like a siren call. With the suitcases opened and dusted off, I watch as Amber comes out of the bathroom with a towel over her hair twisted into a large mass on the top of her head. She swiftly tip toes over to her tall dresser and, extracting items at random, begins to throw clothes into the void of the suitcase. Some items land half inside and half out of it, as though they're trying to avoid coming along on our trip.

Beatrice quickly joins in, carefully folding each piece before finding a suitable spot for it amongst Amber's mess of fabric. Everyone moves around, filling space with noise and luggage with belongings. It makes me smile. My home and my heart are full of sounds, joy, and love.

I'm struck by how different my girls are from one another. Watching from the stairs in silence, I'm in utter awe of them. How I could have created two vastly different people amazes me.

With the chaos of items being thrown into the luggage, it will be astonishing if Amber remembers to pack enough clean underwear for the week. I inch my way up the stairs but hold back. She's almost an adult now. She has to do this herself this time. I've promised myself not to get involved in her packing. If she forgets anything, as hard as it is for me to watch, I have to let her make her own mistakes.

Chapter 13
Amber

Throwing a bunch of bathing suits and tank tops in the mix of clothing to bring to the cabin, I remember that the air is usually a little cooler near lakes and grab my favourite warm, cream-coloured knitted sweater from the back of the chair. Padding over to my dresser, I open a drawer and select a few scrunchies to bring along, throwing them inside a small zippered bag along with some simple studded earrings that will go with everything. I throw in a statement-sized turquoise ring set in gold that compliments my tanned skin.

Most of the clothes I've chosen are either linen white or bright coral as I find they make my eyes stand out the most. I've also packed a nice silk green tank top with detailed embroidery on the top for good measure as it can easily be dressed up or down.

After strapping on a delicate gold anklet to my foot, I pick out a plain gold chain. Both items are simple enough, making it easy to keep on during the whole trip. I grab a pair of thick sweatpants for the cooler nights, as well as jean shorts for the warmer days. At the last moment, I decide to add one sun dress and a pair of dressy sandals to my heap.

Pleased with my progress, I glance at Beatrice, who's still folding her clothes carefully, kneeling on the floor beside the suitcase. Her perfectly folded items fit snuggly together.

When she starts folding her underwear, I have to hold back my laughter. Who bothers to fold their underwear? But then I remember, *oh shit,* I'd almost entirely forgotten to pack some!

At last, it looks like everything is in order.We have everything we need. My stuff is stacked on one side, practically tumbling over, while Bea's side is nicely organized and tidy as expected.

No one expected me to fold everything neatly, but I bet everyone predicted that I'd forget to pack something. Who could blame them? I usually do. But I've made sure to pack lots of options. I'm ready for any weather.

Typically, I dread the way packing for a vacation increases my anxiety levels, making me suddenly have to be choosy with my wardrobe, forcing me to admit which pieces are my favourite, which pieces go with everything or pick out those that are the most comfortable to wear. It's the closest I'll ever get to having a minimalist wardrobe because once we leave, this suitcase will be all I have for an entire week! I needed to choose carefully.

Noticing Beatrice has packed a few books, I scoff. I don't plan on reading anything during this holiday, but I do pack my iPod. I can't live without my music for an entire week—it's essential.

Dad is outside mowing the lawn before we leave tomorrow. Mom had asked him to cancel the newspaper delivery for the week, as well as set up our timer for the sprinkler system to make sure the lawn doesn't dry out while we're away. God forbid we'd come home to uneven patches of yellow grass on the front yard for all to see how unkept and messy the Richardsons truly are.

Stepping downstairs for a snack, I watch Mom busily moving around in the kitchen, unable to stay still, like me. She's filling a large Rubbermaid tub with a few essentials. Reaching the kitchen table, I peer in to see a roll of extra-absorbent paper towels, a container of lavender and vanilla-scented hand soap, a pair of scissors, a few freshly laundered dishtowels, a lighter, an aerosol can of bug spray, and several other useful items. She's always so prepared.

I watch her quick movements and I can't help feeling exhausted by her seemingly unrelenting energy. She'll need a vacation to rest from preparing for her vacation.

"Did you finish packing, sweetheart?" she looks up briefly, just in time to catch me nodding in reply.

"All done and ready to go," I add, smiling brightly up at her, my pride evident in my upturned smile.

"Awesome!" She beams at me. If she's surprised, she hides it well, pretending she had no doubts about my success in the first place.

"I'm all packed as well, but I expect your dad still needs to add a few items before we can zip up the suitcase," she winks at me, and I chuckle knowingly.

Dad always waits until the last possible minute to start packing. In his defence, he always claims to need way less than the three of us seem to need on vacation often going on about how he has no problem wearing the same clothes all week long, stating that a family vacation isn't a fashion show. But the man seems to forget he lives in a house full of girls.

Knowing my mom, I'm sure she's made sure to pack a few extra socks and boxers for him in the zip-up section of the suitcase. She doesn't want to insult him by packing for him as though he were just another one of her children, but she also wants to make sure he'll be taken care of and won't be missing anything.

She used to do that for me too, but she made it clear this time that I had to pack my own suitcase—a *rite of passage* she'd called it. She'd been clear that she wouldn't double-check to see if I'd left anything out. She's trying to let go and I can see how hard it is for her to do so.

Looking out the window, I squint, noticing that the sky is covered with bright, white clouds, not one blue splotch poking out to hint at the sky existing beyond.

The maple and oak tree leaves tremble on their branches like they are holding on with shaky fingers, about to let go, abandon all hope and float away with the wind. The tall pine trees are bending like licorice sticks.

I worry that some of the smaller trunks are about to snap under the pressure. It's almost like the tops of the trees are trying to reach down to the pinecones that fell to the ground in the last sharp burst of wind.

I'm stunned, frozen in place. It had been so warm and sunny the last few weeks that I'd almost forgotten how the hot summer days often bring along the bigger storms. Almost like the weather is at war, constantly fighting for a comfortable balance.

It's impressive really, watching the way those trees bend so low, their limbs almost skirting the tops of the lawn. They sway in unison from one side to the other without breaking. It's almost like they are dancing to the soft melody of a dark lullaby, in a trance, being hypnotized into releasing their hold, giving way to the next season.

A sense of dread creeps over me as I watch from the warm, fully lit kitchen. I can't help but worry that the rest of the week will follow suit. It won't be much of a vacation if the rain forces us to remain indoors the entire time. I've been so looking forward to swimming in the lake, feeling the hot sun kiss my skin, desperate to get a glowing tan. The wind howls against the windowpane taunting me to stop it, but I know there's nothing I can do. The weather is a wild, unpredictable thing, no matter what most meteorologists might seem to believe—it cannot be tamed or explained.

Peeling my eyes from the darkening windows, I make a choice. Rain or shine, I will make the most of this vacation. The prospect of being near water, even if only just for a week, has me feeling like a child on Christmas eve.

After the year I've had, I could really use an escape right now. This trip is coming at the perfect time for me. I won't let anything, or anyone spoil it.

Chapter 14
Beatrice

We drive along the country roads away from town. There aren't many houses out here. I like to imagine that people prefer having a lot of land around their homes, as it offers them some privacy from the nearest neighbours. The strong smell of manure blows in through the car's vents. It clings to my hair. Dad smells it too, and I see him wrinkling his nose in disgust as he turns on the air recirculation to try and stop the car from smelling like a barnyard, but he's too late.

Fallen down, rotten fenceposts line the edges of the fields, doing a poor job of keeping the crops from spilling over into the deep ditches. I catch glimpses of blurry green fields through my window as gravel crunches beneath the tires.

The sound is a constant groan, almost like white noise. My eyelids are getting heavier, the sound of the car is making me sleepy. The glare of the sky makes it hard to look out at the passing scenery.

I'm no expert on farming, but from the looks of it, we are driving by what might grow to be corn one day. Another field is full of long grass that might just be unkept fields. Despite my dad's efforts, the smell inside the car gets stronger as we near a field filled with black and white cows which Dad informs us are called Holsteins. A few farms down we drive by another field, this one home to especially large horses, some running wild through the fields around the property. The sight is amazing and I can't look away.

My earbuds slide out from my ears and I push them back in. The wire keeps getting caught in my loose hair every time I turn to look out the window. I've got a book open across my lap—*Little Women*, a classic. Even though reading in a moving car makes me sleepy, I'm really enjoying it. Other than the Harry Potter books, this will be one of the longest books I've ever read. I'm looking forward to checking this one off my list of reading goals for the year. I'm several books ahead this year already, but I want to see just how many more I can fit in before the year's end.

Normally, I'd be reading as much as possible during the long drive, taking advantage of the time to read a few chapters and get ahead but this time, I'm enjoying the calm drive and just looking out the window. The cabin isn't far enough for any of us to have a chance to get restless or start complaining. Everyone looks quite happy, lost in daydreams as we stare out over the flat land. Fences of trees divide one field from the other, as though the different shades of yellow and green wasn't obvious enough to tell them apart.

The sky has turned a shade darker since we left the house. It will probably rain soon. I hope the clouds will clear up and let some sunlight through. I've been looking forward to reading outside by the lake.

Catching sight of a rundown barn abandoned and leaning in the middle of a field like the weight of the world is on its shoulders, I'm struck by the beauty of the broken-down building. The dark wood structure stands out perfectly next to the golden grass, turning it instantly into a work of art in my eyes. It's no longer a rotting building about to collapse under its own weight, but rather, a place that holds stories that need to be kept, cared for and remembered.

It once kept farm machinery from getting rained on, protecting them from rusting, but now, the building has been left alone and forgotten in the middle of a field. I notice a patch of grass growing shorter around it as though it was unable to get enough sun, probably because of the building casting a shadow on it. A bird rests on the remaining slabs of wood that make up the roof. Still, the barn is holding on, keeping space. It almost seems to have a personality with all its angles, broken parts, and fading panels. It might be falling apart, but it still exists.

As we approach the barn, I feel inspired to capture it.

"Mom, can I borrow your phone?" I ask hastily, afraid of missing the opportunity. "I want to take a picture," I explain, reaching out my hand to collect the phone.

"Of course, hon," she smiles. "Here you go."

I don't have my own phone yet, but I've asked my parents to get me one for my birthday this year. Turning thirteen seems like a good age to gain some independence.

Not that I expect to get that many messages, but just having something normal that everyone else in my grade seems to have might help me fit in better at school.

I quickly lower my window, gripping the phone in my hand. I angle it slightly, trying to capture some of the barn, a border of the grass for a splash of colour, while making sure to include a large part of the sky in the frame. I snap the picture. Happy with it, I click on the gallery see the photo. Expanding the image, I'm pleased to see all the colours working perfectly together.

Minimizing the image by pinching it on the screen, I notice that another picture sits beside it in the gallery. The image is hard to make-out and strangely bright like there's a sunray coming through it. Curious, I'm about to ask Mom about it, but I realize she and Dad are in the middle of a conversation and I don't want to interrupt.

Instead, I zoom in on the image again and instantly recognize my dad's wedding band. His thick sausage fingers are resting casually on someone's shoulder. I startle when I realize that the shoulder does not belong to Mom, but rather to my dad's co-worker, Yvonne. I recognize her blond hair against her shoulder, which almost looks white in the bright picture.

The gesture is innocent enough, I guess. I can easily come up with a dozen reasons why they would have a picture together. They are co-workers after all. And yet, something bothers me. There's something about the picture that makes my skin prickle with shame. Almost like I've opened the door on a private moment frozen in time.

I don't think I was ever meant to find this image, but it's pretty strange that Dad kept it on this phone—the one he fished-out for Mom to use when hers shattered on the floor after her fall.

Mom would easily be able to see that the picture is not of herself. Does Dad honestly not remember that the picture still lives on this phone? Or does he, on some level, want Mom to discover it? If Mom has already seen the picture, why hasn't she said anything about it or deleted it? Maybe there is a reasonable explanation for this picture that they haven't shared with me, but I doubt it.

It's the closeness between Dad and Yvonne that has me holding my breath. I exit the photo app, feeling suddenly grossed out by the phone. I feel like throwing it out the window to protect Mom from ever finding it. Of course, I could just delete it, but then the proof would be gone.

Hesitantly, I quietly hand the phone back without changing anything. I hope Mom won't notice how red my cheeks are. My skin is so pale, almost milky looking, that any splash of colour would immediately give me away like Pinocchio's nose. I'm not good at hiding my emotions, but I've perfected holding back rather than acting on them. Looking down at my skinny hands, the fingers twisted together awkwardly over my bare, pale thighs, I'm shocked by how unhealthy my skin looks. Like I need more reasons to be picked on!

I'm already odd-looking, with gangly arms and legs, large, rounded knees and sharp elbows. I don't need the world to know what I'm thinking all the time, giving away all my secrets, my body betraying me. With my eyes cast down, I take in the sight of my puny breasts—two little mounds of skin that barely poke through my shirt. I don't really need to wear a bra, but I still do, hopeful that I'll grow into it someday.

I feel like the ugly duckling, and I can't wait until I turn into a beautiful swan. At least, I hope I will someday. Not everyone is lucky enough to get good genes like Amber.

I turn my head to look at her. She seems quite happy, bobbing her head along to some song blasting in her earbuds, flipping through her phone updating her various social media accounts. Little red and blue bubbles keep popping up, lighting up her phone with new notifications. It's hard for me not to feel jealous, but then I catch myself wondering how many of those notifications are from friends.

As far as I know, Amber doesn't have all that many friends. She tends to rub people the wrong way. Where most girls her age are always pointing out their physical flaws, Amber is constantly showing off her strengths. She knows she's gorgeous and doesn't feel the need to tamp it down to make anyone feel better about themselves.

I wish I had half the confidence she has. To go through life not giving a crap about what everyone else thinks of you—now that would be a welcome change. I can only imagine how free it would feel to have expectations set so low that you can only go up. It would be a welcomed change to the pressures I face to always be so perfect.

Unlike Amber, I am never allowed to slip up and fail. Not even once. I don't even want to think about how bad it would be if I messed up. My parents have placed all their hopes on me to be the perfect child. It's a heavy burden to bear. The amount of pressure I feel each and every day is enough to make me go crazy.

As part of my parents' expectations, I brush my hair one hundred times a day, wash my face obsessively so I won't get any pimples, brush my teeth for a minimum of two minutes twice a day each day, floss until my gums bleed, and keep my room meticulously tidy. I'm never late, almost never miss any school, and get above average grades. They expect me to be friendly and helpful to everyone, as well as thoughtful, athletic, smart, and funny. It's exhausting.

I've worked so hard to be a well-rounded person. Over time I've barely allowed myself to be a normal human being. Somewhere along the way, I've forgotten that it's okay to mess up once in a while and make mistakes. I find it interesting to see how little people care about what goes on beneath the surface when I appear fully put together. I work hard to hide the scars beneath my ironed clothes. It never stops to amaze me just how well I can pretend or how I manage to fool them all with a simple smile.

In that sense, I've got it way easier than Amber. She just looks like trouble and doesn't care to correct how others might see her. She always says that you can't change how others view you, so why lie to yourself? She does what she wants when she wants to and doesn't care about what anyone else thinks.

I have a hard time with it as her carefree attitude makes my life harder, even on the best of days. At least I'm in control of my own actions. I can keep things close and choose what I show others. But Amber's thoughts and moods are always on display.

It's like she's a rare exhibit at a museum, placed inside a glass case in the centre of a room, highlighting every angle while I'm the mummified pharaoh in a dark corner of the room, wrapped in layers of cloth, hidden from view.

I wouldn't dare to live as exposed as Amber does. I'm totally fine with only showing the perfected parts of myself.

But if I'm honest, I would like a few people to see the real me. It's starting to be hard to breathe under all these layers of fabric I've wrapped around myself. Maybe it's not as safe inside as I thought. Maybe it's time people take notice of who I am beneath it all. I have a voice of my own and I'm tired of staying silent all the time, worried I might trip over my words and embarrass myself. Perfect is overrated and I'm struggling to keep up with it. I'm suffocating here. I'm ready to step out from under my big sister's shadow as there's more to me than meets the eye.

There was a time when following Amber around made me feel safe and protected, a time when I preferred when no one knew me or when I could easily blend in unnoticed, but now I can see how not speaking up for myself made people fill in the blanks and assume things that might not be true about me. It's time to change that.

I'm ready for people to know me and to see me, all of me. I'm terrified but I know I need to do this.

Chapter 15
GEMMA

The car is completely silent. The radio is turned off, and there is just the steady sound of the wheels driving us forward. The girls are both content and calm, each listening to their own tunes, white earbuds snug in their ears. Amber's fingers move rapidly over her phone screen, and I wonder for a moment who she's texting. I've been so out of touch with her lately.

Niall's hands lay relaxed on the top of the steering wheel for once. He's not drumming to a beat from inside his own head but appears peaceful, enjoying the drive. Staring out the window, I'm eager to see the place we'll be staying for the next week. The sun has been trying to poke through the thick, dense-looking clouds, shining a ray of light here and there, giving us hope. But so far it's only teasing us.

The directions to reach the cabin are so simple that I'm doubtful that we'll actually find it. There's no set address and our GPS didn't recognize the location, so instead we had to choose a nearby street and follow Niall's friend's very precise instructions.

'Turn right at the fork by the willow tree. Turn left at the red gate. Turn left again at the blue mailbox. Then go over the small, wooden bridge, and look for a small, printed sign nailed to an old oak tree. Turn right when the gravel road turns to sand. If you've hit the water, you've gone too far.'

The crinkled print-out with the directions lies across my lap, my hands gripping it like it might fly out through the window and leave us stranded in the woods. I have to laugh at the absurdity of these directions. I didn't realize people actually did this in real life. I make a mental note to recommend better road markers for future vacation renters. Otherwise, people might assume they've been sent on a wild goose chase and hoping they get out of these woods and find the cabin before the sun goes down.

My voice is hushed, almost a whisper as I relay the directions to Niall. We can hear the faint sound of gravel as we drive along. The road is getting narrower and the trees denser. We must be getting closer.

I'd quickly given up on the accuracy of the GPS navigation as it can't seem to pick up a proper signal. I'm relying on a good, old-fashioned paper map instead. I follow along our route with my finger, surprised to feel excitement building at the prospect of spotting the lake soon. I'd been doubtful, even dreaded this trip, but now I'm undeniably curious.

I stretch my neck, trying to catch a glimpse of the water through the trees, but the foliage is too thick and completely obscures my view. We pass by a couple walking an old golden retriever. The dog's steps are slow and measured. There's a small limp in one of his back legs. The three of them waddle along, seemingly affected by similar ailments in their hips. Niall steers towards the shoulder, giving them a wide berth. The roof of the car hits a few low-hanging branches as we slow to a crawl.

I ease my window down and breathe in the fresh air. The scent of pine needles and cedar trees hit my nostrils, tickling them and I hold back a sneeze. The faint, familiar odor of lake water hits me next. The air is humid and thick, bordering on tropical. It's warming up.

I try to look up at the sky, but once again, my vision is blocked by trees heavy with leaves. Based on the way my hair is frizzing into wild, unkempt curls all over my head, I can practically sense how heavy the air is, like a thick wall of heat full of static and energy. I wouldn't be surprised if there was a thunderstorm tonight. The ground here is dry, and there's no sign of the rainfall we experienced yesterday. How strange is it that we live only about an hour away from this place and have such varying climates?

"Here we are!" Niall suddenly exclaims, bringing my attention back to the front of the car. He's pointing out as though I might doubt him. "There's the cabin! Do you see it?" he asks me, and my eyes follow his finger.

The girls remove their earbuds and inch closer towards the middle of the back seat, trying to get a better view. Their puzzled expressions match mine.

"Niall, are you sure this is it?" my voice is apprehensive and cautious, just on the small chance this has all been a joke; the wonky directions, the narrow path, and the *piece de resistance*, this atrocious looking shed that he's calling a cabin. Any moment now, I expect him to slap his thigh and laugh at us, pointing, "You should see your faces!" But he doesn't.

Without uttering a word, Niall nods slowly, carefully. He turns to look at me, an apology in his eyes. His mouth twists briefly as though he's embarrassed. He can't be serious!

Unconvinced, I stare once again at the hideous building, my mouth open. I feel like I've been duped, and my blood pressure begins to skyrocket. I want to stomp my feet in protest like Amber used to do when she was little. Such a primitive response to being wronged. I can feel myself losing my cool.

I watch in disbelief as Niall parks the car several feet from the building. I'm still holding my breath, hoping that this has all been a terrible joke, one we'll laugh about for years to come. I'm just waiting for the punchline. Perhaps this is the garage, and the cabin is down below, right on the water? Somehow, I'm doubtful.

We all sit there looking out the window, dread creeping over me as I realize that this is the place we're meant to be staying after all. I swallow and feel my throat closing up. I need a drink. I force myself to breathe. *Don't panic. This is fine. Everything is going to be alright.* I don't sound very convincing, even to myself.

A large pine tree looms over the cabin, making it look like a doll house in comparison. Its branches extend far beyond the other side of the roof, like long claws trapping prey within their grasp. The slipshod roof of the cabin makes me cringe.

It seems there has been no care or maintenance whatsoever to this place in years. The neglect is evident and sad. Such wasted potential.

The wood exterior is in dire need of a fresh coat of stain to keep it from rotting away. The windows, surprisingly all intact, show obvious signs of condensation.

There are yellow strips affixed to the ledge of each window to catch flies—some unlucky ones are trapped already giving the strip a disgusting polka dot look. I can't hide my disdain and feel my mouth scowl as I take in the sights.

"Alright, so it's a little more rustic than Tim claimed, I admit. He might have exaggerated the place slightly." Niall sighs heavily. "A lot, from the looks of it."

I puff out some air feeling irritated. It's a wonder Tim's a respected realtor around here. Knowing he could spin a lie like that, I wouldn't trust him to find my next home.

Clasping his hands together, Niall adds in his most cheerful tone, "We'll just have to make the best of it."

"You've got to be kidding me," I scoff, not bothering to hide my condescension. I hate how I sound to my own ears, slightly frightened but also indignant, as though I couldn't possibly be caught dead in a place like this.

"It'll be like camping, just a little more sheltered." Niall is trying to make light of things, always being his positive self, but this time, his breeziness only irritates me more. "Look at it this way, at least it will be cheap to stay here for the week!" He laughs half-heartedly.

"You can't be serious, Niall," I exclaim, the panic rising once again. My eyes are wide in horror as I stare at my husband. Is he really contemplating that we stay as though all is fine? "Just look at this place!" I'm nearly screaming at him, and I have to take several breaths to calm down. "There is absolutely no way we're staying here tonight, let alone the whole week!" I say with as much authority I can muster, knowing full well that I'm not the one who usually governs our household. Still, I have the right to speak my mind. What is Niall thinking? This is absolutely insane.

To drive home my point, I add, "Even if we wanted to, there's no way all of us can even fit inside this...this shed!" My voice is the squeaky high pitch it only reaches when I'm on the verge of a panic attack.

"Okay, hon. Okay. Deep breaths. Look at me." Niall's heard it too. His soothing tone beckons me to look at his face, his calm demeanour bringing me down. "There, that's it." He kisses the top of my head gently and takes my hand. "Look, I know this isn't what any of us had in mind for our vacation." He glances at the backseat where the girls are looking down at their knees, annoyed, and understandably disappointed. "But I still think we can make the best of it. We came here to enjoy the lake, to get away from the grind of our regular routines, and to spend time together as a family. I would love if all of you just tried it, even just for one night. If it's absolutely horrible, we'll cross it off as the worst night we've ever had, but what if it's not? What if it turns out to be not so bad?"

His boyish wonder and reasoning are contagious and I can practically see it begin to seep into the girls. Suddenly, they are nodding along, his words winning them over. I have no choice but to follow their lead and, against my better judgement, I agree.

"Alright!" He claps his hands, triumphant. "That's what I'm talking about!" Unlatching his seatbelt, he opens the car door and steps out.

Reluctantly, we follow suit.

I'm wearing a long, plain, black maxi dress with a high-low feature, exposing more of the front of my legs than the back. The back of the dress floats behind me, dancing along in the slowly increasing wind.

A small shiver runs over my bare arms and I rub them to warm them up. The air is definitely cooler up here. I should have grabbed my sweater before stepping out of the car. Absentmindedly, I tug at my necklace, pulling it out from hiding beneath the conservative round boatneck design, which allows only a slight peek of my collarbones.

My hair is swept up in a low, messy bun with a few stray wavy strands floating around my head like a halo. Although the dress is basic and void of colour, I feel like I've made an extra effort today. I very rarely wear dresses anymore, but this vacation seemed like as good an excuse as any to wear one. This dress in particular is one of my favourite casual dresses as the fabric doesn't easily show wrinkles and the loose fit hides everything.

I'm grateful that the dress doesn't hug my body, so I don't need to worry about any of my bones showing. I know I've lost a worrisome amount of weight—from stress or the general lack of accomplishment that clings to me daily—but I certainly don't need to draw attention to it. My weight loss is nothing to gloat about.

Making an extra effort, I'd even applied a bit of make-up this morning before leaving, taking great care to swipe a coat of black mascara over my thick lashes and brushing on a bit of peach-coloured blush over my cheeks. I've finished the natural look with a sweet-smelling vanilla balm for my lips. Just as I'd hoped, my efforts make me look put-together, while not trying too hard. It helps me feel more confident, more like the younger version of myself.

My sandaled feet find a bed of dead pine needles. Their orange tint makes it almost appear as if an old shaggy carpet is leading the way to the cabin. The amount of them is astonishing, it's hard to see any sand or gravel beneath. They are surprisingly soft to walk on, dampening the sound of my steps as I meander along behind my family.

A pine needle jabs into my big toe, surprising me. I let out a small yelp and abruptly stop in my tracks to massage my injured foot. Gritting my teeth, I press on, more carefully this time, each step more hesitant than before.

This place was said to have breathtaking views at the back of the cabin, but I'm expecting Niall's friend embellished that description as well. If the front of the cabin is any indication, I'm doubtful that I'll be pleasantly surprised or even impressed by what's to come. I wonder if the derelict appearance of the cabin is meant as a ruse, a tactic to blend into the forest, making it less appealing, discouraging onlookers from getting too curious.

I gaze at the back of Amber's head and reflect on how my daughter puts on a tough exterior for the world to see when she's so much more than that. Her strength makes her seem unstoppable, even dangerous at times. She's often noticed due to her fierceness, but what most people don't know is how sensitive she is.

She's not just one thing. Her edges are sharp and she's quick to put you in your place, but she's also got a kind heart. Like a lioness, Amber would fight against any threat to protect those she cares about, without considering her own safety in the process. She gets that from me.

My eyes swell with tears as I admire her, thinking about how much she's grown lately, and the struggles she's had to get through. She's so resilient. But I wonder if she's thriving or only surviving.

I watch her walk over the pine needles, crushing them under her feet, never once worrying about those sharp needles poking through her sandals. I sigh. She may look all grown up, but she's still a child, oblivious to the dangers surrounding her.

It makes me happy to see that there are still remnants of my little girl in there. Her wonder and desire for adventure can't simply be snuffed out by age. Her eyes take in everything around her, and I wish for just a moment that I read her thoughts. I'm sure they wouldn't be what I expect, but I wish I could hear them all, and not miss anything.

Most of the time, I can just look at her and guess what she's thinking. It's spooky in a way, the link we share, like an invisible thread keeping our thoughts connected at all times.

I imagine it comes with the territory and that most mothers feel this way about their children. I secretly love having this bond with my girls. It keeps me in tune with what's going on in their lives. Although I experience this with both of my daughters, the link is undeniably stronger with Amber. I've just always attributed it to her being my first born, but perhaps it's simpler than that. Maybe it's the fact that Amber's personality is the most similar to mine, therefore, she's easier for me to understand.

I know something's happened between her and Niall recently, but I haven't been able to put my finger on it. Amber usually doesn't hide anything from me, but when I'd asked her about it, she'd remained quiet. We don't keep secrets from each other, so I assume it's not because she's embarrassed about something, but rather, my gut tells me that she's trying to protect her dad. Otherwise, she'd spill whatever was on her mind, without reserve. So, the fact that she's keeping this—whatever 'this' is—to herself worries me. If we end up staying here for the week, maybe the change of scenery and being surrounded by nature will give me the opportunity to talk to her about it again.

Chapter 16
GEMMA

Creaky, uneven stairs moan under our weight and I wonder if it's a bad idea for all of us to be standing on them at the same time. The small porch spreads across the entire front of the cabin. There's barely any room for a rocking chair on here. Some of the pressure-treated boards look rotten through, and some others appear to be bloated after years of being out in the elements. An old, cracked, terra cotta clay pot sits on one end of the porch with a beautiful arrangement of freshly planted deep pink petunias huddled together amongst several strands of Solomon's seal's rich green foliage—a nice touch, but very much like putting lipstick on a pig.

Standing before the locked door, we wait, crammed tightly in the small space like we're on a city bus during rush hour. Finally, Niall locates the key under a decorative ceramic mushroom next to the flowerpot. The figurine is almost unrecognizable.

The long-ago bright-red top is faded to a barely-there shade of pale pink. Beatrice, always helpful, holds the shredded screen door open. The groaning sound of the door makes me jump as a sense of foreboding creeps its way through me.

This is not a good idea. We should leave. We don't need to be here.

Thoughts swirl through my mind. Automatically, I begin expecting the worst, whatever that might be. A dead squirrel in the middle of the floor, a broken window making way for a bird to build their nest in the ceiling, or perhaps even a family of cockroaches feasting in a forgotten overflowing garbage can.

Taking a deep breath, Niall turns the key almost ceremonially and pushes open the door. *Here we go*, I think, closing my eyes briefly, readying myself as best as I can for whatever might come next.

To my pleasant surprise, the place isn't at all what I had expected. It's not a five-star hotel by any means, but it's not as atrocious as I'd first imagined. The simple, tasteful design makes my breathing become more even and I start to relax. The cabin is almost charming in its simplicity.

The flowery scent of lavender fills the space. Beautiful orange and yellow Gerbera daisies stand tall inside a white, porcelain farmhouse pitcher, placed in the centre of a round, wooden kitchen table, tastefully painted in the soothing shade of mint green. The table is adorned with a complimentary assortment of wooden arch spindle back chairs, painted in buttercream, ivory, mustard yellow, and robin's egg blue. The kitchen table sits in the centre of the space dividing the open-concept room into a kitchen and living space. The tension melts away with every step I take.

Yes, I think. *I can do this. This place isn't so bad.*

The walls are painted an off-white, creamy colour, adding brightness and airiness to the space. There are splashes of Dutch-blue flower print designs in the fabric of the curtains and the tea-towel hanging from the stove's handle. A few royal blue plates decorate the walls, adding a cottage-chic feel to the space.

The floors are slightly scratched, rustic, wide plank hardwood flooring covered in a dark stain, which adds warmth to the design. I smile, both pleased and impressed. Whoever decorated this space definitely has style. The kitchen, recently remodeled by the looks of it, has flawless cream-toned cabinets and is host to a large, white, farmhouse sink sitting beneath a deep-set window overlooking the water. There are open wooden shelves above the lower cabinets. Thick, dark butcher block countertops match the shelves above, definitely a popular style for modern farmhouses these days.

Piles of white plates and bowls are nicely displayed beside an array of clear water and wine glasses. Beneath the sink is a checkered blue and white curtain, presumably fastened there to hide the garbage container or something equally unappealing. The drawers have modern, cast-iron black door handles. There is stunning dark wood trim around each window, framing the outside view like a precious painting. A delicate backsplash of pale-yellow square tiles lines the counters, not calling too much attention, but offering some added country charm.

A rusty rake head is fastened to the wall, where large, multi-coloured mugs hang above a small coffee bar area made from an old dresser, complete with cute, matching sugar and coffee containers and a modern coffee maker.

Right off the kitchen, next to an outdated, yet functional white fridge, is a set of double patio doors where there seems to be a decent-sized deck area from which to enjoy the view of the water.

Crossing the floor, I'm suddenly eager to see the rest of the space. My worries are quickly floating away and are being replaced by an overwhelming sense of shame at my earlier critical attitude. I had imagined it would be dark and dreary, but in fact, it's quite charming and clean, while still being welcoming and quaint.

I'm embarrassed by how I initially judged it, because in truth, the cabin is quite beautiful—on the inside at least. My cheeks warm at the thought of my initial discomfort. In fact, I'm pleased with the turn of events. It had been silly of me to react so strongly over the state of this place, almost bringing about a panic attack. To think I'd almost missed out on everything in front of me. My mouth forms a tight line. I'd been quick to dismiss the cabin before even seeing all of it. It's something I do too often, whether for self-preservation or fear of the unknown, I tend to reject things whenever they don't fit within the scope of the life I've carefully built.

As we continue with our tour of the cabin, we discover a minimalist four-piece bathroom with a white vessel sink sitting atop a stunning, small antique mint-green dresser. White towels have been rolled and placed in a wicker basket next to a small pyramid of toilet paper on the bottom shelf of the dresser. A spa-like touch.

The living space is modest, but comfortable. A sofa and several chairs face a small woodstove with a long chimney that stretches up to the ceiling. The woodstove is conveniently placed in the corner of the room, away from foot traffic, leaving enough space for snug furniture placement.

A woodpile sits arranged in a pyramid along with kindling, ready to be put to use. The prospect of reading by a crackling fire almost makes me giddy. I can't remember the last time I've had the chance to enjoy that.

The array of eclectic mis-matched furniture looks like it's either been passed down to the owners or carefully selected at yard sales. Even though the furniture has seemingly been collected over the years, it's obvious each item was chosen with intention as all the pieces manage to complement each other.

The light grey sofa is unimpressive, but perfectly acceptable, showing no signs of droopy, sunk-in cushions. This couch isn't new by any means, but it does have a cozy, worn-in feel to it. A nice mustard yellow chenille throw is draped over the back of the couch, making it homey and inviting. I'm pleased to notice a small bookshelf, stacked with old paperback novels propped-up on the wall next to the couch. Anticipation builds inside of me. I can't wait to survey them for hidden treasures.

Beside the living room and on either side of the single bathroom I'm surprised to find two adjoining bedrooms. They are small in size but absolutely respectable. The furniture in the rooms is outdated and lacks the flair of the rest of the cabin, but there's really nothing bad to say about it.

It's completely functional and tidy. There is no closet space to speak of but that hardly matters. Our clothing can remain in our suitcases for the duration of our stay. In fact, I usually prefer to do that regardless of where we're staying. I find it more sanitary that way—less chances of bringing home bed bugs or something equally unpleasant.

The owners have evidently given a lot of attention to the main area, focusing on making a good first impression. This isn't a hotel after all, but I'm satisfied that we'll have everything we could possibly need during our time here.

That had been one of my initial concerns when Niall had used the word *rustic* to describe the cabin. I'd never in a thousand years have imagined this kind of place. Maybe Niall was right. Perhaps this vacation won't be so bad after all. I sigh, releasing the hold on my expectations, determined to make the best of things, grateful to have a decent head start in that department. Anyone could feel comfortable and pleased to spend a vacation in a well-kept, attractive, little cabin like this.

Leaving the bedrooms, I follow the rest of my family out through the patio doors, stepping onto the deck, steeling myself for the view.

Chapter 17
Niall

I know I've won them over when I hear a chorus of awes and enthusiastic exclamations as we cross the threshold and enter the space. The cabin is a pleasant surprise, beautifully decorated, warm and welcoming. I'm so relieved that I finally allow myself to unclench my teeth and release my fists.

This is perfect. Everything will be just fine.

I can see the relief and approval in Gemma's wide eyes as they dart across the room, taking in the décor. The colours are even calming and appealing. I sigh. Thank God. Only minutes ago, Gemma had almost pushed me out of the driver's seat, put the car in reverse, and left me and this forsaken cabin in the dust, speeding away as quickly as she could.

Now, she's appraising the kitchen finishes, her fingers trailing over the dark countertops, and gently rubbing the fabric of the curtains between her thumb and forefingers. For her, a place has to *feel* good. That's how she knows if she'll be comfortable or not. How it looks is a close, secondary consideration. I'm proud of her for giving it a chance, and I'm fairly certain it's to her liking.

The appearance of the outside was enough to give her a fright, and swear me off from ever making any future vacation plans.

I'd definitely taken a risk, booking a place without first learning more about it, but in my mind, the whole ordeal was an opportunity to have an adventure—a chance to reconnect and create memories as a family. It would bind us together in an even stronger way, like we survived something, somehow.

I'm a little disappointed by how well-finished the interior is, to be honest. I'd sort of been looking forward to keeping myself busy while we were here. I'd envisioned making a few improvements during our stay as a way to pass the time. I'm not used to stopping. It would have given me the chance to brush up on some otherwise dormant skills I'm never truly able to put to good use in our pristine home. Yet, seeing how well-maintained the cabin is gives me the chance to really let go and enjoy my stay here, even if I have to force myself to relax at first.

I hadn't told Gemma, but I'd made sure to pack a few essential tools in a bag just in case we ran into trouble. I'd half-expected the cabin to have been left unattended for months. I'd debated the possibility that the pipes could have frozen during the winter, or that a loose board might be in need of repair and that I could save the day.

From the looks of it, someone has been here recently to give it a proper cleaning. They must be serious about renting it out to families for their summer holidays and, based on my family's reaction, the rent just went up.

The bedrooms aren't up to the same standard as the rest of the interior, but Gemma seems pleased regardless. It is very pretty and cozy inside which is a bonus. We're not here to spend time indoors but rather to enjoy the nature all around us.

I follow the girls out onto the deck, but we barely have time to see anything when thunder cracks above our heads, yielding a surprised scream from Beatrice. The boom is so sudden and powerful that I hear ringing in my ears for several seconds. The hairs on my arms rise and I feel a tingle on the back of my neck.

"Quick! Everyone, get inside!" I yell and urge them back into the cabin.

Rushing inside, we miss the lightning by mere seconds. Even with the patio doors closed, we still hear a loud and alarming crack, followed by what sounds like an explosion making us all jump.

The lightning must have hit a tree nearby. Surprisingly, and against the odds, the power stays on. Thunder rolls angrily above us, making the cabin shake from the noise. We huddle together, taking comfort from our proximity to each other, as if that will keep us safe somehow. Waiting for the inevitable lightning to strike once more, we all stand in the middle of the kitchen in total silence. We wait for what feels like an agonizing amount of time before we hear a distressing pop.

I rush to the window to get a better view. The massive pine tree in front of the cabin has smoke coming out of it and some of its bark seems to have blown off of it. A large gash in the trunk confirms the strike and I stand in awe, glued in place, transfixed as a large portion of the top of the trunk begins leaning towards us, falling towards the cabin.

"Get back!" I scream and I leap backwards, standing before my family, ready to protect them as if that were even possible.

There are several moments of acute silence as we wait, utterly terrified and unsure of where exactly it will land.

With a resounding boom, the tree falls heavily right next to the exterior side wall of the cabin, narrowly missing it. I head back to the window but struggle to see as the fallen tree now blocks the majority of the view. That was so close.

"Holy shit, Niall!" Gemma exclaims, her voice squeaking as though something is lodged in her throat. "That tree almost hit us!"

She begins to tremble as the realization of what could have happened overcomes her. Her hands are shaking as she slowly brings them up to her mouth, attempting to remain calm and steady her racing heart. Tears escape from the corners of her eyes, and she leaves them there, not bothering to hide how frightened she is by how bad it could have been.

I look back and spot the girls standing close together in the centre of the room. Presumably, this is the nearest they've been to each other since they were little. They're almost touching, and I wonder if they'd been hugging only seconds before, but had since let go of each other, because being seen embracing your sibling isn't cool at their age. That would be a rare occasion for sure. I'm almost sorry I missed it.

"It's alright, hon. Everything's fine. We're all safe." Using my most soothing tone, I step towards Gemma tentatively as though she were a stray dog I'm attempting to lure towards me with a stick of beef jerky, unsure if she will unhinge her fury and fear on me or be open to my efforts to calm her.

Her anxiety has been running high lately, with the job search and Amber's suspension, not to mention the end of the school year. An event like this is sure to set her off. I can see her entire body giving in to the fear, letting it have its way with her from the inside out. First, it overtakes her mind, then drains her body. I can see her energy quickly depleting. The spark in her eyes seems to dim. Instinctively, I reach out to her and lead her by the elbow to a nearby chair before she collapses. Once she's settled, I turn to the girls.

"Amber, could you grab the throw blanket and toss it to me, please?" I gesture towards the couch. She hands it to me. Once my wife is bundled and I'm sure she's comfortable, only then do I allow myself to turn back to the window to inspect the damage outside.

With my back turned, I hear Gemma's low, shaky voice, almost a whisper. "We can't stay here, Niall."

I swivel, turning my attention back to her before I've had a chance to hide the irritation splattered all over my face. Her shocked expression frustrates me even more, but it only lasts a few seconds before I rationalize that perhaps I should be more understanding. After all, her anxiety isn't something she has any control over.

But how many times do we have to leave a place or a gathering because she suddenly doesn't feel well or finds it claustrophobic?

How many times have I planned, packed, and driven long distances just to turn around at the very first sign of trouble? No, we can't keep running away. We can't let anxiety control our lives. I force my features to relax. My jaw had been tense. A noticeable throb annoys me as I put on a fake smile.

The girls need this vacation and so does Gemma. Hell, even I need it. Things have been so busy at work lately. I've had a lot on my mind. I need a few days away from home to unwind and not think about all I'll have to do once we get back. The only way to fully achieve that and to let go is to physically remove myself and be somewhere else. Anywhere would have been fine but leaving now would mean the vacation is essentially over. Gemma will be reluctant to book anything else, intent to remain around home. And being so near to work would make it difficult for me to stay away. I need to be somewhere else. But at least being here, even though it's not that far from home, it's just enough of a hassle to get back that I know it would be easier to say no to any requests that might come up.

When we first arrived, I couldn't blame Gemma for being weary. The place had looked like a dump—on the outside anyway. It certainly doesn't make a good first impression. I'm glad I convinced them to take a look inside, or else we wouldn't have seen how adorable it really was.

Things had been looking up when Gemma was taking in all the beautiful touches and comfortable furniture, but this storm, as sudden as it was, has wreaked havoc, undoing all and any progress. We're back at the starting line. The question of staying or not still hangs in the air between us, stifling, sucking all the positive energy away.

Gemma isn't negotiating—she's telling me what we're doing and I'm not having it. We're always catering to her needs, as though she decides everything, molding us into what suits her best in the moment. Well, not this time. Everyone should leave their comfort zone every once in a while—experience new things, discover parts of themselves they've long ago stashed away.

I have high hopes for this week. I truly believe that this vacation is going to benefit all of us if she will allow it. I need to persuade her to stay a little longer, to help her feel at ease in this place—make it worth her while.

However, the storm seems to be working against my best intentions causing an unnecessary challenge. The sky and rain, both violently dark and harsh, seem to be rejecting us. With fury and intensity, the thunder roars loudly all around us and only seems to strengthen as time ticks away. The cabin shakes all around us and I'm a bit concerned about the sturdiness of it. The power flickers and we're plunged into darkness.

"Great," I mutter under my breath. *This is just what we needed—not.*

I stand, determined to make the best of things. Despite the extreme humidity clinging to the air like my shirt sticks to my back, I walk over to the woodstove, and kneel to open the cast-iron door. I grab a few nearby logs and place them inside, reaching for the match box sitting beside the kindling. Lighting one, I wait patiently for the flame to catch.

I can feel the girls watching my every move in total silence. Finally, a small flame emerges from the back, growing slowly but fiercely stronger. The rest of the logs catch fire, the perfectly dried wood emitting a satisfying crackle.

I blow on the fire softly and sit back on my heels as I watch the warm glow, fascinated by the dancing flames. I chuck the burnt match in and close the door as I wait for the warmth to reach the corners of the small space.

My face starts to glisten with sweat. The cabin glows like a pumpkin on Halloween, the light coming off the swelling flame illuminates the furniture at strange angles, casting curious shadows that appear to be moving all around us. It's almost like the shadows are dancing along to the rhythm of the crackling fire.

I wipe my soiled hands on the front of my shorts. Debris and small wood chips fall at my feet as I stand up and turn to face my family.

"Look, I know the situation is less than ideal, but it's too late to go home now." I wave an arm at the window as if to make my point. The sky is now inky black, with intermittent veins of lightning sparking through it.

Before they have a chance to protest, I raise my hand to silence them. Using my most authoritative tone, I add "We'll stay here tonight and reevaluate in the morning. Hopefully the power comes back on after the storm has passed. We will be fine for one night." I can feel them appraising me, trying to figure out how this can possibly work.

Who can blame them? They've always had access to whatever their hearts desired. Gemma and I haven't done them any favours, really. They've never gone without anything. Never without an internet connection, their favourite snacks, electricity, or water. They can always count on their annual shopping trip to replace outgrown clothing, car rides to friends' houses, and home-cooked meals almost every night.

If they're panicking now, it's my own damn fault. I try my best to reassure them that there's nothing to worry about. "We have a cooler full of food and water bottles in the car. And the fire will keep us from tripping over ourselves in the dark."

I watch them mulling this over, still not convinced.

"It could be a lot worse! At least it's summertime and we're not snowed in. We'd have to melt snow on the fire to flush the toilet, but now, at least, we can simply restrict our flushing tonight and grab water from the lake in the morning. If the power does not come back on by then, that is," I add, chuckling.

This earns a scowl from Gemma. I clear my throat and continue, feeling that my argument is beyond reasonable. "All I'm asking for is one night. It'll be just like camping, but even better."

Amber snorts at my last comment. Leaning across to Gemma, I reach for her hand and rub my thumb over the back of it.

"Look, hon, we have a nice bottle of red wine in the car, several bricks of cheese, crackers, and cold cuts. It'll be like a picnic." I try to sound convincing, and I think it's working. I see a faint smile on Gemma's lips. I'm winning her over. "Thanks, hon." Without letting go of her hand, I stand and plant a kiss on her forehead.

Taking a quick glance outside, I notice that the storm seems to be moving down the lake, getting farther from us. "I'll go get the stuff in the car. Amber, can you try to find some candles and maybe a deck of cards? I'm sure this place has one." I smile a charming smile, happy to have gotten my way for once.

One night. That's all I need in order to convince them to stay.

If I can somehow make this night magical enough, then maybe they'll want to continue with the vacation as planned. I really am in no hurry to get home. I'll do whatever it takes to make this trip memorable.

Chapter 18
Amber

Pulling open drawers at random, I explore the small kitchen in search of candles or anything else that might come in handy during our night here. Using my cell phone flashlight to guide me in the shadowed corners of the space, I finally find what appears to be a catch-all drawer, containing an assortment of useful crap: sharpie markers, scissors, tape, some string, an old pill bottle with rubber elastics inside, a small box of plastic snack bags, a plug-in nightlight, and a lighter.

This must be it, I think to myself. Reaching towards the back, scraping the top of my forefinger on the drawer's mechanism, I feel my fingernail momentarily pierce through a waxy surface. Jackpot. I find six, plain, white, unscented tea light candles and some tiny, multi-coloured, shot-glass candle holders in a drawer under the sink.

Placing the candles around the room, I light them one at a time. The cabin looks like a shrine or perhaps even like we're performing a ritual, like a group of witches about to summon evil spirits.

Mom is still wrapped in the throw I covered her in earlier. Despite the increasing heat in the cabin, she's buried under the soft fabric, her feet pulled up on the kitchen chair, leaving only her big toes poking out, barely visible. Her chin is resting on her knees, and her body is still except for her eyes. They are alert and moving around the space.

She looks almost comical, but I know better. She's panicking. It's not hard to tell. There's not much anyone can do for her during this phase of her anxiety. She can't reason her way out of it—we just need to wait it out.

Dad comes back inside, hefting the large cooler through the door,

his boots caked in mud, leaving a trail of it on the floor behind him. He doesn't bother to remove his filthy boots when he walks over to the kitchen and places the cooler on the floor beside the refrigerator, as though it makes any difference where the cooler is in the space.

Placing a hand on his knee, he lifts the lid, releasing a sucking noise as a gush of cool air escapes. He busies himself by pulling out a few items for our dinner, placing them on the kitchen counter in front of him. Sticking a hand directly inside the cooler, he shovels cubes of melting ice in heaps as he roots around the bottom and pulls out a beer bottle. Replacing the ice over the other items, he stands, triumphant, and closes the lid with a snap.

We watch as he expertly twists the cap off his beer and takes a large gulp. My mouth waters. The cool, golden liquid calls out to me. I long for a swig. My parents know I drink alcohol occasionally, but they've never been the ones to offer me any.

Looking over longingly, pondering the best way to ask, Dad catches my eye and a knowing smirk plays on his lips. I feel my cheeks warm, embarrassed to be so easy to read. Without hesitating, he bends down once more, pops the lid of the cooler and rummages through the ice again, extracting a second beer. He hands it to me. It almost feels like a dare to see if I'm bold enough to take it, or maybe even a peace offering for his outburst after my suspension. A simple gesture, to bridge the gap between us. It's all water under the bridge now, his generosity seems to indicate.

Still, I pause, my hand wavering a moment. I risk a glance towards my mom but surprisingly, she nods. Her approval is so faint, I have to strain my eyes to see it. It's almost like she's giving me an out, the option to pretend not to have seen it at all, as though she's ashamed to allow her underaged daughter to drink in a secluded cabin on a quiet vacation with her family. What is she so afraid of? No one is going to judge her for allowing me to drink here. After all, how wild can I really get by drinking one beer?

Decidedly, I grab the cold beer from Dad and twist the top with efficiency, placing the cap in the pocket of my shorts, the sharp edges pulling a thread as I push it down. Bringing the glass bottle to my lips, I feel eyes on me. Everyone is looking at me, mesmerized. Somehow, this feels like a milestone. It's certainly not my first drink, but it's the first time I have one in my parents' presence.

Starting with a conservative sip, I smile in thanks to my parents. They didn't need to do that, but I'm grateful they did. They're hard on me most of the time, but they're still pretty cool as far as parents go. Maybe things will be different during this holiday, a bit more laid back.

Dad snickers softly at my awkward disposition. It's very rare that I'm at a loss for words. It isn't lost on me that his kindness most likely has ulterior motives. He's being overly kind to me in the hopes that I don't snitch to Mom about his angry outburst. I haven't forgotten his reaction when he'd picked me up from school after my suspension, neither had time erased the ugly words he spit at me, making me feel like I was merely the scum underneath his shoe. He'd purposefully said terrible things to shock me and hurt me—to dig at my insecurities with a sharp knife. His tongue had been his weapon. He'd fucked up big time and he was trying hard to smooth things out between us.

We hadn't talked about that interaction since that day, but the wedge it had caused between us was ever-present and growing, like a cavity getting worse with each passing day. Although I could sense that he'd rather forget all about it, my silence is like a dangling threat—just out of his reach, never knowing if or when I'll blab to Mom. I hold all the power and he knows it. He's scared and he knows I know.

Desperate to keep me happy, he's been working hard to make up for his bad behaviour by suddenly acting thoughtful or kind towards me. But I know it's all a show—a way to make me forget. He's trying to stop me from spilling the truth, keeping me quiet with grand gestures.

His eagerness to silence me is the very thing that keeps the memory so vivid in my mind. Why does he care so much about how I perceive him? Why am I such a threat to him? Surely Mom is already aware of this side of him, and me telling her about his outburst would only disappoint her rather than make her run the other way.

Dad should know by now that when you tell me not to do something, it becomes my entire focus and it's all I want to do. Reverse psychology or defiance—call it what you will. Whether it makes sense to me or not, the reason why hardly matters. The sheer fact that he makes such a big deal to ensure I don't spill his secret, the way he's obviously desperate, his not-so-subtle peace-making pleas, those are what drive me to keep messing with him. I can't let him off the hook yet. I have to make Dad regret ever treating me that way. He needs to pay.

At any moment, I could turn the tables on him and share what happened, not caring about the consequences. But I won't. At least, not yet. I want to see how far I can push this—how much he's willing to bend the rules to keep this little incident between us. I wonder how much my cooperation is worth. I picture a puppet dangling on strings in my hand. I wonder just how far he is willing to go in order to keep it hidden.

My arrogance soaring, I tip my beer towards his, clink my bottle to his while maintaining an intense eye contact. *I see what you're playing at*, my stare states. *You don't know who you're messing with*. His face goes slack. His top lip twitches.

Good, he understands.

To the others, it just looks like a pleasant toasting between father and daughter, but as my dad is beginning to understand, he's just added kindling to the fire.

He's just lured me in and made the game more interesting. He's got my attention and I've got his. His slip-up in the car is going to cost him. He'll regret ever disrespecting me.

He's playing a game he doesn't understand the rules to. Turning towards the fire, the flame warms my cheeks and reflects in my eyes. A coy smile forms on my lips. This trip might be more entertaining than I'd expected.

Chapter 19
Beatrice

Sitting by myself in one of the armchairs, I stare confused at the scene before me. Some kind of stand-off has taken place between Amber and Dad. Her thoughts might as well be tattooed all over her face, I can read her so easily. She's never been good at hiding how she feels, never been strong enough to mute herself and tone down her motives.

But that's just Amber. Mom calls her spirited but I say she's predictably unpredictable—an absolute shit-show. She moves to the beat of her own drum, so used to others bending over backwards to please her, no matter how badly she behaves. Our little family unit revolves around her as though the earth's axis is within her. I both hate her and wish to be more like her.

I despise how easily she always seems to get what she wants. She holds a certain power over others; her very presence seems to draw people to her. Like a snake can distract you with its smooth movements and bright colours, making you forget for a moment how dangerous it is, how deadly it can be. How in a split-second, the snake can turn on you—coil its long, flexible body around your neck and squeeze tightly until all the air has left your lungs.

The clinking of bottles startles me out from the horrifying images playing in my head and my attention returns to the room. I watch Amber's smile and shrink in my seat as a cold shiver runs over me. Suddenly, I realize that I'm freezing even though I'm right beside the fire—as though all the heat has left my body. I wrap my arms around myself, trying to keep any remaining warmth from escaping.

I can't believe that just a few moments ago, Amber and I had been hugging. I'd been so scared that the tree trunk might crash through the walls of the cabin and flatten us all that I'd clung to her in fear, but now I hated myself for being so weak. If I'm honest, I sincerely doubt Amber would have tried to protect me. If she'd had to choose between saving herself or me, she wouldn't have hesitated throwing me in front of her to break her fall.

I haven't always hated her. In fact, for most of my childhood I'd admired her like most little sisters look-up to their older siblings. I'd wanted to be with her all the time. I'd even loved her.

She seemed to have our parents wrapped around her little finger, controlling the course of our lives. There was even a time when I'd copied her, talked like her, acted like her, but my parents were quick to shut that down, as though she were a bad influence on me.

Like her behaviour was a stain on me they'd rub raw, trying to wash it off before it went too deep. I think a part of them liked how they had the power to shape me into what they wanted me to be. They said they didn't need two Ambers and that I was perfect just the way I was.

Instead of making me feel special, I started to resent Amber for that. She didn't need anything to make her any more exceptional, it ran deep within her veins. I had to work harder to be noticed. She was mean, shiny, and always planning something—an attention-seeker the world put on a pedestal. I, on the other hand, was forced to kneel at her feet, often forgotten, outshined, and ignored for my need to be loved and approved.

Growing up, Amber would trip me up, placing various objects in my path as though life was a race, and she was determined to win. I'd always played by the rules, but Amber created them as she went. They were ever changing and flexible, like fresh modeling clay, bending and eventually drying up and breaking according to her every need.

I can't really call her two-faced, because she's always very clear about what she's saying or how she feels. I do believe Amber thinks she loves me in her own way. Maybe by treating me like crap she's trying to make me stronger. If this is how Amber treats those she loves, I wonder how exactly she treats those she hates.

Cold in the corner, alone with the shadows that seem to surround me and keep me company, I've had to learn how to be by myself these days. Most of my friends have punished me and rejected me for the simple fact that I'm Amber's little sister and they don't need that kind of drama following them around.

I don't think I've ever felt so cold.

The wood fire crackles next to me, but I don't feel any heat from it yet. Amber's face is turned towards the flame. Any closer and she'd fall inside it. She doesn't fear the fire. I watch, transfixed. I can't help it. Although I may have an idea what she's feeling at any given time, I still don't understand her. I can never predict her next move.

For as long as I've been on this earth, I've been a student of my sister's every movement—a silent watcher, observing from a safe distance, hiding in the shadows, careful not to be seen. In all my years, I've witnessed my sister express hundreds of emotions, watched her lash out and experience emotional outbursts, never knowing when the next one would come. Her moods are as fickle as the weather. I live in a constant state of fear, walking on eggshells, trying not to disturb the ground she walks on for fear that she'll lash out at me.

Amber has never pretended to be something she's not. I think that's what makes it so hard to read her. She's not afraid of danger or failure. In fact, there isn't much that scares her. I'm sure there are things that keep her up at night, but I haven't been able to figure them out yet.

The flames glow in her eyes and it's as though for the very first time I can see her for who she really is. Tonight, she doesn't seem larger than life. She just looks like a young girl with a fire raging inside of her. I feel sorry for her. What happened to her to make her so angry? I can't help but wonder. She's wearing a terrifying grin. I can almost hear her evil thoughts swirling around her head. I wonder if Amber ever feels bad for her actions. I doubt she gives much thought to them before acting them out.

But later, does she ever wish she'd handled things differently? Maybe her process is more thought-out than I think it is. However, I really doubt it. She acts on impulse. Your best friend one minute, your worst enemy the next.

I don't know what my father did to get on her bad side, but I can see fear clearly present in his eyes.

Even my mother's eyes are weary as she looks at Amber. How are all of us so bewitched by one teenager? How powerful she must feel to be at the centre of our attention. The creator of peace or tension, everything depends on her mood. She has everyone following her movements, trying to figure out what she'll do next, only to fall right into her trap. How good she must feel up on her mountain—how entitled. But then, the higher up she gets, the lonelier it is and worse is the fall.

"Girls," my mom clears her throat, as though she's attempting to release some of the very obvious tension in the room. "Why don't you help me grab the pillows and comforters from the rooms?" She stands from her curled position on the chair, stretching a little before sending a challenging glance in Dad's direction. "I think it might be fun if we all sleep in the living room tonight by the fire."

Glad to move from my spot and get the blood moving to my extremities, I walk across the room, careful to leave a safe distance between myself and Amber, leaving her and Dad to settle whatever is going on between them. The air feels thick with tension even though they're both pretending nothing's going on. Mom and I share a worried glance. She lets out a slow breath and we get to work.

Slightly relieved not to be obligated to share a bed with Amber tonight, I quickly rip sheets, pillows, and the comforter from the double bed, bundling it all up in my small arms. The ball of fabric blocks my view a little and I trip, almost slamming my foot on the sharp metal corner of the bed frame sticking out beneath the edge of the mattress.

Barely avoiding it, I readjust the bundle in my arms, pulling up a drooping corner of a sheet and make my way back to the main room. There is a soft orange glow coming from the candles spread out throughout the main area. The reach of the light is impressive. Even the small windowpane from the woodstove seems to have brightened as the night has begun to darken all around us. That, or my eyes have finally adjusted.

Back in the living room, Mom is right behind me with her and Dad's bedding. Dad is busy rearranging furniture, making space for the four of us to set up our makeshift beds for the night. I'm relieved when Mom asks me to place Amber's things on one end of the living room and places hers and Dad's in the centre, making sure to position herself between Amber and Dad. Without any need for discussion, she has perfectly arranged a safe place for us all to sleep, putting herself back in control. What she might not have considered is how she's now placed herself between two raging fires, offering herself up on a platter like a sacrifice in the small hope of keeping the peace.

I settle into the spot Mom assigned for me on the outside, right next to Dad. I try not to think too hard of how dirty the floor might be or what dead insects litter it. The light doesn't quite reach this portion of the room, partially blocked by both an armchair and the bookshelf.

Once the beds are made-up, we move to the kitchen for a plain dinner of crackers and cheese before retreating to our beds by the fire. Without much light to see by and with the rain pounding outside, there's not much else to do.

We are exhausted from our trip and the storm, making it easy to agree to an early night. We don't say anything, but I'm fairly certain we're all thinking it—the sooner we fall asleep, the faster tomorrow will come and we can finally go home.

I'm a little disappointed to be leaving so soon, but we can't stay here without power. Mom has put on a brave face, but I know she's beyond uncomfortable with the idea of staying here any longer than is absolutely necessary. Even so, Dad has put his foot down. He knows Mom won't venture to drive in the dark of night, so by refusing to drive us home, he's left her no other choice but to stay here and make the best of the situation. I wonder how many times Mom has had to swallow her fear and disappointment and adjust it in order to please others. How many times has she bitten her tongue, holding back her words to avoid being seen as difficult, needy, or weak? I wonder how it doesn't eat her up at night, to always do what everyone else wants when her own needs go unanswered.

I wish I could move my bedding to be next to Mom. I would reach out and snuggle into her side, hold her hand, let her know in my quiet way that I'm on her side. But Dad is between us as usual. In a moment, he'll be settled on his back, fast asleep and snoring, without a care in the world. But my mom will lay awake, eyes scanning the dark, her thoughts swirling, keeping her from resting properly. I know this because I'll be doing the exact same thing.

Chapter 20
GEMMA

A soft clicking sound rouses me from a light sleep. Although faint, I hear the subtle noise above the resounding cadence of my husband's snores, as though amplified and undeniable. All night, I'd wished to be enveloped in a peaceful slumber, to allow myself some much-needed rest, but this strange place and the creaking noise of the harsh winds slamming hard against the cabin's ramshackle wood panels just outside, had kept me alert for most of the night.

Now, however, blinding sun pierces through the space and I blink away the mediocre sleep I'd managed to get. I turn my head sideways and smile. Surrounded by my family, I feel whole. Amber is sleeping on her stomach, her head turned away from our little pod, while Bea is perfectly still, mummy-like, lying on her back. She doesn't appear to have moved an inch since falling asleep, or did she sleep at all?

I'd craned my neck throughout the night and had been surprised to see her little eyes blinking in the night. Only the occasional glimpse of moonlight reflecting on her exposed pupils had let me know she was still awake. Understanding the sentiments of why she had trouble falling asleep, it reminded me of when she was an infant. I'd stay up in her room much longer than I'd needed to, just to watch her sleep. It eased my anxiety to know that she was soundly resting and wouldn't wake when I finally moved away, somehow sensing my departure, the sudden gap of heat expanding between us.

Last night, I'd remembered just how small she and Amber had once been, not so long ago. How they'd fit in my arms as I'd rocked them to sleep after reading bedtime stories and the sweet sound they'd make once tucked snuggly inside the soft blankets. Amber would toss and turn, restless, her little legs wanting to escape the constraint of the covers that I'd always find on the floor beside her in the mornings. She'd always release a loud exhale whenever it was time for me to exit her room, startling me into thinking she'd woken up again. It was her way of letting me know she was aware I was leaving but that she'd be fine.

Bea on other hand, would suckle the air, making a cute little noise with her mouth, almost like whenever she'd wanted a bottle. That noise pulled at my heartstrings, willing me to return to her bedside and watch over her, to keep her safe, to protect her from monsters and bad dreams. It was always hardest to leave Beatrice's room. Even though it was clear she was asleep, I couldn't bear the thought of leaving her alone, exposed. Bea is precious—perfect. She's got a kind soul, but I worry she won't know how to protect her heart when the time comes.

Peering over to my left, I see Niall's distorted face, mouth gaping open, features relaxed. His snoring has finally subsided. He must be close to waking up then. His snores are always loudest the deeper his sleep. It's almost impossible to wake him during that stage.

Letting my body rest another moment, I take in the view of the ceiling and the pieces of the room I can see while lying down and notice a painting to the right of the woodstove that I hadn't seen yesterday. It's a beautiful acrylic representation of an iron bird cage with a fluffy blue bird inside. The bird's wings are expanded, as though mid-flight, but the cage door is shut—a trapped bird.

I shiver.

The bird's eyes are simple, deep, black, round dots, but I feel them peering right through me—right into my soul.

What a strange piece of art to have at a vacation home. I suppose the appeal is in the bright shades—a mix of indigo, turquoise, and deep navy. The cage is depicted in a charcoal tone, not so distinct but still very present. The blue bird looks like a rare breed. In a haunting way, the painting is very pretty, and I suppose that whoever picked it wanted to find a nature picture evoking the scenery surrounding the cabin, while taking care to match the colours reflected off the lake.

The paint looks thick and bumpy. I wonder if I would feel the brush strokes, the rise and fall of the thick waves of paint beneath the pads of my fingers if I reached out to touch it. Would my fingernails be able to chip away the large mass, the muted charcoal that morphs into the cage—would I be able to set the bird free? I almost convince myself that I could.

A distinctive hum jolts me back to the room and I can make out the refrigerator's compressor rumbling loudly. The back panel must be in dire need of a cleaning. Then, I remember that clicking noise from earlier and it occurs to me that if the refrigerator has come back to life, then the power must have returned.

Child-like and giddy, I quickly sit up and rise from between Amber and Niall, careful not to stir the covers too much as I stand and tiptoe over to the kitchen. I have to see it for myself and expectantly pull open the refrigerator door, unable to stop myself. The light is on like a beacon of hope. The sight almost makes me cry.

Hastily, I begin to place the items from the cooler on the empty shelves to keep the food from spoiling. Even if we're not staying much longer, the fridge will be able to keep them cool until we're ready to go. The ice in the cooler is all but melted. The carton of eggs has been reduced to pulp, a mushy mess in my hands. I extract the eggs from their useless cardboard home and place them carefully in one of the refrigerator drawers.

I see movement from the corner of my eye and notice Niall sitting up, looking back at me with a sleepy grin on his face. How predictable I am to be the first one up, he must be thinking. It's a hard habit to break—this need to be productive before the rest of the family wakes up to begin the process of getting the day started. With everyone in the way, tasks take much longer to accomplish. More people just make a bigger mess in an already cramped space.

I watch my husband stand, stretch, and stride over to where I'm standing in the kitchen. I release my grip on the refrigerator door handle and lean into him for a kiss. His morning breath is horrendous, and I imagine with growing shame that mine is no better.

Embarrassed, I abruptly break the kiss and turn around to face the window, letting his arms envelop my waist. Even though we've been married for almost two decades, I still like to keep some of the magic alive between us—that includes not letting him smell my morning breath.

"Good morning, gorgeous," he whispers softly into my ear, tickling me in the process. "How did you sleep?" he asks before he nibbles on my earlobe, making me squirm.

"Fine," I lie. "And you?"

"Like a baby." I can hear the smile in his response.

Glancing behind us, I see the girls are still deep in sleep. Niall takes my hand and leads me out of the kitchen and towards the patio doors. The view practically takes my breath away.

The sky is free from clouds, just a rich blue as far as I can see—inviting, providing hope for a beautiful day ahead. Quietly, I slide the door, transfixed by the expansive body of water down below. I step out, my bare feet almost gliding across the deck, and gaze at the glass surface of the lake. The stillness is astonishing and allows an almost unobstructed view of the various fluctuating levels of terrain below the surface. I can see the mixture of colours that make up the different depths of water, the various stones scattered beneath, shadows of fish swimming below, looking for flies, without disrupting the peacefulness.

The complexity of it is breathtaking, like looking at a gemstone—indisputably radiant—a mixture of aquamarine, sapphire, blue zircon, pale erinite, and emerald green. Nature amazes me.

"It's absolutely incredible," I breathe, my eyes unblinking, unwilling to miss any second of this beautiful sight. "I feel like I'm dreaming."

"I'm so glad you got to see it," Niall chuckles behind me. He shifts to stand next to me and leans his forearms on the railing, looking out as he speaks. "This is why I wanted to come out here." He gestures with one arm towards the lake.

"I didn't know a place like this even existed around here," I mutter, still shocked by the clarity of the water.

"I know. It looks almost tropical," he remarks. "Reminds me of our trips down south. Only, this is much closer and a lot more affordable," he chuckles.

"Why is the water so clear?" I wonder out loud, not expecting my husband to know the answer, but he surprises me with a response.

"I think it has to do with zebra mussels or something. Apparently, they eat all the algae and it helps to keep the water clean." He pauses, seemingly pondering something. "Actually, wait here a second." He enters the cabin and returns a moment later with a stack of papers in his hands.

"Look, Tim left us this booklet with information about the area." He flips through it and exclaims, "There it is!" He points to a passage explaining the lake's water clarity.

Skimming over it, we discover that Niall was right in assuming zebra mussels are hard at work eating the plankton and algae. But the water quality is also largely attributed to the large population of trout residing in the lake.

Apparently, water quality is due in part to the amount of dissolved oxygen available per aquatic being. Which largely varies depending on the temperature, which, in turn also greatly impacts the photosynthesis process.

"Seriously? That's remarkable!"

I've never given much thought to how the fish and various organisms living in the water have a direct impact on its quality, which makes me feel quite silly. I find it all rather fascinating to think there are so many things are at work below the surface, mostly invisible to us, all of which are responsible for making this lake as magnificent as it is today. How many things are at play that we're unaware of? The temperature, the plants, the sunshine, the fish—they all have a role in creating this. It's mind boggling.

The pamphlet goes on to explain that Lake Clear is home to rare plants like marsh bedstraw, uplands white asters from the sunflower family, a weed that attracts butterflies called false nettle, and the northern willowherb.

Hearing some groans behind us, we spin around and watch Amber stagger out to meet us, her eyes not quite fully opened yet. Her hair is a knotted mass of tightly wound curls like a lion's mane coiled around her head. Her eyes, which are narrow slits and feline-looking, shine with an amber tint in the morning light, giving her the appearance of a sleepy goddess.

"Holy crap!" She can't hide her delight in sighting the lake. Her mouth hangs open as she approaches the railing. "That's so pretty!" Squealing, she beams up at us and hops in place like an excited child.

It warms my heart to see her so happy. Her features are so beautiful when she smiles—a rare occurrence these days it seems. I don't want to move an inch for fear of ruining the moment. Her joyful shrieks seem to have woken up her sister, for she too is now emerging from the cabin, joining us on the suspended structure, yawning and rubbing her tired eyes.

"Wow!" is all she manages to express when she finally opens her eyes wide, taking in the beautiful scenery.

Laughing wholeheartedly, Niall seems quite pleased with himself. Yesterday might not have gone as planned—the first impression had been a terrible one—but now, looking at this lake, it's easy to see what makes this cabin so special.

"Location, location, location," he jokes.

We all laugh at his realtor joke. Once we're silent again, appreciating the view, he touches my forearm gently.

"Hon, I know you said only one night, but..." he trails off, looking at me with pleading eyes, amusement dancing in them. "Now that the power's back on and you see what this place has to offer..." he lets his words hang in the air between us, waiting for me to pick them up.

Three pairs of eyes look at me, eagerly awaiting my response. How could I be the one to turn them down?

"Oh, alright!" I smack his arm lightly, "Fine, we'll stay." I smile, not quite as bothered by his manoeuvring as I thought I would be.

A small part of me is curious enough to want to stay and explore more of this place. Looking out, I spot a medium-sized boat fastened to a nice wide dock below. Niall had mentioned a boat, I remember now, but that's not really my preference.

Still, I know he'll try and coax me into taking the family for a ride around the lake before we head home. After all, it's not every day we get to tour a lake on a boat.

Peering slightly under the deck, I spy two yellow kayaks resting on the rich green lawn below, just begging to be taken out.

Now, that's what I'm talking about.

Something small, motorless, that glides on the surface of the lake without disrupting it with ripples and waves. With room only for one, a paddle with which I can control my direction, steer it close to the shore and explore the vast life that resides there, or venture to one of the islands sitting across from us in the deeper waters and see what variety of plants grow there. The options are limitless, the temptation irresistible.

We'd woken up feeling reluctant to start our day, but suddenly, it's a mad dash to eat breakfast, all of us eager to reach out and touch that water. As immaculate and still as it sits before us, I can't help but think that if something as small as zebra mussels, algae, and trout can impact the water's clarity, how do boats and human activity disrupt it? If the sun's rays can influence the oxygen levels, what of ourselves will be left behind to change the delicate balance that exists here to create this majestic place? I just hope we leave it in better shape than we found it, but somehow I doubt it. With any luck, the lake won't reject us and spit us out as a punishment for disturbing it.

Chapter 21
Beatrice

We split into two groups. As unplanned as the divide may seem in the moment, the separation is one that often occurs for us. It's like there's this unwritten rule that Mom and Amber stick together no matter what, two peas in a pod, while I always end up joining Dad in whatever activity he's up to. Mom and Amber just get each other on a whole other level. They barely have to talk at all.

It's kind of creepy, actually. People often ask if they're sisters since they look so much alike and whenever they're in near proximity to one another, it's like an invisible thread links them together. If Mom moves to the right, Amber will begin to sway in that direction. I'm not sure if they know how strange it is and yet, I'd give just about anything to be that connected to another person.

My sister used to say she and Mom could hear each other's thoughts. I'm not sure I completely believe her even though I've experienced something similar on a few occasions where Mom seemed to know exactly what I was thinking, but I think that's normal between parents and kids. What Mom and Amber have is closer to witchcraft. Their bond is undeniable and deeper than their shared good looks. I can't say I've ever felt that type of link with either of them. Honestly, I find it hard to keep up with them and their impulsiveness most of the time. I'm just built differently.

What excites them and boosts their energy, usually drains mine or scares me beyond measure. Not only that, but I never really know where I stand with them—if they'll invite me to join in someday or keep excluding me from their private club.

With Dad, however, it's mostly straightforward. I usually know what to expect. I can tell he enjoys spending time with me. I don't have to pretend to be someone I'm not around him. I don't ruffle feathers, I do as I'm told, and I'm too young to talk back to him yet. In every sense, I'm like a well-trained dog to him—a man's best friend.

I reach the end of the dock, my cheap flip-flops slap the wooden boards announcing my arrival. The boat is bundled up under a tent-like protective cover that reminds me of marshmallows. Together, we pull at opposite sides to remove it and reveal the vessel hiding underneath. We stare at it for a long time before finally stepping on board.

The boat is an older model, a pretty blue colour, and larger than I had first thought.

"Look, Bea, it's a Glastron SE 170 with an original Honda motor. Probably a 1998, I'd guess." Dad's grinning ear to ear like a child at the Santa Clause parade.

He's so excited that it seems to bounce off of him as he pads around the dock, a slight jog in his step as he begins inspecting the exterior of the boat before we set off. I watch Amber and Mom lift the kayaks effortlessly and bring them to the water. My fists clench as I see them flexing their tanned bodies, their heads angled towards each other laughing like old friends on their way to cause trouble.

The lake is quiet this morning, but then again, it's barely nine o'clock. We have the place to ourselves, it seems—at least, for the moment.

Grabbing my hand, Dad leads me onto the boat as he unlatches it from the dock. Stepping onto the turquoise carpeted interior, I feel the boat sway beneath my feet, surprising me. The rocking knocks me off balance and I grip the edge of the boat. I quickly choose a seat near the back of the boat, not so much to avoid walking on this unsteady surface any longer but to give myself some space away from Dad.

I watch him step on after me and move the boat under his weight. Steadying myself, I grasp the small railing again, gritting my teeth.

"Will you just look at this thing?!" Dad is ecstatic. "Tim said the boat is 17 feet long."

I nod, but I'm not really interested in boat facts. Trying to distract myself from the shifting balance of the moving water, I look around me. There's quite a bit of space inside the boat, enough for six, maybe even eight passengers.

The seats are made of a white, leathery material. Curious, I skim a hand across the smooth surface. The back bench where I sit has cup holders in the middle. In front of the driver's seat, I spot another row of seats.

I wish I'd chosen to sit there instead, although those seats aren't protected by the driver's window and are more likely to get splashed. Depending on how hot it gets, that might not be such a bad thing. Dad finds several adult-sized, matching blue life jackets and tosses me the smallest one in the bunch. I fasten the clips over my chest as Dad familiarizes himself with the features of the boat and the various switches.

I apply a ridiculous amount of sunscreen to the bridge of my nose and cheeks where I tend to burn. I know I look beyond silly like I'm wearing some kind of cocoa butter war marks, but I'd rather look silly than get scorched. I can just tell the UV index is high today as my skin already has a reddish-purple tone to it.

I'm glad we're heading out early as the sun is bound to get even stronger as the day goes on. There's no wind today. In comparison to yesterday's storm, the lake is mostly still. A small, puffy white cloud would be welcomed here and there to offer a break from the heat of the sun, but it seems that we're out of luck. The air is thick and hot. I'm glad to be wearing my swimsuit under my lifejacket because I'll probably be going for a dip the very moment we get back to the dock.

"Alright, I think I've got it," Dad nods to himself. "You ready, kiddo?" he yells over to me as the motor roars to life behind me.

Instead of straining my voice, which I know would be useless over the noise, I hold up my thumb to let him know I'm good to go.

I'm terrified but also the tiniest bit excited—a surprising new feeling for me. I grab the side of the boat for support, my grip so tight that my knuckles turn white. I don't know much about boats, but this one is the biggest one I've ever been on. We ease out into the middle of the lake starting slow at first and gaining speed the further we get from the shore. We glide over the surface of the water, like a smooth skipping stone, creating swollen wrinkles of waves in our wake. It feels surreal to make our mark on the smooth surface of the lake.

Dad is so excited to get to ride it out. I was surprised to learn this morning that he'd completed the Boat Safety Course when he and Mom first started dating. And so, he still has his proof of competency card. As the card never expires, he's still able to drive motorized boats, but hasn't had the opportunity in quite some time.

He's wearing a light blue microfiber t-shirt, a black swimsuit for shorts, and slip-on Adidas sandals. I only now realize that he's removed his watch, most likely leaving it back at the cabin. It's a trademark for him. Whenever we go on vacation, Dad's not usually in true 'vacation-mode' until his trusty watch leaves his wrist. It's his way of letting us know that he's letting go of work, going with the flow, and seeing where the day takes him, rather than being tied to a set schedule.

Sporting dark, Oakley sunglasses, he looks completely relaxed in his seat. It hits me how naturally he seems to fit in here, taking a boat out on a beautiful lake. As if in another life, this would have been how he'd spent his days—cruising canals, the sun warming his bare arms. Seeing him so at ease helps me loosen my grip a little bit.

I force my arms to stretch out on either side of me, deciding that if I pretend to be comfortable, then maybe I will be—eventually. I really wish I'd thought of bringing my aviators. Instead, I squint as the sun's rays practically blind me as they reflect on the surface of the water like little mirrors—little diamond-like sparkles covering the lake as far as I can see. At this speed, we don't see the clarity of the water as easily, but it's stunning just the same.

We spend the next several hours touring around the lake, crossing it in the centre to reach more ground and line the far edge. We slow down our speed and simply cruise as though we have all the time in the world, which in a way, we sort of do.

I'd lost sight of Mom and Amber when we'd sped away, their figures now little yellow dots on the water. I wonder how they did with the waves we created. Knowing them, they probably enjoyed the challenge. They think on their feet—react rather than plan ahead like me. Waves would have just added to their fun.

Funny how they opted for the quiet, motorless kayaks over the powerful, speedy boat. But I guess everyone wants what they don't have.

This boat is the exact opposite of my personality. It's large, loud, takes a lot of space. It attracts attention and is wide open, inviting people in. It's fast and flashy, so unlike me. And yet, sitting here on the leather seat, feeling my hair floating behind me in the warm wind, I can't help but feel good. I like how it's messing up my usually perfect straight hair. I can almost imagine the humidity and mist from the water getting tangled in it, creating soft beachy waves.

Yet, I know that won't happen. There's no salt in the water, but even if there were, my hair wouldn't change in the slightest. My life, and my hair, are as predictable as death to everyone—set on a trajectory that no one, not even me can change, no matter how hard I try.

The difference between my sister and me is that I choose to accept that fact, instead of spending my days fighting against it. Amber calls it settling or submitting. But I find that choosing the easier path, the conflict-free path, is the better way to go.

This way, at least, I can live my life mostly in peace, be content with the direction of it, and know where I'm heading without any surprises along the way. It might not be a very exciting life, but at least I'm free to live it without everyone breathing down my neck, putting me in shackles to force me into a respectable, boring life, like Amber once described.

She only seems to see the limits, but if she would just stop fighting everything and everyone, Mom and Dad might just give her more space and even begin to trust her. Maybe then she'd start to see the good in life, the beauty, and freedom of it instead of only noticing the boundaries, always tempting her to keep pushing them. She once told me that she feels like a trapped bird with its wings cut off.

She's long ago lost the confidence people had in her. She can't be left alone and trusted to do the right thing. She's like a dog on a tight leash that gets tighter the harder she pulls, and yet, she keeps pulling, to hell with the pain. Just grits her teeth against it, either choosing to ignore it or willing it into submission, like people have begun to expect from her.

She can't help herself—the temptation is too strong. Her mind is always at work, questioning things, pushing her to confront reality, putting herself in dangerous positions just to see how it feels.

But if I were a bird, I'd tape my wings, turn them useless. The cage is a good place for me, and I don't see the point of learning how to fly. I'd rather stick to the path I was born into, not steer away from it.

I don't love pain, and I don't feel like getting lost trying to find myself. I find enough adventure from reading books and that's good enough for me. It might seem less thrilling, but it's safer that way. And that's worth something, for me anyway.

Chapter 22
Amber

The sunshine is warming my shoulders and relaxing my muscles as I close my eyes to fully enjoy the sensation of the rays on my skin. The air feels comfortably heavy, like dense bread baking in a warm oven, making me take a deep breath.

I sigh, happily comfortable in the moment, feeling incredibly peaceful. It feels euphoric to be outside, gliding on the surface of the lake. Almost like an out-of-body experience. The tension leaves my body with every stroke of the paddle as it gracefully slides across the water.

Without distractions or anyone to impress, I feel free to be myself. It's a feeling I've long thought impossible. The clear drops splatter over my arms and twinkle in the sunlight. They make me feel beautiful in my own skin—untouchable and brand new.

Almost like the water has healing powers or a magical ability to fix whatever's been broken or poisoned within me. The water seeps into my skin, leaving a tingly sensation on the surface of my arms. The hairs on my arms stand at attention, undeniably reacting to the light touch, or perhaps noticing the subtle transformation happening deeper inside of me.

I can't help but imagine a sort of cleansing is in process, like this is a ritual of some kind—finding my true self in the middle of nature. Like a sort of baptism, the water is rejuvenating my spirit, or maybe even awakening what's always been there and bringing it to the surface, unable to stay contained any longer.

I've missed this.

Mom looks like she's in her element, too. No big, bright smile plastered on her face, but rather just one of happiness and pure bliss. We've been paddling quietly since we left the dock. We had a few laughs after the boat nearly knocked us down with its waves, but Dad and Bea are far ahead of us now.

I can still make out the faint murmur of the engine in the distance if I focus on it, but mostly my ears seem to ignore any sound but that of my paddle entering and exiting the water. Little splashes landing intermittently on the surface of the water create soft ripples and a soothing dripping sound.

The water is spectacular. I dip my hand in it to gauge the temperature.

Even though it's early in the morning, the water is surprisingly warm to the touch, as though it's been collecting all the sunshine from the last hours, keeping it safely sealed away. There's hardly a difference between the temperature of the water and the air above it.

I'm eager to jump in and discover all the secrets of the lake. You can only learn so much about a place while skimming the surface of it. It's only once you go further—explore the depths of a place—that it becomes a part of you, shifting around you, making space for you to fit inside it, shifting itself to accommodate your presence. Only then can you truly know it and understand it.

I remember when I was younger, our family had gone on a trip to Bermuda. I'd been about eight years old at the time. I remember standing on the shoreline, swaying along with the waves crashing all around me. Mom and I had been holding on to each other. She'd been standing behind me, her arms draped over mine in a sort of hug that also served to help keep me upright. We had laughed loudly every time a wave hit us, knocking us around as it forcefully swept the sand from beneath our feet, upsetting our balance and forcing us to readjust time and time again—relentless.

The ocean never stopped. Even when it looked calm on the surface, the sand was still moving beneath it. We had to constantly fix our position to remain upright, our muscles aching from the effort of standing against the strong current barraging against us, doing its best to knock us down. It was breathtaking but also exhausting.

Sun-kissed, with salt in our hair and on our lips, our curls windblown, and our tired limbs dusted with sand, we'd collapse onto the fluffy white duvet comforter in our hotel room, wrapping ourselves inside it as though it were a cozy cloud.

I remember so vividly, lying on the bed after spending the day at the ocean, how I could still feel the movement of the waves hitting me, pulsing through me, long after we'd left the water. Like they'd imprinted their dance onto me, becoming part of me.

That was when I'd understood that the ocean is alive. It can be beautiful—an escape from reality—but it's also unforgiving. Its angry swells can capture lives whenever they wish to do so. Standing on the shore, the vastness of the ocean just beyond, I'd noticed its undeniable power but also, its subtle but very present fierceness. I'd immediately related to it.

The relentless battle beneath the surface was invisible to those still on the shore but I could feel it deep within me. The continuous fight to remain still—despite being pushed in every direction, assaulted by harsh waves constantly trying to knock me down by the force of it.

I'd never before felt something that expressed so perfectly what was going on inside of me. I was pulled by the constant trial, the fight, the power, the stumbling of feet, the crash, and the crushing strength pressing against my lungs which forced me to take deep breaths. I saw myself in that ocean. In how beautiful it was, how deep it went, but I also knew the destruction it was capable of.

The waves this morning remind me of the ocean, only they don't scare me in the same way. Perhaps because I'm older now, or maybe because the swells here are softer, easily breaking behind us, rather than growing harsher the closer they get to shore. Almost like their fury dissipates with every inch—like breathing—it calms itself down before returning to a more balanced stillness.

The water here is so clear, I can see the shadow of my kayak beneath the surface as the sun rises in the sky. My skin feels prickly, like tiny needles are piercing it and I know that the sun is making my skin darker with each passing minute. I can almost feel the Vitamin D seeping into my skin. Luckily, I hardly ever burn. My olive skin seems to drink in the sunshine and absorbs it into itself, transforming it into a rich, deep tan. Mom's skin does the same thing, creating a healthy glow, making us look like goddesses as we glide soundlessly across the lake.

I sigh happily as I shut my eyes, basking in the peaceful moment, making the most of it. It's so rare that I feel this comfortable in my own skin. Typically, I respond to the environment I find myself in. Where there is tension, I'll react to it threefold, lashing out, acting on instinct, purely in survival mode. But here, the calmness of the lake provides me with a rare stability I'm not used to. I'm enjoying it.

Putting paddle to water, I can't help but stare in awe at all the beautiful colours in the water. Mom has commented on it several times—how it looks like gemstones—and I have to agree.

Even though it's hard for me to live up to Mom's expectations, I feel bad for Beatrice. She wasn't meant to be the last one, but became so by default. All Mom's remaining hopes of raising the perfect children now rest on her shoulders ever since she lost baby 'C' and she knows it. I'm sure she feels it with every fibre of her being.

The doctors never found out why Mom miscarried baby "C". Those things are almost impossible to know as it could have happened for any number of reasons, most of which couldn't have been predicted or avoided. Yet, I know she still blames herself for losing the baby. As though she could have prevented this tragedy, somehow influenced the outcome, relaxed more, exercised more regularly, ate better foods, etc. But some things are out of our control.

Even though it happened a long time ago, Bea still suffers the consequences. For the rest of her life, she's cursed with trying to reach an unattainable level of perfection to make up for the loss of what might have been. But no matter how much she tries, at the end of the day, she's fighting a ghost. How could she possibly win?

Chapter 23
GEMMA

We remain outdoors for the better part of the morning, basking in the glorious weather, until exhausted and sweaty, we finally retreat back to the cabin. Amber and I drag our kayaks out of the lake and pull them onto the grassy edge of the yard, just out of reach of the water to prevent them from drifting off when we're not paying attention. We slump onto the ground beside them, extending our legs as we rest, trying briefly to catch our breath.

I'd forgotten how laborious kayaking could be, especially on stifling, hot days like today. My arms are burning from exertion and from the heat. Stretching my arms over my head, I turn my neck from one side to the other, rotating it carefully. I massage the tight muscles, rubbing them gently to help release any built-up tension remaining after our exercise.

Looking over to my right, I see Amber spread-out next to me on the grass like a glistening starfish and I chuckle. This grassy area is shaded ever so slightly by the roof of the cabin, leaving a blissful cool triangle of grass, refreshing enough when you're attempting to regulate your body temperature. Heading for a shower now would only leave us sweating the moment we got dressed again. I decide to join her and allow myself to fall back into the prickly grass. The coolness is a welcomed respite, almost like applying aloe vera on a sun-burnt back.

"Great workout, wasn't it?" I ask. She responds only with a weak grunt.

"Come on," I beckon. "We need to get out of the sun and hydrate."

Standing up reluctantly, I offer her my hands to help pull her up. We're both feeling drained. I find myself suddenly wishing this place had a hammock for me to relax and swing on while enjoying the shade of a tree.

What a difference the temperature is from yesterday. It's hard to believe that this is the same place. Lake properties tend to be fickle like this though—completely unpredictable. One moment you feel like you're dying of heat, and the next, a storm-front makes you shiver from head to toe and reach for your warmest sweater.

Wasn't it just last night that I'd been chilled to the bone, wrapped under layers of blankets, inching closer to the fireplace for warmth? This morning, we'd been bunched together like sardines in a tin can, the four of us smooshed close. The fire had completely died down, but the heat had lingered in the air, pushing away the expected chill that usually comes with mornings.

It's a wonder we didn't wake up with splitting headaches, complaining and grumpy, peeling off layers, eager to regain some distance between each other.

Stepping into the confines of the cabin, I'm hit by a wall of cool air. It appears that the trees surrounding the cabin are providing a surprisingly good amount of coverage from the sun, keeping the interior nice and refreshing after our morning out in the scorching heat.

Hurrying inside, I find myself desperate to find relief from the rays which I'd welcomed wholeheartedly only a few hours ago. Now, they seem harsh and harmful, like something I should avoid at all costs. My skin is begging to be hydrated. Our excursion on the water had been nothing but a tease.

I grab two bottled waters from the refrigerator and toss one over to Amber. She's found a chair at the kitchen table to sink into. I notice her lips curling in disgust as her thighs stick to the wooden chair when she attempts to move her legs. I decide to give my body more time to acclimate to the cabin's temperature before sitting down in turn. I fear whenever I do eventually sit, I won't be able to muster the energy to ever get up again. I'm completely spent.

Looking at the crumpled sheets on the floor by the fireplace, I imagine what it would be like to take a nap in the gloomy bedroom. Somehow, the thought isn't as revolting as it was only hours ago. I'm sure that once I make myself comfortable in the darkened room, I'll be able to fall asleep easily. After all, I didn't get much rest last night between my racing thoughts, the strangeness of this place, the howl of the wind whipping branches against the cabin, and the insistent creaking of old boards every time one of us stirred.

Combined with the proximity of all of our bodies and Niall's snores, I hadn't stood a chance. I feel the exhaustion all the way to my bones. The idea of sinking into a soft mattress and wrapping myself in a fluffy comforter is definitely more appealing now that I've started to cool off a bit. I'm likely to be useless for the rest of the day at this point, but maybe that's alright. We're here to get some rest after all, right?

My stomach gurgles loudly, interrupting my thoughts. Peering inside the refrigerator door, I find some of the items we've brought along with us that should, in theory, hold us over for today and the better part of tomorrow, but make a mental note that we'll need to locate a grocery store soon to replenish our supplies.

I shut the door, feeling a delicious gush of cool air mist over my face. We always seem to devour more food while on vacation, as though each of us had been starving ourselves for weeks in anticipation of the scrumptious "special food" we indulge in while we're away. Niall had suggested barbecuing some chicken breasts tonight. I salivate at the thought of it.

Looking at the large clock on the wall between the bedrooms, I notice that it's long past one in the afternoon. How time always seems to elude us while on vacation, I'll never know. Our internal clocks seem to be turned off. Nothing keeps to a regular schedule out here, it appears. Startled by the fact that we've somehow all missed lunch, I fling open the refrigerator door once more. Were we really outside all morning? No wonder I'm starving!

Looking at the crisp head of iceberg lettuce and fresh vegetables we brought with us, I begin grabbing items from the shelves, hurriedly assembling a salad to combat my hunger.

"Sweetie, what do you think if I make us a salad for lunch? Something light so we don't ruin our dinner," I explain. "Your dad and Bea will be back soon, I imagine. I'll set something aside for them too. I didn't think we'd been out there that long, but we've completely missed lunch!"

It's really not like me to be so relaxed that I completely forget myself or my responsibility to feed my family. Flustered, I scour the cabinets and locate a thick, wooden chopping board. Placing it on the centre of the island, I grab a sharp knife from the knife block and a vegetable peeler from inside the cutlery drawer and begin attacking the carrots, peeling thin layers off. I then snap off celery stalks and pass them under the kitchen tap to wash away any residual dirt before chopping them into small, bite-sized chunks. My mouth waters at the idea of biting down on the fresh food.

While slicing a red onion, some white juice oozes out onto the board and I use a paper towel to wipe it. The onion's skin has stained the creases in my hands a deep shade of purple. I throw in some freshly rinsed cherry tomatoes, chopped cashews, and a handful of dried cranberries to the mix. Topping it off with some crumbled goat-cheese, I lightly drizzle balsamic vinaigrette over the entire salad and give it a quick toss using some large silver spoons I found.

Finding a serrated knife in the butcher block next to the stove, I slice the fresh loaf of bread I baked at home yesterday morning and set out a stick of butter to soften on a small glass dish. Satisfied with my quick meal, I tidy up the counters and scrub my hands in an attempt to rid myself of the dark dye embedded into my skin from the onion. This will do to tide us over until dinnertime.

Lunches in our family are usually more of an after-thought—thrown together leftovers, scavenging the pantry for something to put together—whereas dinners, in comparison, are usually quite the elaborate production.

Typically, I strive to serve three course meals at least four or five days a week, almost always starting with my famous and savoury, thyme-infused, home-baked bread, sliced and ready to be dipped in expensive olive oil. This is followed by an array of perfectly roasted, seasonal vegetables, colourfully arranged next to a generous portion of marinated and grilled meat of some kind—well-seasoned and tender, of course—with a side of grains or fluffy mashed potatoes.

I always try to pair the meals with a nice glass of red wine and a decadent dessert. I tend to prefer a chilled cup of fresh fruit, but ever since the girls have taken an interest in baking, they sometimes supply brownies or something equally rich and chocolaty. Not that I mind at all, but we just can't have such calorie-filled sweets around all the time. Balance is key.

For tonight, I've brought along a rather large, seedless watermelon to enjoy. I find the promise of a refreshing fruit after devouring salty, charred meat smothered in barbecue sauce is the perfect way to end our dinner.

As I'm placing the salad bowl and basket of sliced bread on the centre of the table, I hear the sound of a motor approaching. I smile, knowing that Niall and Bea have returned just in time for our lunch, as though I'd planned it that way.

Stepping onto the deck, I wait for either of them to meet my eyes so I can gesture for them to join us inside for a bite to eat. Just as I'm reaching the railing, I notice Niall grab Bea's arm quite aggressively, his grip firm and insistent.

I see my baby girl turn, apparently as stunned as I feel. Bewildered by the scene unfolding before me, I watch, helpless as Bea attempts to pull her arm out of his grasp. When he jerks her arm hard, forcing her to look at him in the eye, my breath catches in my throat.

What the hell is going on? I want to yell out to them, to bring his attention away from Bea, to distract him or perhaps just to let him know I'm watching, but I can't find my voice.

Looking from my perch, I suddenly feel out of place. Heat rushes to my neck and I worry about getting sick. Looking down, I notice Niall and Bea in the middle of what appears to be an intense conversation. They are so close in proximity that people on the other side of the lake could easily mistake them as being in some kind of lovers' embrace. But from here, I have a clear view of Niall's snarl.

He seems intent on keeping his voice low. Frustratingly, he's barely moving his lips, making it impossible for me to decipher what he's saying. Squinting, I try my best to make-out the words escaping out of his mouth, but I can't focus. My heart is beating so hard in my chest, it's shaking my entire body just enough that it makes their figures appear less focused and slightly blurry.

There's something familiar about Niall's stance. I realize that I've seen him like this once before. That time had been by mistake. He'd acted totally fine afterwards, pretending it had never happened.

But when I'd insisted, he'd begged me to let it go, promising it would never happen again. He'd explained at the time that he'd simply slipped-up and lost his patience.

That altercation had happened shortly after Bea turned two, if I remember correctly, just weeks before I lost baby "C". I can't help but wonder now if it had possibly been the catalyst for the miscarriage. My baby getting out as though it sensed something I'd only just begun to understand.

I watch, horrified, fixed to my perch on the deck as Niall stands over Bea in a looming, imposing manner. It's confusing and terrifying to watch. I quickly scan the deck, but there are no stairs leading down to the water from here. In order to reach them, I would need to go through the front door and circle around to the back. But by then, their tense 'discussion' would be over.

Feeling hopeless, I watch as Niall's laser-like stare bores into Bea. There's a certain desperation to his posture. A sort of fear mixed with anger. A dangerous combination for anyone, let alone my husband, the father of my children. In this moment, like so many years ago, I feel repulsed by him.

I'm afraid of him and what he appears capable of doing in this very moment. He likes to play the part of the provider and protector, but right now, in his desperate attempt to conceal whatever disagreement he's having with Bea, he's a stranger to me. My role as a mother has always been, and will forever be to protect my children first, and at all costs.

Chapter 24
Niall

Releasing Bea's arm, I instruct her to keep quiet about the ordeal. I tell her to head upstairs and join the others while I tie the boat to the dock. Going through the motions of securing the boat, I begin to chastise myself. What the hell was I thinking? What if Gemma had seen me? It would all be over.

Running a frantic hand through my sweat-soaked hair, I can't help but feel unhinged. I'm not myself lately. Maybe it's this damn heat that's making me irritable and unstable. Is this a mid-life crisis type of reaction? No, not likely. It's probably due to the fact that I've been stamping down these feelings for years, until finally, they are beginning to burst out of me like fireworks—loud and unpredictable.

What is it about my teenage daughters that they know just the right buttons to push to piss me off?

Swearing through my teeth, I figure I better remain down here a while longer, at least until the fury leaves my body. I feel hot all over and not just because of the sun beating down on me. I wish I'd brought a hat along to shield my head. My receding hairline, although practically unnoticeable to anyone else, suddenly feels exposed and painful as an overwhelming need to scratch the itch overcomes me. Damn it. I must have burnt my forehead. Pressing a finger to my temple, I wince. Yup, definitely burnt. I'll be lucky if it just stays red and irritated and doesn't turn to blistery agony.

I find some reprieve from the sun under a nearby tree and stand beneath it for several minutes, forcing my breathing to return to normal. When did I get so temperamental and quick to anger? My entire life I've worked so hard to steer away from that impulse, burying it deep down, never intentionally reaching for it. Like a ghost, it haunts me, appearing before me when I least expect it.

But now, the girls have been summoning it, slowly figuring me out. I'm not sure how much longer I'll be able to hide it. They've forced it out of me, and I don't know how I'll ever manage to snuff the life out of it again.

I've kept my rage a secret for as long as I remember, always understanding that it was a reaction best kept hidden. Control was a necessity as unpredictable events seemed to trigger it. There'd been a time in the past when I'd been pushed to my ultimate limits and had lashed out unforgivably in front of Gemma. I still regret how I acted that day. I thought for sure she'd divorce me right then and there.

To my surprise, she'd bought my lies and forgiven me. She'd wanted so badly to believe I was good to the core that she'd chosen to turn a blind eye to any unwanted behaviours.

I'd never loved her more than in that moment. For she had seen the darkest and deepest parts of me and rather than run away, leaving me, she'd taken my hand and assured me that this was something we'd figure out together. I'd been so grateful for the grace she'd provided, but I wasn't stupid. I knew that I could never slip up again. Gemma is kind, but she's no fool.

I admire the way she decides how she will react to things, as opposed to being surprised by them. She always says that we can't control what happens to us, but we can control how we react to it. It's one of her favourite quotes by Brian Tracy. I only wish she'd abide by it more often. Her capacity seems stretched to the max these days, jumping at every sound, getting worked up over every little hiccup. She used to stuff it away, barely let it affect her, but something's changed.

I struggle daily to suppress my immediate responses and process my feelings before they begin to show. But Gemma has done it, for me—for us. She's saved our family from being torn apart.

I need to hold it together for her and tamp down these unwanted emotions. I can't afford to have another outburst like this.

I've been wound up so tight lately with work and Amber's suspension that I feel like a spring about to fly off in any direction. The stress has been accumulating and, like an overflowing cup, the contents are seeping out, bringing my worst self to the surface— exposing the ugliness residing in the depths of my soul. The darkness is threatening to come out, begging to be released. And dammit, it had felt so good to let it out, to give into it, even if just for a little while. But the triumph of allowing it to consume me had then burnt me like a flame.

The gratification had been quickly snuffed out by the heavy shame that descended on me and instantly made me feel like shit. If I could just hold on to that powerful feeling, without the rage linked with it, that would be ideal. But unfortunately, they seem to go together. I can't have one without the other.

My old man was like that too. Except, he didn't have as good of a handle on his anger as I do. What I've seen him do with his fists still haunts me today. It was a different time back then. Most men I knew believed in the same kind of discipline. His behaviour was viewed as someone with strict character who valued order. It was never considered abusive. We never complained about it because that was just Dad. Most of my friends were experiencing similar things, so we didn't really talk about it.

My father demanded respect with closed fists and harsh words, spat out of his mouth like darts through the heart. His strong hands could grip limbs so hard that they left imprints of black and blue bruises on my skin that lasted for days after. Hits to the head and face whenever we got out of line were normal forms of punishment back then, and even though I knew this, I'd still manage to earn myself a few spankings whenever I disobeyed him. Nowadays, parents do it differently. We're hardly allowed to touch our kids without attracting attention from authorities or concerned neighbours. Our children seem to rule over everyone these days.

I've always struggled with disciplining the girls. My go-to methods were seen as unorthodox or ancient, according to Gemma. So, I've been content to leave most of that responsibility for my wife to manage.

She's got more patience than I do in that department and as she spends the most time with the girls, it just makes sense. She understands them in a way I never will.

Shaking off the residual anger still lingering, I take a deep breath, steeling myself. Leaning against the rough bark of the tree, I feel the coarse surface scratch my bare arms, irritating my tender skin. I don't remember if I packed any aloe, but I'm sure Gemma has a tube of it in her toiletry bag.

She's always over-prepared, always ready for the unexpected, almost like she plans for illness or injuries. Our kids might be growing up, but my wife will always carry an assortment of medical supplies with us anywhere we go. "*Just in case*," she often chants in her sing-song voice.

Becoming a mother has forced her to settle into this structured, prepared being, always anticipating and planning ahead. The mere thought of it exhausts me—I couldn't be bothered. But then again, I am grateful for this new responsibility she's adopted since the girls were born. Now, I never need to worry about forgetting anything, because chances are, Gemma will have already thought of it for me.

Pushing myself off from the tree trunk, I start making my way up the little grassy hill towards the cabin. A subtle movement draws my eyes to the deck, causing my steps to slow down. I start, stopping dead in my tracks.

Not a face, but rather, the glimpse of a dark mane of black curls leaving the door frame and entering the cabin. Gemma had been standing on the deck. Most likely she'd been waiting for us, anticipating our arrival with a meal prepared, as usual.

As the realization dawns on me about what this could mean, I blanch. The hairs on my neck rise.

My first thought is that she saw me. The second is that she knows what I did to Bea, and I'm screwed. My third thought is that she'll most definitely leave me.

I can't let her do that.

Chapter 25
GEMMA

Eagerly, I wait for Beatrice to step inside the cabin. When she does, she's smiling brightly, and I'm immediately taken aback. Why would she pretend to be fine when clearly something major has just happened between her and Niall? Astonished, I watch her move around the cabin, her movements fluid, showing no signs of the tension I'd witnessed only moments ago.

Amber, who, gratefully, hadn't witnessed the scene on the shore, offers Bea some lunch and the girls begin sharing their experiences of the morning. They're both acting so normal. From my position by the patio doors, I watch silently, confusion spreading over me. Had I imagined it? I had been quite high up on the deck after all. Maybe I was more dehydrated than I'd realized, and it had caused me to distort what I'd observed.

I replay what I'd seen but struggle to shake the look Niall had in his eyes. I'm positive that I didn't imagine that.

Approaching Bea carefully, as though she's a wounded animal I'm trying not to frighten into scampering off into the deep woods, I quietly observe her every movement, trying to gauge her frame of mind. Attempting to be subtle, I search her face for any signs I might have initially misinterpreted or missed entirely. Nothing is amiss.

Her face is free from tears and animated as she gives a detailed account of the many beautiful islands they explored on the lake. I blink and give my head a shake. Am I losing it? Have I gone completely insane and made this horrible thing up in my twisted mind?

I know I didn't get much sleep last night and I am slightly dehydrated from the sunshine this morning, but am I really capable of making something like this up?

I grab a chair and join them at the table, still wary. I've hardly spoken a word since witnessing the altercation at the shore. Trying not to be too obvious, I steal glances at Bea, trying to get a better look at her arm. She's very lively as she talks about the boat and the waves, her arms moving continuously as she speaks. It's hard to get a clear view of them as they're constantly in motion. But from what I can tell, there doesn't seem to be any sort of visible bruising or finger marks. Still, I'm not entirely convinced. I'm surprised to realize that it never even occurred to me to suspect that Niall is capable of something like this. Because I have no doubts now that he is.

Bea's demeanour sends me for a loop. If she wasn't so convincingly content and joyfully expressing herself, I would have met her at the door and demanded to look her over, inspecting her arms for any possible injuries. I had every intention of confronting her the moment she walked in to get her side of the story while Niall was still at the boat, but watching her stride inside with an air of confidence I so rarely see in her, has left me mute. I'd desperately wanted to hear what Bea had to say before my husband's presence might influence her narrative.

But then she'd come in like everything was fine, as though she and Niall had spent a pleasant morning touring the lake. She genuinely appears to be happy. The contrast between what I'd observed down by the water and her apparent cheerfulness now are so at odds with each other that the quick switch is giving me whiplash.

A low throb begins at the base of my neck and I bring my hand to it in an attempt to quiet it down. Massaging the spot, I can feel the soreness underneath. I'd injured it quite badly when I'd fallen down the stairs. Was it really only a few weeks ago that I'd blacked out from the shocking pain and temporary lack of oxygen? Perhaps the fall caused more serious damage than I'd first thought.

I'm still pondering these thoughts when Niall finally walks through the door, seemingly his usual self. His face is flushed with sweat and too much sun, but he's beaming with a genuine smile plastered across his face—evidence that he enjoyed his excursion this morning. He's bursting at the seams to tell me about it, I can tell. But, good manners win out and he goes to the sink to wash his hands and splash some water on his face before joining us at the table for a very late lunch.

"This looks incredible, hon," he says appraisingly, looking right in my eyes, his hand reaching for mine on the tabletop.

There doesn't seem to be any trace of avoidance in his body language. If anything, he's conducting himself completely normally. Spooning a healthy amount of salad onto his plate, he joins Bea in recounting their adventure, and follows it up by asking Amber about her kayak experience.

I watch quietly as my family enjoys a lively retelling of this morning's activities. We make plans to visit the Bonnechere caves tomorrow.

Lost in thought, I rip apart a soft slice of bread, popping a piece of it into my mouth in lieu of offering any significant input to the conversation, not trusting my voice to be calm if I were to speak. I feel my heart rate increasing. I still can't make sense of what I'd seen by the water and it's really eating at me. I wish I could simply blurt it out, ask them directly and put them on the spot. But I know I won't. Instead, I try to piece together the scene and try and figure out if maybe I'd seen it wrongly.

The sun had been straight above me, shining down and reflecting brightly on the water's surface like thousands of little diamonds. I hadn't been wearing sunglasses, so it's possible the sunshine had momentarily blinded my vision. But then, I wouldn't have been able to see anything. That's not the same as changing what you see.

I'm still questioning my sanity when Bea looks over at me, her eyes sparkling. "Can I have some more salad, please?" she smiles sweetly, holding up her plate.

Bewildered, I force a smile and nod. "Of course, sweetheart. Have as much as you'd like."

If everyone wants to pretend like everything's fine, then I will too, even though I find it hard to do. Perhaps I'm wrong in what I thought I'd seen?

Lunch is over swiftly and without any hiccups. Once finished, we clean up and settle around the cabin to read or listen to music before heading back outside to enjoy the sun's golden hour. It's strange how normal this all is.

I rub my head, wondering if what I'd seen had been conjured from my own imagination. Everyone seems relatively fine, so why stir the pot? Maybe it's best if I just let it go for now and enjoy what's left of the day.

There's a lot more activity around the lake now. Several boats are speeding by, their motors purring along as they skip over waves made by others. Some of the boats have someone tubing or skiing behind it, yelling gleefully as they attempt to hold on and not fall into the water.

A group of young adults lounge on a pontoon boat. Their hysterical shrieks and giggles can be heard across the lake. Another boat with a flat deck carries a family of five. They wave over to us, and we wave back.

Our girls are swimming in the lake, now perfectly warmed after a day of sunshine. Their bare bellies can be seen below the water. They look like little silver fish lures as they dive under the surface, reaching the soft sand at the bottom with their hands and practicing handstands, letting gravity and the pressure of the water hold them upright.

They used to play in the water like this for hours when they were younger.

Niall and I would sit on the dock, watching them, grins on our faces, I can't help but observe that we must look like the perfect family to everyone passing by.

Removing my cardigan, I place it behind me on the dock and extend my arms backwards to help support me as I tilt my head back and stare up at the sky.

Clouds have appeared since I'd last looked, just little puffy white ones, no threats of rain in them. There are hues of gold, varying shades of pink, and purple scar-like scratches lining the sky as the sun begins its descent.

The girls splash in the water and laugh. The sound is beautiful. I can't remember the last time I've seen them like this. This place seems to bring out the child in all of us. With a focus on rest and play, responsibilities placed aside for the time being, it's nice to let go and enjoy everything around us and all of its beauty.

Returning my gaze forward, I smile but I can't help wondering. The water's soft swells move to the beat of passing boats and swimmers, constantly adjusting and morphing to the foreign movement. The lake appears to reject the disturbance caused by all the commotion and activity. The water keeps knocking, trying to regain its calm exterior, to maintain its facade.

The waves, subtle as they are, are hindering the clarity of the lake that we'd all witnessed this morning. I can't help but see it as a punishment for our disrupting the calmness.

From above, perched on the porch of the cabin, the water had seemed so clear, I'd been able to see fish, stones, and the multitude of shades of colour in the lake.

But now, as I sit on the dock with the sun slowly going down, dipping behind the adjoining higher landscapes, the bright orb appears to be swallowed up by the large expanse of water. The ripples and unsteady rhythm making the lake not so clear. The busier the surface, the harder it is to see the bottom.

Distractions, laughter, splashes, and glimmering diamonds of sunlight are causing a sort of mirage, obstructing the view of what lies beneath the surface. I dip my foot in the water, my pink nail polish lost in the movement of the water. Lifting my foot out again, drops of water fall back into the lake as the air hits my exposed foot making me shiver. The air feels colder now.

I reach for my cardigan and pull it back over my shoulders, suddenly chilled.

"Well, I guess I better get started on dinner," Niall announces as he stands up abruptly.

"Right, dinner," I say absentmindedly. I'd all but forgotten about it. "Alright, girls. Time to get out of the water and dry off for dinner."

They moan in protest but quickly join us on our ascent back to the cabin. Dried off and freshly clothed in cozy loungewear, we wash, chop, and toss vegetables together in the kitchen.

As the girls set the table, I pick up the watermelon I'd carefully selected at the grocery store, the one that sounded hollow and full of juice. Placing it on the cutting board, I grab a sharp knife and slice through the centre, cutting right through the rind and flesh at once.

The fruit pops under the pressure. It requires almost no effort for me to slice it in half, its flesh resting face up. Carefully flipping it over, I begin to cut even slices and arrange the triangles on a plate for later. The pink watermelon juice spreads over the cutting board like diluted blood, staining the light wood's surface and penetrating the grain.

The sight of it unsettles me and for a panicked moment, I stare at it unmoving, my reactions delayed. With trembling hands, I hastily wipe the juice with nearby paper towels, but the stain remains.

"Damn it!" I chastise myself.

Pursing my lips, I inspect it. I won't be able to remove that stain now. The cutting board is still usable, obviously, but no longer in perfect condition. Distracting myself, I continue with my tasks as it occurs to me that, similar to the cutting board, I may be able to wipe away unpleasant memories like what I think I saw between Niall and Bea, but even so, a dark stain remains in its place as a constant reminder that not everything can be swept, repaired, or cleaned back to its original form.

Shaking my head, I resolve not to dwell on this any longer. If Bea and Niall both seem reasonably alright, then maybe the problem is me, not them. I pour myself a generous amount of Pinot Noir in a delicate glass and shudder at the resemblance to blood.

What the heck is wrong with me? My mind is wicked.

I need to focus on better, more positive things. The fall down the stairs has really messed me up, perhaps in more ways than I'd care to admit. It seems to make me think the worst of those I love most.

I feel constantly paranoid, anxious, and guilty. I take a sizeable gulp of wine as I step outside on the deck to look over the lake.

The barbecue is lit and the meat sizzling on the grill is releasing a delicious aroma in the air. The lake's afternoon activity has begun to quiet down as people head home for dinner.

While the meat is cooking, Niall prepares a bonfire, gathering lawn chairs around it. With a nice view of the lake, I imagine we'll spend most of our evening gathered around it.

There are many clouds covering the sky now. They are effectively blocking out the stars, and yet, some still manage to cut through the thick masses and reflect on the surface of the water like millions of tiny sparkles. I breathe a sigh of relief as I see the lake finally returning to its original calmness. The panicked waves from earlier are like a faraway memory. Perhaps it will all be okay after all.

Chapter 26
Beatrice

Tossing and turning beneath the sheets, I hear Amber grunt next to me in bed. The double mattress should be large enough to accommodate both of us, but Amber is lying face down, her legs spread wide, leaving me with almost no room on my side. Usually, I'm perfectly happy to lay on my back as I don't tend to move much during the night, but my legs seem to have a mind of their own tonight.

Spasms and muscle aches from hours sitting in the boat are catching up with me. The swim should have helped to get them relaxed again, but my legs just won't settle. My mind is also racing from the day's events.

I still can't believe how easily Mom believed me when I'd plastered a smile on my face and claimed that everything was fine.

She'd been so eager to believe my lie, so willing to push aside any doubts about her husband. She'd avoided bringing anything up, steering clear of any confrontation, even though she'd clearly known something had happened. It was as though the very idea of Dad doing anything wrong clashed with her ideals of our perfect family. Instead of broaching the subject and risking making things uncomfortable, she'd simply turned the other way. Mind you, I'm partly responsible. I'm still not entirely certain why I insisted on pretending that everything was fine. I can feel my body tensing as shame fills me, quickly moving to anger.

Would she even have believed me had I exposed him? She'd taken in my fake smile and chosen to ignore what her gut must have been telling her. She'd taken my upbeat demeanour as proof that her suspicions were wrong. As quickly as the doubt had crossed her mind, she'd pushed it far away. She'd so easily ignored the signs, pushed unwanted thoughts aside, choosing to see only the good even if it wasn't real. It's a skill that takes time to perfect. She has a lot of experience in that department. She's been doing this for years.

I keep waiting for the day when she'll notice me. For the day when she'll come to my rescue, put me first, ahead of Amber and Dad. And yet, as hard as I try, I just can't see it. It's a sad life when you don't feel wanted by those who made you.

I know Mom wanted me, or so she claims. She knows her lines by heart. Though they alter slightly over the years, the message remains the same. She loved the idea of the 2.5 kids, the beautifully decorated home, the successful husband, but after she got it all, it wasn't quite like she'd expected.

Beautiful daughters can become a pain to their mother as they grow up. Amber and Mom dance a tango of jealous rivalry when it comes to being admired. They used to share the spotlight, passing the baton back and forth, relishing their equal, glorious good fortune.

I shake my head. How vain they are at times! It's like they think nothing and no one can touch them, that everyone else in the world is below them, looking up to appreciate their natural beauty. I envy them more than I want to admit. But I also pity them. When you're that stunning, you can't really ever hide away.

I've found my place in the shadows and made peace with standing behind Mom's and Amber's bright lights, even though I find myself blinded by them at times. I've chased it often, as one does with bright things, only to be pushed aside and deemed unworthy. Without meaning to be, I was cast away, deprived of any attention from others, as if I were a dark thing scavenging the dirty floor for crumbs and scraps to eat. Always seeking and eating, yet never satisfied. So, I'd turned to books.

If I couldn't be the pretty one or the desired one, then I could be the smart one and do my best to have perfect behaviour at all times. I chose to be calm, constant water while Amber would be the raging ocean. I'm the warming fire glowing at night, providing reassurance and light to see by, while she is the blaze that destroys the house.

Although, after today, I can't help but wish I had a little bit of Amber's spark in me.

I rub my arm where Dad had grabbed it only hours before. It's sore. He'd been insistent, his grip strong and unyielding. The fury in his eyes is one which I've only ever seen in Amber. There's a dark side to my father that I'd never witnessed before today.

Closing my eyes, I wish for sleep. But my mind keeps tormenting me, refusing to let go of these thoughts. I'm not sure how yet, but I'll have to let them go somehow or risk going insane from trying so hard to keep them caged.

Turning towards Amber, I begin to wonder if I could share my secret with her. There was a time when we were close, more friends than sisters, when we'd enjoyed each other's company.

Today at the lake had felt like these old times. A tear slips from my eye and runs down my cheek, landing inside my ear. I don't move to wipe it. I miss being a child and not worrying about all of these things. So much has changed. As time goes on, it's becoming abundantly clear that I'm not wanted here. I don't belong.

Amber wouldn't understand. Would she even listen to me without making a snide remark? Would she believe me? Probably not. She'd probably tease me about it, expose me, and make me regret ever confiding in her. Keep your friends close and your enemies closer, right? Well, my enemy lies right next to me.

While I lie like a soldier, waiting for battle, alert, and listening, Amber has her face down, smothered in her pillow, without a care in the world. It's as if she knows on some level that I pose no threat to her, that I won't ever hurt her, because she's the lion and I'm the lamb. She rules the house, and I have no choice but to obey.

But that look in her eyes last night bugs me. Her delight in aggravating my father is proof that something's going on between them. Even if it's unclear yet, there's definitely a rift between them. An irreparable one, it seemed.

Amber had drawn her line in the sand, so to speak, drawing boundaries not to be crossed. Dad had watched, half amazed at her strength, and half in absolute disdain of her arrogance. No doubt wondering how he's come so far only to allow himself to be undone by his own daughter.

It must kill him a little inside every time Amber gets away with something.

He lets it slide most of the time, returning the balance, obtaining control over the situation so that he can again feel on top. But the older Amber gets, the more she understands, and the more dangerous she becomes. If she's the lion in the family, then she rules over all. Lions don't have natural predators as only humans hunt them.

Amber might think she's obtained immunity, now high up on her throne, but she should watch her back. She sleeps easy now, but she's let down her guard. She's forgetting that the best defence she can have against any threat is an ally.

Today I witnessed what happens to Dad when he feels like control is slipping through his fingers. He works so damn hard to keep a tight lid on things, but he is beginning to unravel. Something has changed recently.

He's not controlling his emotions well. They are slipping right out of his firm grip. Instead of suppressing his feelings, as I assume he's always done, he's allowing them to bubble up to the surface, exposing them for all to see.

But I doubt he'll allow this to go on for much longer as it would ruin the image he's worked so hard to perfect over the years. He won't let anything, or anyone expose him for who he really is.

And yet, now I know. I'm the wild card he wasn't expecting—the silent one who usually doesn't cause trouble. He hadn't anticipated that I would confront him on the boat.

I'd seen the shock and the fear in his eyes when I admitted that I'd discovered proof that he'd been cheating on Mom, and I knew with whom. Dad uses his strength, his body, and his voice to intimidate people and get them to do as he pleases. It's an old technique—ancient even.

But to me, the louder he yells, the more I see him losing control, the more holes I can poke in him and see his true character eager to be released. I'm just not sure I want it to come out. It's ugly, and quite frankly, it scares me.

But how can I go on pretending now? How does Mom do it? Surely, she must suspect it. Wouldn't she know on some level that he's been unfaithful to her? It would be all over him, in his scent, or in the subtle changes in how he touches her.

I shudder. I'd prefer not to think about this too much. I have to consider the possibility that Mom doesn't know. That this would destroy her. She'd feel like such a fool. How can Dad do this to her?

She's dedicated her entire life to serving our family. She doesn't deserve this, or rather, he doesn't deserve her! She's committed to us—to a fault.

She's lost parts of herself in the process, lost her fire. But maybe it's still in there, deep inside, like coals glowing red, waiting for fuel to ignite them back to their full fury.

Turning my head, I stare at my sister. We're so different, she and I.

Amber is loud and makes her presence known. Dad also likes to dominate the space he's in, whether it's with a bellow of laughter or a firm handshake. I'm the silent observer in the family and in ways they don't understand, I hold all the power.

I've been watching them all, studying them, for years. I know the expressions on their faces. I can read them like a book. I blend into the shadows and go about my days mostly unseen.

When they think no one is looking, that's when they let their guard down. They've ignored my presence for so long that they don't even sense when I'm in the same room.

I could be holding a knife to their throats, and they'd never even hear me coming. Their skin doesn't prickle when I'm near, the hair on the back of their necks doesn't stand up when I walk by. That's exactly where I want them—unassuming and feeling safe. How could someone as unimportant as me do any real harm to them? How could a lamb ever hurt a lion?

Chapter 27
Amber

A gentle rain patters against the window. The comforter covers me, the fluffy feathers weighing gently over me. I have no desire to get up as the air is chilly on my face. Yawning, I readjust my position, sinking deeper under the covers, resisting the urge to pull the comforter over my head and hibernate a little longer.

The darkness outside caused by the looming clouds isn't helping me to wake up. How is it possible to wake up from a night's sleep feeling more exhausted than before?

Turning over in bed, I realize that Beatrice isn't lying beside me. She must have gotten up already. I can't say I'm surprised. I tend to sleep in longer than her. Still, it's strange that I never noticed the covers shift or the mattress lift when she left. Then again, Bea has a way of going about unnoticed. Rubbing my eyes, I wonder what time it is.

The rich smell of coffee wafts through the open bedroom door and only then do I become aware of faint murmurs coming from the kitchen. A spoon makes a *tink* sound against a ceramic mug as someone stirs their drink. The air is filled with the scent of sugar and bread, immediately reminding me of cake and effectively rousing me from the last bits of sleep I'd been clinging to. *Pancakes!* I guess, my mouth already salivating.

Hastily, I rip the covers and duvet off of me and throw on a grey crewneck sweatshirt to cover my rising goosebumps. I'm still in my pyjama shorts when I pad over to the kitchen. It seems that I'm the last one up this morning, as usual. I'm greeted with excited cheers, a good morning hug from Mom, and an apprehensive smile from Dad.

Bea has her nose deep in a book. She must have grabbed one from the little bookshelf in the living room. Her legs are curled up beneath her as she sits slumped in one of the armchairs next to the fireplace, isolating herself in every possible way. She always sits like that, with her legs tucked in. I think she started doing that when she was little, afraid some creatures or ghosts might slide beneath her and graze her legs when she wasn't paying attention. The fetal-like position must be reassuring to her, curling up in a tight ball—a way to protect herself by making her body as small as possible, or perhaps as invisible as possible.

She's an odd duck, that girl. Constantly yo-yoing between wanting to fit in and be seen and hiding away.

It's sad to watch sometimes, how hard she tries to please everyone—her desperate attempts to be liked by all. I struggle to understand her most days.

Some sisters seem to share a rare, unbreakable bond, as though they are joined at the hip, two peas in a pod—inseparable. Their love for each other trumps everything else. But with Bea and me, our relationship is more like oil and water, or fire and ice—it just doesn't mix.

Looking out the window, I see that the lake is rippled with thousands of circles where drops of rain land on the surface. It's nothing like the other morning. It's amazing how unpredictable and changeable the temperature is by the water.

I remember whenever it would rain when we were kids and we'd complain about being cooped up indoors, Mom would pull out an old craft box that she usually kept hidden away from our curious little hands, the glitter perfectly contained. Each time we had access to this treasure box of goodies, we littered the kitchen table with its contents, scattering stacks of colourful paper and rolls of shiny stickers, extracting an assortment of stamps with letters or pictures on them, the ink pads long since dried up.

The craft box also held a bottle of liquid school glue, white and gooey that we would squeeze enthusiastically, before sticking mis-matched, chopped up pieces of craft paper together, adding buttons or old beads, and leftover ribbon from Christmas onto it, creating unique masterpieces. This box would entertain us for hours.

Within it, there was also a cardboard box containing wax crayons, with every colour we could imagine along with a beautiful princess-themed colouring book. I could always tell which drawings I'd done because I very rarely coloured inside the lines. Often, my hand appeared to have a mind of its own.

I would drag my favourite red crayon across the page, covering everything in its passing. It didn't matter to me if Snow White's dress was meant to be yellow and blue, or if the lines served to preserve some shape to her dress. My hand gripped so tightly around the crayon, it's a wonder I didn't break it in half as I covered the page.

Bea, on the other hand, was always painstakingly precise when it came to her drawings, as she is with most things, I suppose. A rule-follower to a fault.

I would wait what felt like hours before getting a turn with the colouring book. My sister would carefully select each colour, making sure to be as accurate to the characters as possible, darkening the extremities and shading the middle to give it depth. Ever the perfectionist, she would cry if ever her hand slipped and created a rogue dash across her drawing, claiming it was ruined.

Come to think of it, I guess the difference between us has always been there. It seems more obvious now in retrospect. I smirk despite myself as I think of how much my drawings must have bothered Bea. Mine were usually covered in bright, angry red dashes across the page and rippled with rips where I pressed a little too hard.

She must not have understood my technique, maybe even chose to ignore it completely. To her, my attempts might have appeared messy and disturbed, whereas hers were usually perfect renditions of what she'd held on to in her imagination. She preferred fairytales, castles, and ball gowns, but I tended to focus my energy on the evil queen, the poisoned apple, and the hunter.

If you pull back the curtain on fairytales, most of them are darker than they first appeared. They are warnings dressed up in pretty dresses, silenced by catchy songs, camouflaging the reality of what they're really saying just below the surface—that the evil lives within each one of us. We all have the capacity to play the villain in our own lives. Anger and revenge have strong desires to be known and released. With the right motive or the right opportunity, they might just get that chance.

Chapter 28
Niall

It seems like we've only just arrived at the cabin and now we're already leaving it to go exploring. The large tree trunk that was hit by lightning on our first night lies helplessly on the ground between the car and the cabin. One of its sides is completely stripped with shreds of bark scattered all over the carpet of pine needles.

I can't believe how narrowly it missed hitting our car. It's astonishing, really. Another few inches to the left and the entire front of the vehicle would have crumbled like cardboard under its weight. The front windshield would have no doubt shattered into a thousand tiny shards of glass all over the seats, rendering it unsafe to drive. We would have been stuck here until a tow-truck could come collect us.

I let out a sharp breath, all at once scared by how close we came to losing our car and grateful that we're all alright. I feel sad to leave the lake and boat behind, but it's a rainy day, so it works out great that we'd planned on visiting the Bonnechere caves today.

The drive is short, barely twenty minutes, and the road is peaceful. It seems that most people have opted for a quiet day inside rather than getting outside and exploring. I feel a twinge of pride at the fact that my family is up to venturing out today despite the rain, as though we're all determined to make the most of our vacation, rain or shine.

The parking lot hosts several vehicles containing other brave families willing to step out of their comfort zones to discover something new. The rain isn't unpleasant, only spitting now as we make our way to stand under a large wooden gazebo to meet our tour guide. Tim had included brochures for local sites to explore in the welcome package. Amongst the sparse few was one for the caves, indicating daily tours every twenty minutes, starting at 11 a.m. We're right on time.

Exiting the car, we follow several other visitors to the entrance gazebo at the edge of the parking lot, following each other like a line of ants.

"Welcome everyone! My name is Trevor and I'll be your guide today!" He dramatically makes eye contact with each one of us before continuing his well-rehearsed speech. "Has anyone ever visited the Bonnechere Caves before?"

His energy is contagious. He seems to genuinely enjoy his job and appears to be around Amber's age. Since the caves are closed for parts of the fall and winter seasons due to flooding, this must be Trevor's summer job.

He's wearing a long-sleeved forest green dress shirt and khaki cargo pants as his uniform. As a few people timidly raise their hands, Trevor nods and proceeds with his speech.

"The caves were discovered back in 1853 by Alexander Murray, a surveyor who, while in the process of creating a map of the Bonnechere river, noticed what appeared to be subterranean channels. The first ever exploration of the caves happened almost a hundred years later, in 1955 by Tom Woodward, a WWII Veteran..." The kid explains that this guy apparently wrapped a rope around a tree and slung himself down a sink hole.

I remember parts of this story from our last visit here, but it still strikes me as either an incredibly stupid or brave act—the outcome determines which.

I'm doing my best to listen, but my attention keeps shifting to Amber. She seems particularly interested in what Trevor's offering. And I don't mean the historical information. There's no doubt the kid is good-looking, and he presents himself well, but he seems to be capturing her attention more than anyone else here. I can tell he's also noticed her because he's stumbling over his words, coughing at random, his voice wavering. Amber's stare, both enticing and intimidating, demands all of his attention. Trevor doesn't seem to know if he should fear or approach her. The strange standoff makes me cringe uncomfortably.

Amber knows what she wants, there's never a doubt about that. The thing is, what she wants isn't always what's best for her. As her father, it's my job to keep her safe, even from herself. It's obvious that there's chemistry between them.

Fleeting looks, batting eyelashes, both offering each other their full attention. Amber had already been the most excited to visit the caves as she loves adventures, but Trevor is the cherry on top.

I observe them from the back of the group. Their subtle, silent, and flirtatious conversation is betrayed when Trevor's cadence switches from a rehearsed narrative of facts to a more engaging tone, as though he's trying to mask his excitement at her undivided attention.

"Alright, well, let's get started, folks!" He waves for us to follow him and turns to walk down a narrow, corridor-like path of trampled grass with long grass swaying on either side, resembling moving walls.

"The tour will last about an hour," he informs us, twisting his head slightly to allow his voice to carry behind him.

Stopping in his tracks, he turns abruptly to face the group, halting us all in our stride.

"Because the caves are below the water level, the temperature inside is about ten degrees," he informs us with a concerned frown, but after looking us over, he seems immediately reassured. "Ah, good! I can see that everyone's brought along a light jacket, so we should all be comfortable." Clasping his hands together, he offers a contagious smile. The short walk has helped him regain his professional demeanour.

He's working hard to keep focused, I can tell. He's doing that thing where he's trying to avoid looking directly at Amber, as though she were a solar eclipse and would damage his vision if he did. I can tell all he wants to do is look at her, wanting more of that intoxicating stare, but surprisingly, he wills himself not to.

Instead, his gaze intensifies on everyone else. His fists clench at his sides from the effort and restraint it's taking him to ensure he keeps his tone even and remains calm. His attraction to my daughter is evident.

I shake my head, annoyed. I don't like this. I'll have to separate them before this goes any further.

Trevor starts the tour under a second wooden gazebo which shields a display of ancient fossils from the incessant rainfall. He describes each one, explaining how the limestone we're about to walk through was dumped there by layers of mud buildup during the Ordovician time. Baffled, I stare at the geological time chart pinned behind Trevor, his voice zoning in and out.

The Ordovician time was over 500 million years ago, even before the dinosaurs! It's difficult not to be impressed by Trevor's knowledge as he picks up rocks and explains the differences between the various invertebrate creatures, detailing their findings of gastropods, horned coral, pelecypod, and curled shelled cephalopod fossils. I won't remember these by the time we end the tour, but none-the-less, I'm amazed.

After the short demonstration, Trevor guides us to the entrance of the cave. The dark, mouth-like opening entices us to enter it. Gripping a banister, I step onto the secure boardwalk and fall in step behind the girls, as the access point only allows one person to enter comfortably at a time. There are several electric lights installed on the ceiling of the cave, making it easier to see ahead. Still, within seconds of entering the cave, I'm surprised by the vast darkness spreading ahead of us. As well, just as Trevor warned, there's a noticeable temperature drop.

Following the pack, I see the rock glistening in the faint light coming from Trevor's headlight. He speaks as he walks, his voice clear, not nearly as echoey as I recalled from the last time we were here.

I reach out my hand and touch the wet surface of the rock. It's not slimy per say, but definitely moist. Wiping my wet fingers on my pants, I lift my head and notice a low, narrow tunnel to the side.

Amber has noticed it also.

Trevor halts the tour and invites whoever wishes to venture inside what's called the Spelunkers tunnel to do so now. He explains reassuringly that the tunnel loops back around and will bring them back to the tour.

Starving for an adventure, Amber doesn't hesitate as she decidedly walks down the dark tunnel. Someone with a headlamp walks ahead of her, lighting the path. We watch their bodies disappear, a muffled echo resounding in their wake. Some of the other visitors are taking pictures in the dim light of flashlights or head lamps provided for the tour. We're completely surrounded by rock. The air is cold and damp, but we breathe easily.

"Congratulations!" Trevor announces suddenly. "You're now officially certified "spelunkers" which means you are now real cave explorers!" he cheers, inviting the rest of us to join him in the celebration.

When she makes her way back out of the tunnel to join us, Amber's coat is streaked where drops from hanging stalactites have landed on her shoulders. Her eyes sparkle, obviously thrilled by her experience. This kind of outing is right up her alley.

When we reach a larger cavity in the cave, Trevor instructs us to turn off all our lights. Even though I've done this exercise in the past, I'm still taken aback by the absolute darkness surrounding us. It's astonishing how much we rely on tiny pinholes of light in normal times. But here, every ounce of light is snuffed out.

Our eyes may be open, but they are unseeing, leaving us to rely on our other senses.

The only sounds I can hear is of our own breathing, drops of water dripping in the distance, or the odd shuffling of feet as someone readjusts their position. Grouped closely with strangers, the silence makes me uncomfortable. After a minute or two in complete darkness, Trevor instructs us to turn our lights back on to continue with the tour.

As we walk along the narrow path, Trevor teaches us further about the stalactites hanging overhead, explaining that the natural structures are produced by slow drips of water containing build-up from minerals. The pointy formations come from rainwater mixed with carbon dioxide, which, mixed with bat excrements, drips onto our coats. Apparently, the largest stalactite they have here measures just over a foot long.

The tour explores about one third of the totality of the caves, as it's the only part safe enough to host visitors. About halfway through our tour, we hear the faint murmurs of distant conversations as another group enters the caves far away.

Amber is disappointed to discover that the bats that hibernate inside the caves during the winter months are away during the warmer season. I, for one, am grateful. Bats scare me, but I won't admit it out loud.

I can tell that Bea is also glad for this. The mere mention of the furry creatures has her practically pinned up against the wet wall of the cave, as though one might materialize before us at any moment. She couldn't get far enough away if she tried.

In the beams of the electric lights, I'm struck by how young she is. I can't believe I'd lost my cool with her. She'd driven me so crazy on that boat ride that I'd snapped. It was inexcusable, I know. I feel bad about it now. I'm just grateful I didn't leave a mark.

Chapter 29
Amber

My gaze lingers on Trevor's face as we leave the caves. That adorable grin of his had reached deep inside my soul. I try to position myself near him so I can ask for his phone number. I want to see him again, even if I have no idea how to make that happen. I assume he lives locally, but it's not that far to make a potential relationship impossible. Besides, I'm sixteen now. I'll be getting my driver's license any day. I'm really digging his nerdy look and I also like the fact that Trevor doesn't go to my school, therefore he doesn't know about me or my reputation. He's a blank slate—a fresh start.

Decidedly, I make my way over to him, going around lagging visitors. He's occupied at the moment, answering further questions about the cave's discovery, but his eyes find mine. I see a spot of pink on his cheeks, but he maintains the conversation without any hiccups.

Sensing he's about to finish, I step closer but feel a firm hand on my shoulder.

"Come on, Amber. Let's go." Dad's voice is low, but effective. I have no choice but to follow him.

Reluctantly, I walk back towards the parking lot, dragging my feet. Every ounce of me wants to turn around for one last look at Trevor. I'm dying to know if he's watching me as I walk away, but I resist the urge. I walk on, my stride switching from hesitant to decisive.

I'd been silly to imagine a relationship with a guy I'd just met. I know nothing about him, and it isn't likely I'll ever see him again. Better to not drag this on any longer. Looking back would etch his face in my mind forever and increase its importance, eternally searing his memory as 'the boy who could have been more'. I refuse to allow that to happen. I know myself and my weaknesses.

I know to others I often appear cold and indifferent on the outside. People might assume I go about life largely unaffected and unmoved by my emotions, but I'm not impenetrable. I feel things deeply. My heart bleeds instead, preventing my tears from escaping outwardly. I feel every ounce of the pain of separation and disappointment. The hope that had risen within me is quickly extinguished as I struggle to breathe. I feel it all, but it's impossible to tell just by looking at me. I'm good at hiding it.

It's no wonder that I often lash out inappropriately. It's from holding on too tightly to feelings, afraid of releasing them to the world. But the effort of holding everything usually overwhelms me, accumulating until it's unbearable and I can no longer manage effectively or even pretend to control it.

Before I realize it, the pressure from withheld emotions bursts at the seams, like a dam where the concrete foundation has cracked beyond repair, allowing water to burst through, causing irreparable damage.

I need air. I need space. My feelings take up so much room within me, I might as well be composed of them—no organs, just emotions. As though they alone are what keep me alive—dreaming, hoping, and fighting. To have an opportunity, as small as it was, for the potential of love and to have it snatched from before my eyes is almost too horrible to bear. I know I will probably lash out later. But for now, I manage to breathe through it, but just barely.

I close my eyes and push his face far from my mind as quickly as it entered it. It's the only way to save myself from exploding. Still, I can feel the familiar rage building inside of me.

My instinct is urging me to defy my parents and return to Trevor, just to talk. The unfairness of being denied this somewhat insignificant experience is almost worse than disappointing them. I consider my options for a moment, but decide to step inside the car and strap myself in, a pathetic restraint for the time being.

I feel as though my emotions are so strong that they will propel me out of this car and towards Trevor, almost without conscious thought. I know I'm being dramatic, especially about a boy I've just met and never talked to, but it's in my nature. Dad hadn't explicitly forbidden me to speak with Trevor, but he'd taken away the opportunity, which is just the same. His disapproval or reluctance to let me speak to Trevor is the very thing pushing me to do just that. But for whatever reason, this time, I let it go. The fight's left me. I just don't have it in me right now.

Dad's been strange and unlike himself lately. He's not as relaxed as he usually appears. His movements are stiff and unnatural, like he's holding himself back. His smile is tightly stretched across his face and his eyes are practically slits from the strain of pretending. He's watchful and observant. I'm not sure yet if he's trying to discover something, or if he's trying to see if people have found out who he really is. He's acting paranoid. I bet he's trying to hold back his emotions like me. I can almost see the smoke coming out of his ears as he works so hard to keep it together.

The drive back is silent. I stare out the window, lost in thought as Bea listens to music on her device with her eyes closed. I know she's not sleeping but she's escaping in her own way and blocking out the rest.

I don't know when she became so mature. It's like she grew up overnight. It's hard for me to believe that she's turning thirteen this year. I worry about her. Is she tough enough to survive all the drama that comes with becoming a teenager? I'm not so sure.

I find it difficult to read her lately. There's been a shift in her demeanour recently. At times, she seems to have built walls around herself. I've noticed her getting harder around the edges, growing thicker skin. Like she's becoming tougher. Not stronger per se, but callous and bitter—uncaring. As though, for the first time, she's realizing that life isn't full of rainbows and unicorns or that the sunset isn't made of peaches and cream, but a fire warning us of tomorrow.

She seems more alert, prepared for anything, always on guard. I'm not sure what she's getting ready for, but I can feel the shift radiating from her.

She sits up straighter these days and doesn't miss much. Sitting in the shadows, she's constantly observing. Patiently waiting for something, only I have no idea what.

It seems like we've all reached a point in our family where no one trusts each other as completely as before. Bonds have been severed and our confidence in each other has been broken like brittle sticks of wood.

What this means for the future of our family, I don't know, and I don't really care. I'm tired of pretending to be the perfect little family. I'm more and more convinced that such a thing doesn't even exist. Everyone has secrets. Sometimes the power lies in hiding secrets. Other times, you reign by exposing them.

Chapter 30
GEMMA

The cabin is dark when we return, and I worry that we've lost power again. I haven't gotten used to this place yet or familiarized myself with all its dark corners. There hasn't been enough time to notice the distinctive way the light seeps in through the windows or where the sunlight lightens the floor slightly in one particular spot, muting the veneer on the oak planks, or the way the boards creak when they're stepped on.

I've barely paid attention to the direction in which the light breeze blows the kitchen curtains, or the rhythmic sound of the clock mounted on the wall. I don't yet know this place as intimately as I know my own home. Yet, there's something about this cabin, a certain familiarity that automatically makes me comfortable.

Although the building is a far cry from being as pristine as our home, there's something comforting in the finishes. The way the warmth of the wood mingles effortlessly with the painted and mismatched furniture seems to automatically put me at ease. It's almost like I could step out of character—make a mistake or a mess—and it wouldn't be the end of the world and wouldn't define who I am. It would simply be a mess. Nothing more, nothing less, and easy to clean up. Many people live in homes with this sense of comfort amongst the disorder. The very fact that nothing matches is the appeal.

It's how it was intended, purposefully eclectic. It's so far from the design of our own home where everything is white, crisp, and glossy. I could eat off my floor at home, but I wouldn't dare do that here. And yet, I'm perfectly happy to drape my coat over the back of the wooden chair and remove my shoes.

I love the feel of the oak floors on my bare feet. I feel a freedom I haven't experienced since being a child. Running wild in the grimy driveway, sand crusted between my toes, the soles of my feet blackened by dusty roads. My face and clothes caked with mud or dirt and holes in both knees, and my elbows bleeding from a recent fall, those had been some of my best years. My smile was always stretched wide—I'd been blissfully happy. No matter how often I'd fallen down, I never hesitated to get back up again.

I'm not sure I could say the same nowadays.

Thinking back to my fall in the stairs, I'd stayed lying helplessly on the floor of my own house for what had felt like hours. Paralyzed by shame as much as by the pain.

How weak my body has become! A body that had once created life, who'd once jumped over fires in the yard, these legs that had propelled me across a multitude of creeks to reach the other side of a small ditch, running into neighbouring fields. The soles of my feet had been rough and coarse, and I'd been proud of that fact, thinking it made me stronger— fierce. Proof of a thirst for adventure I'd quenched.

Yet I didn't feel parched—that wasn't me anymore. I was older now, wiser. Wasn't I?

Everyone has seasons of longing for past selves, or memories of youthful energy, childish dreams, and ideals. I knew better now. Back then, I'd been a wild thing. I'd allowed the wind to direct my every step, blowing me around like a dandelion seed. My feet would run without stopping, my mouth, once opened, was never closed. My skin, forever with a coat of dirt or mud upon it, made me unrecognizable at times. Every day I'd become someone new.

Set in my ways now, or willed into them, I have to leave that past life behind. It's painful to think about the little girl I used to be. How I'd feared nothing and lived every moment. Over the years, my childish ways and innocence opened doors that should have been bolted shut. There was no way back.

I thought that building walls around me would help keep me safe, but somewhere along the way, I opened the wrong door and invited fear inside like a secret lover in the cover of night. I've let my anxiety move in and now it's impossible to kick it out. I'm too scared to face it, so instead, I avoid it and pretend it doesn't exist.

Since we get back from the caves well past lunch, we decide to have a late dinner. The rain is still falling hard outside, drenching the earth, so I opt to make a simple pasta dish instead of a barbecue. I don't have much at my disposal, so we'll need to find a store tomorrow to make it through to the end of the week. I'm running out of ideas of what to make for meals.

Shivering, I feel the same chill I'd felt when we first arrived. None of the oppressive heat from yesterday lingers. All the warmth has been snuffed out by a dampness that seems to reach deep into my bones.

Heading to the bedroom, I change hastily into cozy, warm clothes, stumbling and losing my balance as I hurry to fit one leg and then the other into lined sweatpants. Pulling on some dry socks, I find myself looking forward to a nice, quiet evening by the woodstove. Maybe I'll even read one of the books I've picked from the small collection available. I know Bea won't mind a night in either, but I worry about Amber. How will she entertain herself tonight? She has a tendency of getting into mischief whenever she's bored.

Coming back to the living room, I'm surprised to see my family sitting together, all waiting for me to join them. Laid out on the coffee table is an old deck of cards, fanned out and ready to be picked. The cards are frayed at the edges, but otherwise intact.

"Want to play a game with us?" Niall looks up, hopeful. "We're playing Crazy Eights." He motions for me to take a seat next to him.

"Thanks," I say as I curl up beneath a throw blanket.

The fire is lit, and the glow is glorious. I feel groggy, covered by all this warmth. Our trek through the cave this morning and the air pressure from the rainy weather and grey clouds have caused a dull headache to throb behind my eyes. I rest my head on the couch pillow.

"You guys play, I'll just watch," I answer after a while. I relax into the soft cushions, letting my head loll, a soft smile on my lips, watching my family playing a card game.

Vacations have a way of bringing people together.

This is easily a situation we could replicate at home, but yet, I know for a fact that we never will. We may mention it here—how fun and simple a game it is and why don't we play this at home—but we'll never carry this moment back with us. These games, just like the relaxing atmosphere will unfortunately remain here, waiting for the next family to come visit and appreciate them. There are things we do on vacation that we wouldn't dare do during our usual routines, as though we become other people while we're away.

We drink more, speak our minds without guarding the words that leave our mouths, and eat constantly, our bellies seemingly endless pits—insatiable. We spend most of our time outdoors if the weather permits, but the moment we return home, the spell is broken. Just like that, there is a shift in the atmosphere. We return to our old habits, shutting ourselves indoors, finding chores to occupy our time. We're constantly interrupted by phone calls, to-do lists, or well-meaning neighbours stopping by for a quick chat, but all we want is to be left alone with our thoughts.

Out here in the middle of the woods, no one knows us—we're left mostly to ourselves. There isn't much to do, which is surprisingly nice as it forces us to rest. We stretch out outings to make them last longer, knowing they are few and far between. We have a newfound appreciation for our clothes, since we have only packed a limited portion of what we normally have access to at home. In the same way, the food we eat seems to have more flavour as we savour it, appreciating every bite, careful not to waste any. It's almost like we trigger some dormant internal understanding that we may never again return to this place, therefore it's our duty to make the most of it and enjoy all it has to offer.

No longer surrounded by the usual, mundane things, it's easier to notice the different elements. They leave imprints on my mind in a way my regular days at home don't seem to do. I can almost recall every detail of our previous trips, down to the meals we ate on which days, simply because it broke the pattern of our everyday lives at home. It provided excitement, unknowns. It felt refreshing.

"Ha! I win!" Amber exclaims, a fist punched in the air in triumph. I smile. I can't help it. I haven't seen her enjoy herself as much as she has this week in a long time. She seems right in her element. I wish I could hold onto this moment.

I notice a flash of something spreading across Niall's face as he watches her. Contempt mixed with an equal amount of disgust. Quite truthfully, the expression is so quick that I almost missed it entirely. I shiver as I think back to what I'd witnessed on the dock earlier. Before today, I'd almost pushed it completely from my mind that Niall's features could arrange themselves so disturbingly. But of course, I'd seen them do so once before.

227

His face returns to his usual smile within seconds, the terrifying snarl disappearing completely before anyone else witnesses it. Amber shows off her cards and Bea picks up the rest of the deck to shuffle the cards. They have no clue that something more sinister is at play. Uncomfortable, I grip a fistful of the throw blanket to stop my hands from shaking. My gaze wanders across the table, shock and fear blending together. Bea is smiling into her newly drawn hand, but Niall's expression is eerily calm, intentional and practiced, and yet there's nothing calm about it.

Even though he'd quickly rearranged his features, I still see the lingering hate in his stare. In an instant, it's like the glass before my eyes shatters. All the previous illusions I'd once had of my husband evaporate in a cloud of smoke right before me. I can no longer separate his face from the fear I felt when I noticed his stare. This isn't the man I'd fallen in love with all those years ago. This man is a stranger.

I recoil slightly in my seat, feeling like a gush of cold air has swept in and settled between us, pushing us further apart like two blocks of ice floating on water, drifting further away from each other. I recognize now that what I thought I knew about my husband had all been a charade, a series of masks he's expertly been wearing this entire time, expertly switching one for another according to the situation. I'd been so trusting—so blind. He'd always been in control of his emotions, his life, and me.

Until now, it would seem.

The mask he's chosen isn't fool-proof—I've seen what's underneath. His smile is plastered on and fake—his eyes seem hollow and dark. I flinch.

I recognize this face. It's an old mask he's shown me once before. Only this time, the surface is cracked, allowing me to peek behind it and see the truth.

Chapter 31
Amber

I let myself sink into the soft mattress and pull the comforter around me. Bea is settling in next to me, but her mind seems restless. I feel like we've been making progress in our relationship these past few days. There seems to be some kind of treaty between us, an unspoken, mutual understanding that we are now on the same team. As though we're both consciously willing to push aside our differences, put down our weapons, and make peace for the greater good. By now, it is certain that we are never going to be the same, never going to see eye to eye on all things, but we seem to have decided to accept each other for who we are. There's a freedom in that.

Bea has let her guard down a little. She even laughed at one of my jokes at dinner. She's still her usual composed self—not-a-hair-out-of-place Bea—only now, she's a little more laid back.

I like it.

It's been raining all day. I can hear the droplets hitting the roof, falling repeatedly, almost becoming white noise. I yawn. The steady rhythm is making me sleepy. My legs feel tired and achy. I reach down to press my thumb into my thigh muscles to help ease the dull, throbbing pain. The barely-there throb is irritating. I sigh, feeling old.

With the lights off inside the cabin, the place is completely dark but for the warm glow coming from the living room woodstove.

I can hear the low murmurs of my parents' voices beyond the room, and I'm surprised by how comforting that is. I remember when I was a little child and I'd fall asleep to the sound of them talking in the room next door. How safe I'd felt—reassured by their nearby proximity. Back then, we had a much smaller house and the wall had been thin enough to eavesdrop on their conversations—a skill I would develop and rely on through the years.

Bea is lying still on her back as she usually does when she sleeps. She's always fallen asleep this way. From the moment Mom wrapped her in a sleep sack when Bea was just a few months old, she'd conformed to this position, never altering from it. It was as though sleep only came to her if she laid in this position, flat on her back, arms resting limply on either side—completely unmoving.

Mom always jokes about how differently I had slept as a young child, always fighting against the garment, pushing and pulling it until my arms were finally released from their fabric prison. Even then, I'd needed space, to be free—to break out of the shell constructed all around me.

Mom laughs about it now, but I know that at the time she was often exasperated at my resourcefulness, always getting out of the sleep sack as though I was a secret agent on a mission. I must have driven her crazy—never letting her rest. She could never be assured I'd remain peacefully asleep in the bed she'd so carefully tucked me into.

I like to imagine that I was making my mark on this world even as a child. I've never liked feeling smothered by blankets, finding them constricting rather than comforting. Mom likes to wrap her body in throws and thick sweaters, and wind scarves around her neck, but I prefer when my skin is bare. I find that it helps me breathe easier.

Bea's breath is uneven and fitful tonight. Her eyelids are closed, but I can see her eyes moving restlessly beneath the thin skin. I purse my lips and furrow my brow. My sister doesn't usually let things affect her too much. She likes to hang back, observe at a safe distance, and not get involved. As though she's afraid of getting her hands dirty, she remains in a place, far away from it all.

Even as kids, I'd been the one jumping in muddy puddles, splashing it all around myself. The murky liquid would get everywhere—in my hair, on my face, inside my boots. I'd have to sit on the front steps to remove my boots and pour the muddy water out before placing them to dry on a rack. Mom always had spare splash pants for me and yet there would very rarely be a clean pair ready to be used.

I loved squeezing the mud between my fingers, letting it get underneath my fingernails, the tint of the dirty water coating my bare arms.

It was practically impossible for me to resist passing up the opportunity to jump in a puddle on the way to a store. Mom would have to pull me away, tugging at my little hand, desperately trying to save my newest pair of shoes. Depending on the day, she'd either do her best to physically restrain me, or let me have a go at it and laugh along with me—defeated, but choosing the high road, relating to my impulse.

Bea has always been the opposite. She hates getting dirty—would cry anytime sand stuck to her hands, demanding to be washed right away as though the very idea of being dirty scared her—an anxiety inside her from a young age. She couldn't stand getting her clothes stained and would fret and obsess about the tiniest drop of mustard landing on her shirt, insisting that she needed to change before she could move on to the next activity.

It seemed we were always waiting for Bea to change. Her laundry hamper would pile up sky high, toppling over inside her closet filled with barely worn clothes. It drove Mom crazy. Bea could change her clothes fifteen times a day just in order to maintain the idea that she was clean. She always wanted to put her best self forward, whereas I never felt that need. I was never going to be perfect, so why kill myself pretending to be?

Bea's breathing is raspy, her chest lifting rapidly. I wonder if she's having a nightmare. Her brows are furrowed, and her lips are curled. It's an expression I've never seen on her face before. It's almost like she's getting ready for a fight rather than reacting from fear—a mix between anger and vengefulness.

I force myself to stop moving as I observe her curiously. Placid Bea—she'd never hurt a fly. She's lived her entire life to please others, ruffling as few feathers as possible. Watching her now, I can see a little bit of the flame that burns in me sparking to life within her. I smile—an ember of pride rising in me.

This vacation seems to have released something in her she'd repressed for a long time and is only now setting free. Finally, a sister I can hang with. I watch her keenly as she lets her guard down—her true self coming out in her unconscious. This is not the person she portrays for everyone else—the one desperate for love and acceptance. Instead, here is a strong girl who's ready to fight for what she wants.

Vacation Bea had started to unspool before my eyes like a loose thread being pulled from a sweater. She's slowly and steadily coming undone, breaking out of the cage she's built around herself over the years. It's mesmerizing—like watching a chrysalis turn into a butterfly. I find myself drawn to her, excited for her.

Watching her now, her face twisted and angry, it's almost like she's fighting an internal battle with herself, trying to hold some part of herself back. The strain of it looks excruciatingly painful. There's a war happening just beneath the surface. Maybe she's always been fighting silently—a quiet warrior. I've just never paid enough attention.

When I'm struggling with my emotions, I let them all spew out of me, freeing myself from the burden. I reject my feelings as a part of myself, refuse to hold them tightly against my heart as the pain and the strength are much too great and too heavy for me to carry on my own.

With every step, I rage, scream, cry, hit; anything to let it out. But Bea holds it all inside of herself, lets it fester and grow into something I can't even imagine.

On the outside she's calm and collected, but what if there's always been a storm raging inside of her? What if I've just been too loud and all-consumed by my own outward fight, too self-absorbed by my own war to notice she'd been fighting one alongside of me this entire time?

I shiver despite the warm duvet spread out over my body. There's nothing to laugh about here. What's going on with Bea is real. It took a while for me to notice, but she's on her guard, even as she sleeps. She doesn't feel safe even surrounded by her family. An overwhelming sense of unease rushes over me. Perhaps Bea's threat is closer than I'd thought.

Bea's face and body are rigid—she's ready for an attack. Her face contorts into an unrecognizable expression. It would almost be funny, except that I notice her hands. Her fists are clenched so tight the knuckles are white. The amount of self-control she must have to keep hold of her hands, keep the storm brewing internally, rather than letting it seep out is unfathomable. I can't help but wonder how long until the dam breaks and all hell breaks loose? I'm not sure I'll want to get in her way if that happens. And I'm almost certain now that it will.

I can feel it deep within every fiber of my being, deep in my belly. *Trust your gut*. Something is coming.

Chapter 32
Beatrice

Warm morning light shines through the window, covering my arms. Even with my eyes closed, I can feel the warmth spreading over my body. I'm sweating beneath the duvet. Amber's body feels like a furnace next to mine. I stick a leg out to let the morning air cool it off, but the air feels stale.

Kicking off the heavy comforter, I open my eyes reluctantly. I'm exhausted. It might be due to the heat or maybe it was the dreams I had last night that kept me stirring and fitful. I yawn loudly, covering my open mouth with my hand as pungent morning breath drifts into my nostrils making me recoil.

"Gross," I complain of my own body odour.

With my jaw shut all night, teeth grinding, and saliva festering with nowhere to go, stress hormones, and fear added to the mix, the result is quite atrocious.

Humans are disgusting, I conclude.

In my t-shirt and pyjama pants, I tiptoe quietly out of the room, pulling the door shut behind me. Amber tends to sleep in later than the rest of us. My mom claims it's due to a growth spurt—teenage years or something like that—but she's always needed more sleep.

I expect the sudden craving for more rest will overwhelm me soon enough as I get older, but I can't say I'm looking forward to it. I'll be thirteen next week and I've yet to get my first period. A few girls in my grade have had theirs and have now developed breasts, capturing the attention of all the boys in the class.

It's funny how having boobs can affect social circles, dividing who's popular and who's not. As though we have any control over when our body develops, or like it has anything to do with our personality. Often before falling asleep, I find myself wishing for boobs like Jennifer Carter's. She's only thirteen but looks sixteen now thanks to her recent development.

I heard her in the change rooms once saying her bra came with an underwire and padding because sport bras just didn't cut it anymore. She would parade her new body for all to see, making us instantly jealous and envious of her recently developed curves and the status they gave her, not to mention all the attention she received from boys.

I can't help but crave the same for myself. My tiny boobs barely make a dent in my swimsuit. I look boyish, straight as a board, no curves to show off. Amber was a late bloomer too, but she turned out just fine with the perfect ass-to-boob ratio, with just enough soft curves to feel feminine without the daily struggle of fitting into skinny jeans.

I try not to have unrealistic expectations about the way my body will transform in the next few years. There's no stopping the natural process of things, but I wouldn't mind getting a bit of Amber's good fortune in the looks department.

Mom and Dad are huddled around the kitchen table, sipping from obscenely gigantic cups of coffee. I hadn't noticed those cups when we'd rifled through the cupboards, but they are comically large. They remind me of the ones seen on *Friends*. I've always wanted to drink from one, but I suspect the drink's warmth would evaporate too quickly for my taste.

I like my hot drinks scalding to the point where I practically burn my lips when I take a sip. My mom has adapted to enjoying lukewarm coffee, a habit developed by necessity, not by choice, from years of running after us. I wonder if she actually prefers it this way or if she just tells herself she does.

"Hi, darling!" Mom's voice is light and airy, like the curtain blowing softly over the kitchen sink. A slight breeze is making its way inside the cabin, and I breathe in deeply, taking in the freshness of the air.

"Hi," I yawn sheepishly, instantly reminded of my putrid breath. "Sorry, morning breath." I cover my mouth hastily.

"Do you want some orange juice?" Mom starts to stand, ready to cater to me, but I motion for her to sit back down.

"I can get it, Mom," I tease. "I'm almost thirteen now, remember?"

"Right, of course. What was I thinking?" she chides herself gently, laughing.

I grab the juice carton from the refrigerator and a glass from the cupboard and pour liquid sunshine into it until it reaches the rim. I carefully pick up the glass and bring it to my lips to sip the top before attempting to walk across the kitchen, not wanting to spill even a drop.

"So, what's the plan for today?" I inquire, partly dreading spending yet another day confined in tight quarters with Dad, but also curious.

"Well, it's quite beautiful out," Mom points out. "I thought we'd just hang out around here and enjoy the lake."

Mom had been reading a book when I'd stepped out of the bedroom, but she'd quickly abandoned it the moment I'd crossed the room, ready to give me all of her attention. Poised and content to serve, she eyes me eagerly, as though me drinking orange juice is utterly mesmerizing to her.

I feel myself shrink in my chair under her stare. She doesn't seem to be looking for faults, but I can't help feeling awkward under her gaze. Forcing myself to return it, I notice that her eyes are watery, and I feel my body relax.

She's probably just nostalgic, remembering the past years, like a movie playing the highlight reels before her eyes as she watches me intently. There's a twinge of regret in the way her mouth curves downwards and I begin to worry.

Catching herself, she shrugs it off and plasters on the smile I know so well. The 'everything's fine and dandy' smile that I've come to recognize as her fake smile. Looking across the table, I realize that Dad hasn't once looked up from his phone. He hadn't even bothered to greet me when I sat down next to him.

My body feels warm and my nose wrinkles in disdain as I watch his eyes scanning the words on his phone, completely absorbed in the screen as though it holds the secrets to the universe.

He often gets like this when he's working, his lazer-focused attention effectively muting any distractions. I wonder if he's reading a new message from Yvonne. I have to push down a snide remark to keep it from erupting out of me as I watch him, suddenly seeing him as a small, pitiful man.

My mom is a goddess next to him. What is she doing with a loser like him? Why does she let him mistreat her and cheat on her like this? She deserves so much better.

Glancing back at her, I see her studying her coffee intently, lost in thought, with that same smile fixed on her face. I press my lips together, forcing the exasperation to remain hidden. I want to reach out to her across the table and brush my hand over hers to reassure her and let her know that I see her, all of her. Unfortunately, after years of this, Mom's coping method has been to pretend she's fine and act like she's never known anything different than the life she has right now. It's as though she's forced herself to forget what true happiness feels like.

Just once, I'd love to see my mom let loose, abandon all pretenses and just allow herself to feel and be her own person, no matter who it might upset. She lost sight of who she was before she became a wife and mother.

My mom's former self now resides in her stories, inside the bulging photo albums now gathering dust on the shelves in the living room back at home, and in the colourful garments packed away in boxes inside her closet. That Gemma died when Amber and I were born.

Rather than simply adding a name to her person, she'd exchanged it for another, *wife*, then later, *mother,* losing her name and herself little by little when she married Dad. He'd chiseled away at her, turning her into his own ideal of perfection and into an exemplary wife he could be proud of. She'd never really been loved for who she was, but rather the potential he'd seen in her.

Dad is probably not entirely responsible for Mom's transformation. I'm sure that on some level, she allowed it to happen, maybe even convinced herself that she wanted to meet his expectations and didn't always fight back against them. Perhaps she thought it was the only way to get what she wanted out of life, that there wasn't enough space for Gemma, *the woman she'd been* and Mom and *wife, who she was now*. To her, it seemed they couldn't all exist within the same person.

There were times when I was younger, when Amber was off at school, and it was just me and Mom at home. There were rare and special days when Gemma would resurface from the grave. When a song would blast through the speakers and my mom would pull out her old garments from that hidden away box in the closet, draping shiny fabric over me, colours flying everywhere as we danced and twirled with abandon, as though we were the only two people alive in the world.

For hours, we'd laugh until our cheeks hurt, and our bellies cramped. We'd eat ice cream for breakfast and pretend the floor was lava. Those were the best days. I would get lost in the glimmer of Gemma and hope some of the shine would stick to me.

But then something would change.

Almost as quickly as she had appeared, Gemma's spark would dim, as though a cool breeze had swept through, making the flame flicker, threatening to snuff it out at any moment. Before I knew it, Mom would be back, gathering scarves and dresses in her arms, methodically and quickly, on a mission to erase any trace of our fun, or of Gemma, I never knew which.

I remember watching her mechanical movements, relentless in her efficiency as she swept up the beautiful mess we'd created together, only to put it all away in a dirty old cardboard box stuffed inside a dark closet where I wouldn't see it again until the next time Gemma came out.

I longed for those days. They were such a bright contrast to the rest of our time spent in discipline, order, academics, and classical music. I would sometimes get glimpses of Gemma at bedtime, when Amber and I would snuggle beside her and she read us stories from some of her old books. She always entertained us, enthralled us with her storytelling by creating different voices for each character. The books came alive and the pictures she described would remain with us long after bedtime. It was quite the production, and she was very good at it.

Unfortunately, that spirit died slowly over the years, becoming a monotone reciting, the story coming out as flat as her smile. Gone were the days of grand elaborations, sidebar comments, exclamations, and spontaneous laughter. Just a dutifully read passage, reading exactly word for word, black and white, what appeared before her eyes on the pages.

Without any room for imaginative passages, there was no more stories from her childhood, no more glimmers of Gemma. Instead, we learned to expect plain, steady, and predictable Mom.

I assume most people would delight in having someone like Mom, someone reliable and dependable. It's true that we always know where we stand with her. She's clear, concise, and fair in her discipline. Whenever we mess up, she just has to look at us a certain way to make our bodies unwillingly retreat back into ourselves and march our way up the stairs to our room.

We know the drill.

Day in and day out, the predictability I'd once relied on, one I'd even yearned for, I had begun to resent. I desperately missed the spontaneity of Gemma. I missed the fire and the possibilities. Somewhere deep inside, Gemma was still there, concealed by layers of responsibilities, expectations, regrets, and grief. Gemma was buried deep.

Looking at my mom I can't help but feel sorry for her. Sure, Gemma wasn't always reliable. Her emotional outbursts left me rattled for days by their sheer force and intensity. My soft-spoken mother would roar like a lion whenever Gemma would come bursting out of her, but very quickly, as fast as a blink, Mom would return with her placid tone, reassuring touches, and stillness that would throw me for a loop. What had happened to her? Why was she holding back parts of herself so tightly that she was willing to extinguish her fire?

Was she afraid of her own strength and unpredictability? Maybe she rejected her impulsiveness and spark to the point of hatred and had built fences around herself. Built up walls in the form of structured routines and repetitiveness in order to control her days so she wouldn't have to feel the highs and lows.

But who can live like that? That's barely living at all. To me, it seems that Mom is only surviving her life. I think I'd rather die than relive the same days over and over.

Chapter 33
Niall

When I woke up this morning, my phone was lit up like a Christmas tree. Emails from clients suddenly needing me to put in offers on houses that have been sitting on the market for months. Claiming they'd had a change of heart and grown attached to the place and simply had to have it. The small bungalow my clients had originally dismissed, claiming it was puny and pathetic, was now charming. A few of the emails were from Yvonne regarding other properties. With every new message from her, I feel my chest constrict with building excitement. Her subtly suggestive, yet professionally written email doesn't fool me. She wants me.

Being away from me seems to have sparked renewed interest in her as I'd hoped it would. I'm enthralled by the messages, reading between the lines, getting turned on by the underlying meaning between the words, making of them whatever I please.

Absentmindedly, I munch on toast smothered in honey. Crumbs fall like confetti on my shorts in celebration of my triumph. I'm glad to see Yvonne practically begging to have me back in her arms. She thought she didn't need me anymore, that I'd fulfilled my purpose, scratched her itch—or so she'd claimed when she'd ended our affair.

Yet, her recent messages seem to suggest otherwise. She hasn't flat out said it, nor would I expect her to. We need to be careful, but I know what she wants and it's clear from the increased beating of my heart that I'm more than willing to fulfill her wishes.

Sensing eyes on me, I look up to find both Bea and Gemma staring me down. Gemma wears a strange, waxy smile stretched so wide I worry her lips will crack under the tightness, while Bea stares unflinchingly, sending daggers in my direction. She knows exactly what I'm doing and is obviously disapproving. She's become a threat to my secret relationship. I refuse to let my almost thirteen-year-old daughter expose me and destroy everything I've worked so hard for.

When she'd confronted me on the boat, I hadn't been expecting it. It caught me by surprise and I didn't have a chance to come up with a believable lie. I'd always suspected Gemma might get curious about my whereabouts or even peer over my shoulder to read my messages as a kind of passive check-in, but I'd never considered that my youngest daughter would be my demise—not in a million years. But Bea had discovered irrefutable evidence.

A few years ago, I'd brought the girls to the office with me whenever Gemma had any appointments. I'd let them play around on the computer, checking out the various listings I had going at the time.

They'd both met Yvonne on several occasions. It was difficult to forget someone as stunning as Yvonne. She'd made an impression. She could pierce a hole in your heart like a worm and wedge herself inside you. Yvonne demands attention. The girls had been mesmerized by her larger-than-life presence.

Peering up from my phone, I feel sweat start to form on my hairline. Bea threatens me with her stare, glaring at me with intensity. She's shooting daggers, silently accusing me of breaking up the family, of hurting her mom, of being an ass, whatever the mood *du jour*. She's not usually so transparent. I guess it's inevitable that she's becoming more like Amber every day.

Great, like we need two of them, I sigh and resume looking at my phone. I decide to ignore Bea's accusing glare. She can judge me all she wants. She's just a child. She doesn't understand adult things yet.

She couldn't possibly comprehend my needs or desires to be wanted by multiple women. It's impossible to resist. Gemma just isn't the same as she used to be, especially not after raising the girls. I used to cherish her, call her my precious gem. She'd been my world. But her shine had gradually begun to fade over the years.

She is so dull now she's lost all her charm, so much so that she is practically unrecognizable. She is shades of grey when she used to be radiant, full of light and colour. Even her wardrobe seems to have transformed from a rainbow to a stormy cloud. It has been quite depressing to watch.

Some people might resent me for not sticking by her and waiting it out, as though there was still hope for things to return to normal. Yet, I know she isn't getting out of this. Not easily anyway.

Whatever evils she is fighting, they are there to stay. They are as much a part of her as the girls are, clinging to every fiber of her being. Darkness from the miscarriage had snuffed out all the brightness and made a home inside of her. I'm afraid it might just kill her to even attempt to wrench it out of her as it's intertwined itself so thoroughly to her. To untangle it would be to reshape Gemma's entire person. Even if I did manage to remove the darkness, would there even be anything left of the old Gemma?

I hadn't seen her in years.

The woman my wife used to be had practically been erased from my memory. All that was left was an old tape I sometimes played in my mind when I'd find myself longing for her. I missed who we'd been back then when all we'd had to worry about was our own happiness.

However, I couldn't ignore the many benefits of how predictable this new version of my wife was. She was floating through life, looking straight ahead, never deviating from the path. In many ways it seemed easier for her this way. It caused the least disruptions and she was better able to manage her emotions. I'd used this to my advantage. We've settled into our roles over the years and things were working like a well-oiled machine. Only, there's no heat and certainly no more passion. Our love is not even lukewarm. More like stone cold—practically non-existent.

This arrangement of ours, what we call our marriage, is a farce, a contract for the betterment of everyone. I need a wife to keep up my image and reputation in the real estate business and she needs a provider to be available to care for the girls.

Brushing the crumbs from my shorts, I let them all fall to the floor. I don't care when they get cleaned-up. I just know that it's not my problem who does it or how it gets done. I rise from my seat and stretch.

"I think I'll head out to the lake," I announce suddenly. "This heat is making me groggy," I yawn as punctuation.

Amber, unsurprisingly the last to rise this morning, shuffles into the kitchen and pops a bagel in the small toaster, switching the setting to three to ensure she won't burn it.

"Hi, sweetheart," Gemma greets her. Amber only grunts in response. "The water's hot for coffee," Gemma indicates helpfully, guiding her daughter in her dazed state using only the soothing sound of her voice.

The girls have always had sharp hearing when it came to Gemma's voice. It's like a superpower, as though they are connected on another level that I can't fathom. It freaks me out at times. Gemma once told me she feels so connected to the girls that it's almost like they can communicate through telepathy. She's reassured me on many occasions that this is a normal phenomenon between mothers and daughters, and that she used to do it with her mother—not that this gave me much comfort.

"I think I'll go for a swim too," Amber mutters.

The toaster pops, the sound of the mechanical spring echoes in the small cabin. She grabs the bagel slices hastily, carefully trying not to scorch her fingers, plopping them onto a plate and drags her feet to the table where there are remnants of cream cheese and butter.

"That's a good idea. Maybe after lunch, we could head to the store to pick up a few items," Gemma suggests hesitantly. "We're running low on some things," she offers as an explanation. "I started a list on the counter. Let me know if there's anything you'd like to add to it before we go." Gemma looks up at me, waiting for me to contribute to the conversation.

I stare at her, wondering why the hell I'm still standing here talking about something as mundane as groceries while part of me is visualizing Yvonne bent over my desk, her panties down to her ankles, her toes curling, her hands gripping the edges of the desk, begging me to go deeper as I thread my fingers in her hair and pull her head back.

I shake my head to mentally erase the image and force myself to return to the present. Right. This is what life is like for me now. Groceries. How thrilling.

But being the devoted husband I am, or at least that's the role I'm playing, I smile brightly at my wife, thank her for her thoughtfulness, and let her know I'll add a couple of items after my swim. She smiles sweetly back at me, and I can't help but feel disdain. I've lost all respect for her. She has no backbone, constantly bending to my every whim. She's so eager to please me, and yet, she's so far from the mark, it's laughable. Thinking that I'm content with her presence alone, or with her attention, her *sacrifices* as she once put it—it's pathetic.

She has a way of twisting things to make herself appear like a victim of my choices. As if staying home to raise the girls wasn't a choice we both made together, instead of one I imposed on her as she often claims.

If I recall correctly, when her maternity leave expired, she'd been beside herself trying to get comfortable with leaving her daughter with a stranger so that she could pursue a career. She'd been on the fence, unsure if there was even a point to it. But now, her song has changed its tune. She is resentful of the choice she'd made all those years ago, blaming me for forcing it on her. She seemed to be under the impression that she could change the plan, roll the dice again, and try her luck at another path. But she'd made her choice.

I intend on keeping her in this spot for as long as possible. She may think she has a say, but it's all part of my plan.

If I flat out rejected the idea of Gemma ever returning to work—if I'm anything but encouraging of her pursuing work—then I will very quickly become the bad guy. She would begin to view me as controlling and limiting her success. But by encouraging her, listening to her lamentations about wanting more for herself, acknowledging her fears, and even entertaining a round of mock interview questions to 'help her' practice some skills, I'd played my part as the doting husband well.

There hadn't been much to worry about. When each job prospect fell through and the opportunities thinned out, I made sure I was there to pick up the pieces, just as I'd planned. She needed a reminder of my role as provider and her place as a housewife and mother. Any illusions of anything different needed to be squashed and never entertained again.

Chapter 34
GEMMA

My swimsuit fits snuggly around my waist, the elastic material stretching over my bony hips. I haven't purchased a new one in years. There just never seemed to be a point. It's not like I'm trying to impress anyone or have anything to show off. However, this old, faithful one might have seen its last days. Other than the thinning fabric, there are visible signs of wear and tear just below the armpits, where my arms have frequently brushed the stretchy fabric, the repetitive movement causing pilling on the surface of the suit.

The black, one-piece suit is now faded to a charcoal colour from being washed often and from the chlorine its endured over the years of swimming in Grace's inground pool. No matter how many times I've washed it, I can still detect the distinct smell of chlorine on it.

With my head cocked to the side just over my shoulder strap, I inhale deeply, letting the scent coat the inside of my nostrils. I just love that smell.

Normally, I detest swimming in lakes, due to a long-standing fear of catching the infamous swimmer's itch and the inevitable possibility of one of my feet brushing against the slimy scales of a passing fish or floating algae. The thought of either event occurring is frightening enough to quickly propel me away from the water before my toes have even sunk into the sand.

But thankfully, Lake Clear is known for good water quality and of course, its clarity. There should be no risk of any ill-intentioned monsters lurking in the water here.

It eases my anxiety somewhat to be able to see underneath the surface. I push myself further out of my comfort zone and force my body into the water. My slow steps disturb the water as the muddy ground shifts beneath my feet as I trudge deeper, away from the shore. I'm surprised to see the sand particles settle back to the bottom of the lake, almost like they are eager to return to their rightful place, afraid of getting swept away in the current of my slow and easy walk.

There aren't many boats out this morning as we're, once again, outside earlier than most locals. Trying to make the most of our time here, we've been enjoying the lake as often as possible. The weather has been unstable, so whenever it's been nice, we've spent our time outdoors, hanging out in folding chairs, perched on the dock or settled in the shallow water at the edge, dipping our feet in the water to cool off.

The humidity today clings to my skin like plastic wrap. I have to keep wiping water on my forehead to cool off. The skin around the crown of my head feels sensitive under the harsh rays as I unsuccessfully attempt to stave off a sunburn.

The large oval open-back design of my suit doesn't offer much protection from the sun's unrelenting rays and I've absentmindedly forgotten to apply sunscreen to my back. I keep turning to face the sunshine in a weak effort to save my back. However, the heat is quickly becoming unbearable. Beads of sweat dribble down my hairline and drip uncomfortably into my ears.

The surface of the water is misty. There are visible waves where the surface of the lake is evaporating into the air. I see no other alternative but to dip my head back allowing my hair to be soaked entirely, before I wring out the excess water sealed in the locks.

My wet hair is heavier, but the welcome relief is almost instantaneous, although not long-lasting. I lean back again and lie idle on my back, allowing my hair to once again swirl in the refreshing water as I let myself float. My ears are just below the surface of the lake so all I hear are the intermittent splashes the girls are making as they swim lazily in the water, chattering away like they haven't done in years.

Niall left a short while ago hoping to reawaken his dormant long-distance swimming ability, claiming he needed some exercise after all this sitting around and lounging. Without him next to me, it's blissfully peaceful. I don't have to worry about looking perfect or peering over my shoulder and catching the disappointed looks he assumes I'm too stupid to notice. I don't usually have time to reflect on the negative energy he emits whenever he's near me.

I sigh happily. Everyone is doing whatever they please and I'm feeling perfectly content. The sun shines on my face, but the water is cooling me at the same time—it's the perfect balance of both worlds. It's still and quiet but for the distant splash or bubble resounding in the water. It feels blissful. I could easily fall asleep, but I don't dare.

I would do anything to stay in this moment a while longer, but without warning, a loud, shrill scream breaks through the surrounding calm, jarring me out of my dazed state. Suddenly, I no longer feel any of the previous warmth, only coldness. A mother knows her baby's cries. The scream came from Beatrice.

"Mom!" The cry pierces my heart, almost knocking the breath out of my lungs.

Her desperation echoes across the water, ringing in my ears, pulling me towards her.

Somehow, I'd managed to drift to the very middle of the lake, putting some distance between myself and the cabin. Instinctively, I begin to swim towards the scream, my body propelling itself forward with the grace of a dolphin. I glide over the surface in one of the most remarkable breaststrokes I've ever performed.

The fear of algae and scaly fish swimming around my legs evaporates like the lake's surface. The drive within me, one I had thought dead and gone, is revived. I feel alive, terrified, and purposeful. For so long, my girls have managed well with minimal help from me, rendering my role in the family almost obsolete. But now, Bea is injured—she needs me. I would do anything to take the pain away from her, but damn it, I can't deny how good it feels to be needed.

Reaching the dock, I heave myself up. My muscles scream from disuse. I'd assumed I'd lost all strength built up over the years from endlessly rocking my babies, expertly maneuvering strollers and yet, it's still there. I run towards the grass where the girls sit, water running off my limbs, my legs moving even though I've lost all feeling in them in my panic. Alarmed looks greet me as I approach, and I instinctively fake a calm I don't feel seconds before reaching them.

If I pretend to be calm, they will relax a bit, which will help the situation overall. Beatrice has been known to overreact to injuries, but who am I to know her threshold for pain? Amber and I tend not to be bothered by pain half as much, used to constantly bumping into things, clumsily and brusquely. We have things to do, places to be—a little scrape won't slow us down. But Bea, she bruises like a peach. She's soft and fragile like a rose petal. Her skin tears easily and the blood flows dramatically. Where her character is placid, her injuries tend to always be ghastly and exaggerated in comparison.

I remember once Amber had scraped her arm while falling off a high branch in a tree, and it had barely bled. But Bea could trip on her own feet and blood would gush out, requiring immediate aid, perhaps even stitches. My heart aches as I take in the scene.

Bea's cheeks are streaked with fresh tears, her eyes swollen from crying. She's holding onto her right foot, and her face is contorted and puffy. It's obvious that she's in agony.

I kneel beside my daughter and barely feel the sharp shards of dry grass poke my knees. My hair drips down my back, the sun already at work drying the roots.

With careful hands, I lift her injured foot from her grip to inspect it more closely. Several one-inch cuts on the bottom of her foot are oozing with bright red blood. I reach for a nearby towel and wipe the sole of her foot gently. The cuts appear to be surface wounds but the number of them is frightening. I can't wrap my head around what could be sharp enough to cut her like this. Did someone throw a beer bottle in the lake and it had shattered on the bottom?

"Looks like zebra mussels," Niall's sudden presence behind me startles me.

I look back in alarm. I hadn't noticed him approaching us, but he must have heard Bea's cries from wherever he'd been in the lake, just as I did. Guilt immediately fills me. I shouldn't have allowed myself to drift so far from the cabin. I'd been so entranced by the subtle waves, the soft gurgles of the water, and the drifting clouds above that I'd momentarily forgotten my responsibilities. Surely, I could have prevented this somehow...

"They're everywhere here; on the bottom of the lake, the dock, even on the rocks." Niall continues with his theory as he bends over to inspect Bea's foot more closely. "Yeah, I think that's most likely what happened." A look of sympathy crosses his features as he looks back at Bea's tearful face.

Turning to me, he adds, "We should probably have bought some water shoes. I didn't know how many zebra mussels there were here, but when you start looking for them, they're literally everywhere." He grimaces, and I feel myself shrinking, thinking that I should have somehow known. This was all my fault.

"Is she going to need stitches?" I inquire, but Niall simply shakes his head.

"No, no. I don't think so. Just clean out the cuts as best you can and rest your feet for a few hours," he instructs Bea. "You'll be able to walk sooner than you think. I've seen worse cuts from those pesky things, you'll be just fine."

My husband stands tall, comfortable once more as he assumes his place of control. He's back in charge. Bea looks horrified at the idea of getting a needle in her foot, the mention of stitches turning her face a ghostly shade of white.

"Okay, hon, let me pick you up and carry you to the cabin to rest your foot." Niall bends over, effortlessly lifting Bea and begins the short climb to the cabin. She looks so tiny in his arms.

Grabbing the few scattered items left behind, Amber and I quickly follow behind them. My heart aches for Bea. Her scream had been ear-piercing and alarming. It had shaken me to the very core of my being. I'd acted on adrenaline alone, but now it was rapidly escaping me. My body was beginning to shut down and a headache had started to throb furiously between my eyes, courtesy of the sun and the scream. I long to lie down for a nap, to just shut my eyes for a while and forget about all of this.

When my children suffer, I feel it deeply. I physically carry their pain as if it were my own, as though it was me who had cut my foot on zebra mussels. It's exhausting and I have to keep reminding myself that I'm fine, I'm safe. But the alarm bells have been rung and their echoes resonate so loudly that it will take a while for the noise to subside.

Chapter 35
Amber

The cabin quickly turns into a makeshift hospital room. My parents' undivided attention is on Bea. She is seated on the couch with her injured foot propped up on a cushion. The distinct smell of antiseptic clings to the air as bandages are applied to the sole of her foot and fastened in place by a sock.

They work quickly, moving around in silence like experienced teammates during a sport's game. How many times have they worked side by side like this? There is a systematic order to their movements, an understanding between them of which roles to take. I'm surprised to find it somewhat reassuring. They keep me out of the process, leaving me to watch from the sidelines of the kitchen.

I'm quite relieved by this as I wouldn't even know what to do if they asked me to help.

I took first aid as part of a babysitting course, but the basic elements are lost to me. I reacted completely unexpectedly, freezing in place, seemingly mesmerized. I feel a giggle starting in my throat and I cough to cover it up.

Inappropriate responses to stress are my go-to. I'm an expert at it. I never react well to important things but when it comes to emergency situations, I'm utterly useless. It's like all my emotions hit me all at once and I lose the capacity to think. My brain shuts off and allows my body to react however it pleases, often by laughing nervously, which unfortunately makes me seem insensitive and cruel.

I turn away from them to cover my mouth, willing my shoulders to quit shaking as I do my best to stifle the laugh that wants to escape. Breathing deeply, I don't remove my hands until I have composed myself.

Before turning around, I open the refrigerator in search of a distraction, but find the shelves rather empty. We had planned to go to the store later. I turn around and cross to the bedroom to change out of my swimsuit, leaving damp footprints on the floor behind me. The trail will either dry up with the afternoon heat or be swept away by my mom before it even has the chance to evaporate.

Shutting the door, I can let my mask fall. Keeping my poise is hard work. Here, behind the closed door, I can finally let my features relax as I dig through the suitcase.

The heat that's accumulated inside the small space is oppressive. I grimace at my clothing options. They are all wrong; either too tight, clingy, or warm. There don't seem to be any suitable options for this humidity.

My hair sticks to my face and I swipe it up into a messy bun, knowing full-well that stray hairs will fight against the constraints of my elastic, creating a hideous, curly, lion's mane. But I couldn't care less.

At the moment, all that matters is cooling down my body temperature. At last, I select a light and airy white eyelet sundress deciding that it's the least likely to stick to me or overheat me. As I pull it over my head, the bun catches on the fabric. I feel the mass of hair fall in slow motion down from the top of my head to the side, but I leave it alone. I can't muster the energy required to fix it yet. My arms feel so heavy at my sides, that the strength needed to fix my hair seems monumental in this heat.

Grabbing some pretty, gold, strappy sandals, I take a peek at myself in the compact mirror from my make-up bag. My tan is coming in rather well, giving my skin a nice glow. Once the sweat disappears and I no longer resemble a melting wax candle, I might actually look beautiful—sort of goddess-like. My white dress gives the appearance of a pretty, modern toga-inspired outfit with the flowing material shortened to fall just above the knees. The gold sandals provide just the right refined touch to my look.

As I step out of the room, Mom looks up from her crouched position beside Bea and shuts her eyes tightly. She smacks her forehead. She'd forgotten all about the necessary grocery outing. I see her pleading eyes stare at Dad, and he nods back at her.

"Alright, Amber. You and I will go get some food while Dad and Bea stay behind." She sounds exasperated by the task ahead.

Mom's squinting and absentmindedly rubbing her temples. She must have a headache again. She's been getting them so often since her fall down the stairs.

I worry that maybe there's injuries we're not yet aware of. I'm lucky to hardly ever get them, but she's told me how awful hers are—a black-out kind of painful.

She should really stay back and rest, but to send Dad to get food for us would be the equivalent of him sending me to buy building supplies. He'd get it done, of course, but it would inevitably take him twice as long as he'd most likely get lost wandering down the wrong aisle. It will just be simpler this way. I'd offer to get the groceries by myself, but I don't have my full license yet and I don't know the roads here.

We grab our purses and head out to the car. Sidestepping the shattered bark shards from the fallen tree, treading over the remains carefully, we finally make it to the vehicle. Once our seatbelts are fastened, Mom leans forward, resting her forehead on the steering wheel, stealing herself.

She seems to be feeling several emotions all at once, something I'm all too familiar with. I don't pry and don't push her. Instead, I just sit patiently and wait until she feels better.

Gathering herself, she sits back into the seat and starts the car, her gaze out the windshield. Due to the cover of the tall trees, the radio signal doesn't reach us until we're back on the main road. Mindful of my mom's headache, I turn the dial low, just enough to fill the silence but not loud enough to irritate her.

Thankfully, we don't have to go far before we find a corner store. It might not be the cheapest option, and I'm sure that if we drove a little farther, we'd find a larger grocery store, but with everything going on, this will have to do.

I know the prices will be higher than they ought to be, simply because convenience stores are placed strategically to lure and entice people passing by. Being visible and easy to access is half the charm, and it's hard to deny the convenient proximity to the cabin. They know they will get us because we won't risk getting lost and venturing out of the confines of our holiday perimeters. The bright advertisements plastered on the windows leave little hope of finding fresh produce, but alas, we park and decide to try our luck anyway.

A small bell above the door announces our arrival, making me shrink in humiliation. Yet, surprisingly, the corner store isn't as terrible as I'd imagined it would be. The tacky exterior doesn't continue on the inside. Just like the cabin, the interior of the store is surprisingly larger than it had appeared, stretching deep into the back. The store even has a produce and dairy section, and offers a good variety of pharmacy products.

I spot prepared sandwiches wrapped in plastic, safely stored in a refrigerated unit along the back wall. There are quite a few varieties, most of which I would actually consider eating. The store is noticeably clean, spacious, and well-lit. Nothing like the dark, old campsite corner stores I've been to where you'd be hard-pressed to find anything beyond chips, pop, or candy.

Grabbing a shopping basket each, we begin to fill them with items, finding that our appetites are ruling the search. The store is well-stocked with basic staples—bananas, apples, fresh yellow corn, eggs, milk, and cream. There's even an entire shelf dedicated to breakfast cereal. At every turn, I'm amazed by the selection available in such a small store. I'm browsing their stock of granola bars when I feel a light tap on my shoulder. Turning around I meet with Trevor's semi-familiar grin.

"Oh! Hi, Trevor!" I say nervously, trying to act cool. "How are you?" I manage.

Tucking a strand of unruly hair behind my ear, I feel self-conscious under his gaze. I'm also suddenly aware of how the wire basket handles are digging uncomfortably into my forearms with the weight of all the items I've crammed inside it. I shift the basket slightly down my arm, trying to balance the weight better, but notice large indents on my skin and move it back quickly before Trevor's sees.

"I thought that was you!" he says, a shy smile on his face. "Listen, I'm glad I bumped into you," he begins. "My friends and I are having a little pre-Canada Day party tonight at my parents' place on Cherry Island." He stops, assessing my reaction, but I simply nod, waiting for him to continue, not sure where this is going.

"I wanted to know if you'd like to join us," he adds and I feel stupid for not anticipating this.

I open my mouth to come up with an excuse but then a few girls appear at his side. One is slightly taller and leaner than me, her shiny brown hair rests in soft waves on top of her shoulders. The fringes are pulled back with a wide, sixties-inspired white headband, highlighting her big brown eyes. Her red top with white polka-dots is tight and dips in a sweetheart neckline.

Her friend is an equally attractive blond chick with thick, brown eyebrows, the kind that every girl in my high school strives for but fails to replicate. She has lips so plump they can't be fully natural, and yet, somehow, they suit her face, giving her appearance an Angelina Jolie likeness. I realize too late that I'm staring and snap out of it to their playful giggles.

"This is Renee," Trevor points to the brunette, and then to the blond."And Eve."

"Hi, I'm Amber," I muster, my voice cracking at the end, almost like I swallowed a fly when I opened my mouth.

The girls exchange a look and then Renee addresses me. "You HAVE to come out with us tonight! It's going to be epic!" She winks at me, conspiratorially, as though I should know what she's insinuating. A thrill of excitement passes through me at the prospect of whatever she's suggesting.

Playing it cool, I ask her, "Sounds great. What time?"

Squealing, Eve informs me that Trevor will come get me at the cabin by boat at around eight.

"What's at eight o'clock?" Mom's voice startles me, pulling my attention away from the intense stares of the three before me. She'd silently drifted over to where we'd gathered, expertly eavesdropping without being noticed.

I turn to her and vaguely relay the information. I see her mull over the details in her mind, observing my eager eyes. Just like Renee and Eve had shared a look, conversing in silent agreement to invite me to join them, my mom and I share a similar stare now.

"I think that would be fine," she finally says, a small smile playing on her lips.

I'm so grateful, I could hug her, but I simply smile widely, practically feeling the sparkle in my eyes as I look back at her in appreciation. I never expected her to agree to this. It's so unlike her. She usually runs these kinds of things by Dad before committing to anything. It's rare for her to make decisions on her own anymore. It feels good to see her taking charge like this.

Renee takes down my cellphone number in her phone so she can text me tonight before she and Trevor head out to collect me. I'll have to text her the cabin's address, but they seem to have an idea of which one we're staying at already. Being locals, they know which places are rentals and which have permanent residents.

"Great! So, I'll text you later tonight!" she says as they exit the store.

"See you later, Amber!" Trevor waves on his way out of the store, triggering the bell chime above the door.

My cheeks burn as I replay the moment. I'm going to a party tonight! I can hardly wait.

Feeling the basket tilt, I attempt to steady it, only to notice that my arm is practically numb. The achy muscles are stiff from holding the same position throughout the entire conversation with Trevor and the girls. I'd been so captivated by how beautiful and friendly they'd seemed, that I'd completely forgotten I'd been holding the basket.

For someone who usually struggles to connect with others and very rarely makes new friends, I'm struck by how easy this interaction had been. I'd felt welcomed into their little group right away. It was refreshing to feel a sense of belonging, even amongst relative strangers.

My heart pumps quickly as we pay for our over-priced items. It doesn't slow down the whole way back to the cabin. Eight o'clock can't come fast enough.

Chapter 36
Beatrice

I'm not brave enough to risk putting weight on my foot for fear of the stinging pain that would surely accompany it. My leg weighs a ton. I lost feeling in it, propping it upright for the better part of an hour. I haven't dared to move from my position since Mom and Amber left, not trusting Dad to catch me should I fall. Besides, Mom and Amber will be back soon enough.

My foot throbs like it has a heartbeat, but the pain has dulled some, maybe because of the numbness settling in or just from time passing. The cuts stopped bleeding almost the moment we entered the cabin, but they hurt like hell. I hadn't had a chance to take a proper look, but what I had seen had been similar to half a dozen bloody slashes across the sole of my foot, not too deep but surprisingly painful.

I've been struggling to stay focused on a book I'd grabbed at random from the bookshelf to keep myself occupied as I wait for my foot to feel good enough to limp on. Shifting uncomfortably on the couch, my bladder screams in protest. Frowning, I shut the book, tossing it carefully beside me on the couch.

Using all my strength, I place both palms on the soft cushions as I attempt to lift myself from the sinking seat. Reluctantly, I extract myself from the comfort and restraint of the couch and wince at the sting of pain radiating from my foot. Suddenly, the bathroom seems too far out of reach. Grimacing, eager to relieve myself, I brave the pain and make my way slowly to the bathroom. I make it without too much of a hassle.

Dad glances up nonchalantly from his seat in the kitchen, still bent over his phone. He hasn't moved since Mom and Amber left either. Rather than interacting with me or vaguely attempting to make me feel better, he's cowardly used Mom's absence as an opportunity to text his lover this entire time, simply choosing to ignore me out of spitefulness. Or perhaps he's just plain forgotten I exist.

In the bathroom, I glance at myself in the mirror and notice puffy purple bags beneath my eyes. My skin is so pale that I look ill. I run my fingers through my hair and curl my tips at the strands, which feel equally unhealthy. It's as though the sun has scorched it, ripping away all of the nutrients instead of giving it a rich glow like it always gives Mom's and Amber's locks.

Staring at my reflection, I notice the faint outline of a bruise on my arm where Dad grabbed me the other day. I'm surprised to see a mark, but grateful for it somehow. It makes the whole ordeal feel real, not just something I made up.

I allow myself to imagine walking out of the bathroom in only a tank top, my bare arms exposing the results of his anger clearly visible on my skin. I allow myself to imagine his face when he'd notice the bruise. I picture him gaping like a fish out of water, the blood draining from his face by how bad he feels. But that will never happen.

Dad wouldn't admit to being in the wrong. It's not likely he would even notice the bruise. He's avoiding me at all costs. He's not even scared of me or of what I might spill to Mom. Perhaps he should be.

Instead, he just seems annoyed that I'm breathing the same air as him. I'm a constant reminder to him that if I decide to speak up, I could easily undo all he's worked for in one fell swoop. As the keeper of his secret, I hold my head up and remind myself that I'm the one who holds the power here. My eyes shine darker for a moment as I mull this over. I kind of like having this hold over him.

The air in the main room is sticky. I want to open a window or the patio doors just to allow the air to flow in a little, but then I risk making it even warmer in here. I wipe away the beads of sweat that have been collecting on my forehead and catch a whiff of the musty smell of my perspiration. Repulsed by my own stench, I swivel around and return to the bathroom to apply a fresh coat of deodorant, as this morning's application must have dissolved in the lake during our swim. The white powdery product coats my underarms, but then immediately clumps into tiny balls as though my body heat is melting it. I wipe it away with my hand and wrinkle my nose.

"Useless", I mutter, irritated at having fallen prey to false advertisements of long-lasting freshness.

When did I start smelling so bad? I realize all at once that this must mean my body is changing. My hormones are at work—the pungent smell is proof of that. Things are changing around me, but the biggest transformation is happening within me.

Grinning, I allow myself to hope that this will be my best year yet. I resolve to never again bend over backwards to please everyone else. I'm my own person after all. I have my own likes and dislikes, unique opinions and dreams. I've restrained myself for long enough. No more taming. I'm ready to roar.

I'm still in the bathroom when Mom and Amber return from their outing. When I step out, I half-expect everyone to immediately notice the transformation I've experienced, to spot the sudden confidence, and maturity I'm exuding, but I may as well be invisible.

Everyone is busying themselves rooting through the grocery bags Mom has piled on the counter. She is taking out the items painfully slowly, pulling them out one at a time. The plastic bags crinkle loudly and break up the reflective state of my thoughts, forcing my attention back to the cabin and the stale air. I need to get outside. Surely there will be a soft breeze to provide some relief, even for just a moment. The sun is no longer in the centre of the sky, not scorching us like little ants beneath a magnifying glass.

Limping towards the patio doors, I feel a twinge of guilt. I should probably help Mom and Amber unpack the food and put it away. But I keep my head up, determined not to let the *should haves* and *could haves* rule me any longer. I don't *need* to do anything I don't want to do.

It will take practice, but that's how I want the next phase of my life to go. I want to make my own choices and pursue my own desires. I will say *no* more than *yes*.

It will be difficult to fight the deeply rooted need to please and to be agreeable, but in the end, it will be worth it. I am determined to find my voice again.

I lost it a long time ago, hiding behind the shadows of those who had the confidence to stand taller, or speak more loudly than me. It became second nature to remain quiet, guard my thoughts, and be obedient, but where did that get me? Instead of gaining respect, others now see me as a push-over, someone who is easily manipulated, a wallflower they could stomp on and it would hardly even matter.

As I cross the room, every step sends a fresh flash of pain up my leg, making me wince. Reaching the patio door feels monumental, like planting the flag at the top of a mountain I've struggled to climb.

My grip is tight around the handle as I pull it open and step out on the deck. A soft breeze greets me, a blissful reward for my perseverance. I feel wild and free. For the first time ever, I'm making choices for myself, without any motive other than to satisfy my own needs. It's new and refreshing, but a little frightening. Electricity seems to course through me as I sense this foreign new strength, a new power source building inside me.

Grinning stupidly, I turn to close the patio door but freeze as I notice Amber staring at me from the kitchen.

I usually try hard not to give her any attention, but now I look right at her. I'm struck by the hardened expression plastered on her face. Confusion envelops me for a brief moment as a shadow of regret lingers in her eyes, immediately replaced by bitter anger.

Her lips are pursed, and her gaze has shifted from my eyes to my exposed biceps. Glancing down at my arms, I see what's caught her attention. The faint, yet undeniable outline of a large handprint covers most of my upper arm, the mark now tinted in varying shades of blue and purple. I bite my lower lip, suddenly nervous.

My earlier eagerness to expose the bruise is instantly erased and replaced with shame. I'd been so keen to escape the constraints of the small, confining space and get outside as quickly as possible in search of fresh air, that I'd failed to consider the consequences or the people who might be affected by this revelation. I feel both embarrassed and entitled. Why should I be the one to hide or feel guilty? I've done nothing wrong.

Horror and shock splash over Amber's features, the bright light dimming slightly from her eyes. No sound comes from her lips, but I can almost see smoke coming out of her ears as the gears work in overdrive in her mind. Mom is oblivious, busy stocking the cupboards, and Dad still has his nose deep in his phone.

As though in a trance, Amber and I stare at each other, neither one of us daring to move as an invisible current of electricity escapes her and bolts right to me, making me step backwards, as though I had been physically struck. Her look is piercing, questioning and furious. Yet, somehow it's clear to me that I'm not the intended target of her wrath.

During our entire silent exchange, Amber has been clutching a family-sized box of cereal, bending and crushing the flimsy cardboard, gripping it firmly in the air. The sight of her tightening grip makes me shiver as I recall my father's large hand holding my arm in a similar fashion only yesterday.

272

Suddenly aware of her hand, Amber drops the box back on the counter, as though scorched by it. Determined, but light on her feet as if she's aware that discretion is key in this kind of situation, I watch unblinking as she follows me outside.

With the door carefully shut behind us, we walk in silence to one end of the deck, draping our arms over the banisters in practiced unison. No matter how different we may appear to be, we're still sisters after all. Stitched together in the same womb, raised by the same parents.

It's remarkable how we can come out looking and acting so distinctively different from one another. And yet, standing here, next to Amber, I realize for the first time that we're not all that different after all. I've grown up significantly in the past year and have since matched her height. Pretty soon, when my boobs finally come in, I'll probably be able to fit in her hand-me-down clothes.

We stare out over the lake, taking in the sights for a moment. Amber's face is twisted. There's no peace in her expression, a contrast to the view before us. I imagine her mulling things over. She appears torn and confused. I open my mouth but find myself unable to find the words to shed some light on the situation.

Sensing my struggles, she swiftly takes over and interrupts me before I've even begun. I'm grateful she's taking on the older sister role and shielding me from discomfort in this small way.

"Dad did that to you?" She turns to stare at me, pointing at my arm as she waits for me to confirm her suspicions, her gaze never leaving mine.

Her stare is intense and her eyes red-rimmed. Her lip quivers as she's trying to identify a lie or any ounce of truth in my reply. Surprised by her directness, and the accuracy of her assumptions, I find it best to simply nod. There isn't much else to say anyway.

I startle as Amber takes in a sharp breath, shutting her eyes following my admission. The air shifts between us, giving me permission to spill my guts, and I'm surprised to hear my voice, steady and unwavering as I recount my discovery of Yvonne's picture on Mom's phone. How it had led to my confrontation with Dad. How he hadn't denied it, or shown any sort of remorse whatsoever. And how instead, he'd tried to intimidate me with force, bruising my arm with his firm grip.

"Bastard," she hisses through clenched teeth.

She slams the top of the banister, causing the length of it to reverberate beneath the force of her strike. Attempting to bring it back into stillness, she grips it firmly with both hands, dipping her head between her arms. Taking a deep, shaky breath, she closes her eyes once more and tilts her head so that it's parallel to the deck boards.

"I'm so sorry, Bea," she whispers, her voice hoarse and full of emotion.

I don't quite know how to respond, so I stay quiet. Gazing out to the water, I take everything in. I've shared my secret, and instead of feeling better and relieved, I feel apprehensive. Amber's not the most rational person, especially when it comes to emotions. I'm surprised to realize that a small, selfish part of me had hoped to see her become this upset about my situation.

Now that she knows, I worry about what she might do with this information. She can be dangerous with the right fuel to ignite her spirits. Always looking to pick a fight over mundane things, what will she do with this kind of damaging and potentially life-altering information?

Her anger doesn't surprise me in the least. In fact, I'd been counting on it to some degree. What's got me puzzled however, is the fact that Amber has apologized to me, as though this entire thing has been her doing.

What does she have to be sorry for? Before I can ask, she answers for me.

"I'm sorry I didn't protect you from him." She stands up straight once again, resolute in whatever decision she was considering when her eyes had been shut. She's ready to ignore the doubts, the fears, and the risks.

"It's okay," I offer timidly.

"No, Bea. It's not okay. It's the furthest thing from okay."

Her head shakes in rage. I can almost feel the heat radiating from her skin, only inches from me. I want to pull my hands from the railing before I get burned, but I fight the urge to do so. Instead, I plant them firmly, unwilling to move. Stubbornness and courage rising within me.

I'm touched to see how deeply she cares for me. I'd never known Amber to take her big sister role to heart, but it was clear to me now that she did. For her to respond in such a way, to be so affected by this, fills a deep need inside of me to be protected and loved by my big sister. She has my back and will help me get through the obstacles before me. It's what I've always wanted—a true sister, a friend, and a confidant.

I smile, grateful for the sudden, monumental shift in our relationship, but I can't help feeling a little disapointed that it took Dad physically hurting me to get her to pay attention to me and offer her unwavering loyalty.

"Don't worry," she adds. "You're not alone. I'll protect you from him. I won't let him hurt you ever again. I promise." She turns and looks me dead in the eye, sealing her words.

I feel them leave her mouth and penetrate my ears, settling inside my brain. It takes me several seconds before I understand the serious implications of what she just said. Rather than experience the dread of fear, I'm surprised to feel a jolt of excitement.

Yes, this is what I want.

The feeling is almost too much for me to stand. I feel myself growing eager, jittery at the prospect of the damage the two of us are capable of inflicting. I can hardly contain it. Shivering with exhilaration, I barely manage to nod to confirm my understanding of the ramifications.

Amber might be unpredictable, determined, wild, and fierce, but she's no liar. When she makes a promise, she never, ever breaks it. And that's exactly what I'm counting on.

Chapter 37
Niall

Lifting my eyes from my phone briefly, I startle when I catch sight of Amber and Beatrice deep in conversation on the porch. I can't remember the last time those two confided in each other. I've heard that raising girls, teenage girls especially, can be less than pleasant at times. Between the incessant, high-pitched, and mind-numbing girl-talk, or the ever-changing hormones, the high importance put on their appearance, and the obsession with getting the latest products, it can be downright hell for fathers.

I've also been warned that daughters, who'd once idolized you and held your hand so tightly you feared it might tear it off, could turn on you in the blink of an eye and paint you as a villain.

Pretending not to be bothered by this sudden change of events, trying my damnedest not to be paranoid and imagine that they might be plotting my demise, I return my attention to the kitchen in an effort to distract the looming thoughts swirling in my head.

I stand to help Gemma sort through the remainder of the bags. She claims to have only stopped at the corner-store, but the massive number of bags littering the small cabin gives me pause. Distracted by the prospect of the girls sharing secrets, I mistakenly place the milk inside the cupboard. Gemma chuckles at my misstep and gently chastises me for my inattention. I laugh along to placate her, but inside I feel like melting wax.

Worry is an overwhelming sensation, a creeping one—subtle but all-consuming. It begins with thoughts that first appear innocent and untouchable, easily contained, but then fear starts to manifest outwardly, unpredictably, and noticeably in gestures, ticks, body heat, perspiration and an increased heartbeat.

Recently, due to the increased pressures and stresses at work, I've come to understand anxiety as less of a sensation, and more so a way of being. It can be impossible to manage.Although there can be short term benefits, such as the ability to think quickly and make decisions, for the most part, it can be quite paralyzing.

It takes over my entire body, locking me in place, rendering me immobile. The thoughts pour into my head, my legs and arms become concrete, and I am unable to feel anything else—it's completely debilitating. It makes me act and think in ways in which I have zero control, absolutely no say in the way in which I react, which can sometimes come out in angry outbursts.

I feel wrinkles on my forehead. Worry lines, no doubt. I need to get myself together before I completely go overboard and lose it again. Maybe the girls are talking about something entirely different, something that has nothing to do with me. Yet, somehow, I seriously doubt that.

Glancing out the window, I see the girls hugging now and my pulse intensifies. My legs get wobbly, like rubber hands, struggling beneath my weight. Suddenly, the floor doesn't feel like it is strong enough to support me. I sink into a nearby chair before my legs give out as the floor feels like it's tilting. *I'm doomed.* They haven't looked over this way once, never hinted at what they've been talking about. But I have the overwhelming sense that I know exactly what it is. I can feel it.

I could try and spill my secrets to Gemma before the girls do. If it comes from me first, then we might stand a chance of getting through it. But, what if I'm wrong? What if the girls aren't discussing my infidelity or my rage? Then, I'd be screwing myself by revealing what I've been up to.

It occurs to me that this might be their intention. They want to see me sweat. They want me to worry. I doubt they'd want to get their hands dirty. They will probably go on acting like everything is fine, letting me stew as I wonder and worry if and when they might let something slip, undoing everything I've done to keep it a secret. All my efforts to keep this from Gemma would be lost. My reputation would be ruined and my integrity questioned.

I can't let that happen.

I won't allow my own daughters to destroy all I've worked for over the years.

These girls, *these kids*; they have no idea who they're messing with. If they're stupid enough to say something, they will leave me no choice. I'll have to make them pay.

Chapter 38
Amber

Back inside, Beatrice and I make our way to our room to change for the afternoon. Bea's foot isn't as sore now and she's no longer hobbling around. I watch her dig through our luggage and pull out a pair of cheap flip-flops. On the other days, we'd just headed to the water barefoot, but with cuts on the bottom of her foot, the thin soles of the sandals will protect her just enough.

Looking through my things, I pull out my cellphone and turn it on. Within seconds, a new notification lights up the screen with a text from a new number. It's from Renee. Excited, my thumb hovers over the screen before I press on it to read the full message.

"Hey A. It's Renee. Trevor will come to get you @7. Cya soon!"

I send her a thumbs up emoji. I'm so excited for tonight, I can hardly stand still.

After selecting bleached denim shorts and a loose, white, beaded tank top, I head outside towards the dock with Bea following slowly behind. We walk in silence down the grassy hill, carefully gauging how Bea's foot is holding up to the pressure applied to it on the strange angle we're forced to walk.

Thankfully, she makes it down without too much effort and we settle down at the edge of the dock, dipping our feet in the water. I lie down on the sun-faded boards and let the sun's rays caress my face for a few moments. There's wind in the air now. It's warm but persistent. The little hairs around my face, those I didn't manage to secure in my high bun, are floating around and tickling my nose. Turning my head to one side, I try to shield my face from the wind.

I'm still fuming from what Bea told me earlier. Yet, I can't say I'm entirely surprised to hear about how Dad acted. It was just a matter of time before his true character started to show through. A classic Jekyll and Hyde situation. How he can pretend to be one person with others and another with us baffles me.

My mother is either clueless, blind, or in denial. I seriously doubt my father is that good at hiding his rage all the time. What if mine and Bea's recent ruffling of his perfectly combed feathers wasn't actually the first time? What if he's always been like this and we're the ones who were blind? Have we been ignoring the facts and refusing to see what was happening right in front of us?

The thought germinates in my mind as I mull it over, trying to see if it holds up. For Mom to be aware of Dad's penchant for aggressive, almost violent behaviour, to dismiss his actions as normal, possibly even warranted, makes me fume.

Perhaps then, it's her we should be angry with. For hiding this knowledge, or for not protecting us from him. For ignoring what she knew, for playing a part in it, for being complacent to his methods of parenting. Even if she disagreed, her silence can be viewed as a nod of approval.

Shaking my head, I turn it towards the sun, my closed eyelids warm beneath the rays. The sunshine feels good on my skin. When I open my eyes, I see the glow of a warm and dark tan developing like tiny sprinkles of diamond dust on the surface of my skin. This usually brings me joy, but in this moment, I find none.

I can't bear the thought that Mom might have always known what Dad is capable of, that she might have neglected to share her knowledge, thinking she was protecting us when, in reality, she'd put us in even greater danger by hiding it. If this was true, then she'd been lying to us all for the sake of keeping up the image of the perfect family.

Is a reputation that important to save?

If the truth somehow got out that our family is anything less than exemplary, I can only assume that all hell would break loose. The solid walls built around us over the years and everything within it would crumble to ashes and be utterly destroyed. It would be like it never existed.

How long will we need to wait for the existing cracks to weaken the walls? Will the walls crumble one by one or all at once? Perhaps the demolition needs a helping hand or a nudge in the right direction. Maybe the process should be sped up rather than being dragged out as it currently is.

Our family's demise is approaching, slowly and menacingly, but I'm not known for my patience. I disapprove of lies and omission of facts. I disdain tales and secrets festering right under the surface.

Sitting up again on the dock, I look over at Bea. Her skin is red and burning. How different two sisters can be—the colour of our eyes, the shape and style of our hair, and even the pigment of our skin. While my skin cherishes heat, even transforms it into beauty, hers burns under it, her body rejecting it almost as soon as it starts to penetrate it.

For years, we've been polar opposites, like yin and yang, but this new truth has united us. It doesn't matter how we appear physically. That's not what binds us as sisters. Rather, it's our promises to each other. In caring for each other, in the tiny little details where our lives cross paths, or in the subtleties in which we understand one another without speaking.

I'm sure Dad is sweating buckets in the cabin right now. Worrying about my and Bea's renewed friendship. Our differences used to work in his favour, pitting us one against the other, drawing our attention away from his shenanigans with our small childhood dramas.

It probably infuriates him to know that he underestimated us when he let his guard down. I doubt he even considered that we would be drawn closer to each other based on our shared experiences dealing with his turbulent moods. He must be angry with himself for ever allowing us to be alone together.

Until now, I hadn't noticed how hard he'd been working to keep us apart.

I expect he'll try to separate us again, but even if we're separated as a means for him to control us and keep us quiet, we're still sisters. He can't take that away from us. Even if we're apart, our bond won't ever break.

For a moment, I worry about going to the party tonight. Should I cancel? Bea might need me here. Even if Mom is around, it might not be enough to deter Dad from trying something. He might pull Bea aside again, corner her, muddle her mind with doubts and threats.

I'm sure I'm letting my wild imagination get carried away, but I can't ignore the sense of trepidation that consumes me. Shivering, I wonder how far he's willing to go to keep his secret safe.

Chapter 39
GEMMA

The heat today is intense. I can't seem to cool off. I thought remaining inside the cabin was my best option to shield myself from the sun and humidity, but it seems to have collected all around me, practically suffocating me.

The air inside is palpable and stale. The open windows offer little to no relief. In fact, they seem to mock us with their gaping mouths, sucking in more hot air, twirling it around the small space, plastering my stray curls to my forehead.

The sky is mostly clear today, except for several slow-moving clouds floating about, as though they've been brushed on a canvas with a paintbrush. The translucence of the clouds allows for slices of blue sky to peek through, offering no protection from the harsh sunshine.

It's laughable really. What is the purpose of a cloud if not to provide shade and rain? Today, the clouds are useless, only present to add a whimsical appearance to the sky, for dreamers and artists to gaze upon. It strikes me that not everything needs to have a purpose all of the time.

The heat isn't the only reason it feels unbearably warm in the cabin. Tension was running high in the small space.

Niall had risen abruptly from his chair only moments ago, almost knocking it over in the process. I'm not sure why, but he seemed magnetically drawn to the patio doors. He'd been so intent on rising to get a better view of the girls that he hadn't bothered to cover the menacing look in his eyes.

The sudden way he'd stood up had startled me and all I'd been able to do was stare. I'd been watching from afar, not daring to move a muscle or risk making any sudden movements for fear of bringing attention to myself. Niall observed the girls so intensely, it bordered on predatory. I'd tried to trick myself into believing that he's spotted something of interest in the lake that required his immediate attention, but I knew better. It had been clear as day that Niall had felt threatened by something.

His fists had been clenched so tight that it had turned his knuckles white. He'd leaned forward, hunched over, as though this will help him to hear through the glass doors. Covered by the shadows of the cabin, he'd moved his lips slightly, mumbling to himself with his nose practically pressed against the glass.

There had been a deep V visible on the back of his shirt, where sweat had soaked through, starting between his shoulder blades and reaching all the way down to the small of his back. But he'd been too deep in thought to notice.

Alarm bells had begun ringing in my head as I'd surveyed the scene unfolding before me. I'd tried to make sense of it and couldn't help but see Niall's intense concentration as worrisome. He seemed completely oblivious to my presence. I pose no threat to him. I'm simply a watchful, silent observer.

Standing in the middle of the kitchen, with half a dozen cabinets open, their shelves spilling with newly purchased items, I'd been camouflaged by my surroundings. It had been as though I hadn't even been there. Niall, so used to seeing me bustling about in the kitchen, unpacking, sorting, and shelving items, had barely registered my presence. Either that or he'd blatantly ignored me. I hadn't been sure which was worse.

My heart had sank at the thought of being invisible to my husband.

We'd been so close once, united by marriage if nothing else. It had taken me a while to realize how conflicted our views on parenting were, until we were in the thick of raising our kids. I'd often felt lonely and isolated when it came to making decisions regarding the girls.

Being left to make most decisions regarding setting boundaries, or choosing appropriate disciplinary actions, I often felt the pressure that came with the responsibility. As the official monitor of emotional outbursts and our family's social planner, the expectations on me to keep everyone in order often left little room to focus on myself.

I'm the housekeeper, main chauffeur, only cook, nurse, teacher, and errand runner. An exemplary wife, a good, caring sister, and much, much more.

Titles are often used to measure a person's success, status, or rank, and people work hard to obtain them. I used to place so much importance on them, striving to be the best in each of my roles. I thought it would help me feel more in control of life and help me gain more respect. Instead, my many titles were no more than cumbersome links of heavy chain wrapped tightly around my ankles, nipping at my skin, slowing me down, or holding me in place, constricting and limiting me.

I've seen it happen again and again. People get promoted and responsibilities build up to match a thickening wallet. We throw celebratory parties and special dinners to recognize the achievement as a way to share the excitement of the honour. But often, the stepping stone is more like a trap door. Priorities get blurred, lines get crossed, marriages are put to the test, and families can fall apart under the increasing pressures of the job. The excitement of signing a new contract or accepting a pay increase overshadows the fact that you were signing away your soul.

Not that people shouldn't push themselves, develop their skills, or add experiences to their repertoire, but maybe there should be a list of potential risks that accompany the rewards. At least then, people would know what they're putting on the line when they sign their names. As insurance, I might recommend keeping a copy of the key to the shackles we choose, that way, we have an escape plan.

If only there was a way to dip your foot into the wealth or the fame, to taste the life you've always envisioned for yourself, but without significant risk.

That's what Niall's been doing this entire time. Our whole marriage has been nothing but a charade. Just a show for everyone else to enjoy but us.

It used to benefit me, at least financially. The prestige wasn't bad either. But playing along with this sham we call a marriage is beginning to cost me my happiness and my sanity. To be quite frank, I'm not entirely sure it's worth it anymore.

My hold strengthens on the carton of eggs and my index finger pierces through the cardboard, cracking an egg in the process. Yellow yoke oozes out of the carton, snaking down my arm before splattering onto the floor.

I curse under my breath and snap out of my trance. My thoughts float right out of my head but seem to linger in the air around me. They make it impossible to ignore the doubts and regrets that consume me. A fleeting moment of strength bubbles up from deep within, urging me to stand up for myself, propelling me towards a future I've scarcely ever allowed myself to entertain. I tend to reserve my longings for a different life to some of my darker evenings, spent in solitude when Niall is away at the office or whisking away that blond woman he thinks I don't know about.

I've remained discreet regarding Niall's affair, refusing to admit to him that I'm aware of it, deciding instead that it suits us both. It satisfies his urges while getting me off the hook. I long ago stopped being interested in intimacy with my husband, rather finding joy and fulfillment in raising our daughters.

In a way, the love I'd once had for Niall got transferred to our children. They are my world and the source of my happiness. And yet, only a month ago I'd been so desolate, so desperate to find a vocation outside the home, feeling completely useless and unwanted by my family. I'd been willing to find purpose elsewhere in hopes of proving my importance, even if it meant leaving them behind, feeling like I'd failed them, and breaking my heart in the process.

On some level, I'd known getting a job wasn't truly going to make me happy and that being there for the girls is my calling, but I couldn't help it. I was desperate for Niall to see me differently for once. I craved his admiration, wanted his respect above all else, but would have settled for his undivided attention.

Getting a job would have provided me with some independence, perhaps even helped me gain some confidence. Maybe even enough to finally leave him. I think that on some level, he'd known that this was my intention. It wouldn't surprise me if he'd had something to do with my multiple, unwarranted rejections.

I might never know the truth. Maybe I am washed up and worthless as Niall seems to think. With my daughters all grown up, I feel lost.

The sun is quickly setting below the horizon, dipping behind the hills across the lake. The girls come in for a simple, fresh salad dinner that we all devour in silence. Everyone seems to have something on their minds.

After dinner, Niall and I wash the dishes as Amber gets ready for the party. It had taken some convincing for Niall to allow her to go to Trevor's party—after all, we are on a family vacation, and she barely knows the guy. But as both Niall and I had briefly met Trevor, he'd finally agreed to it, with the condition that she be back by midnight.

In the distance, the faint murmur of a boat motor rumbles, the sound moving closer to the shore at the bottom of the hill. We peer out looking below, eager to catch a glimpse.

There are two silhouettes aboard the boat, and I vaguely recognize the second as Renee, the girl who took Amber's phone number at the corner store.

A flutter of excitement twirls inside of me in anticipation of the fun night ahead for Amber. My youth had been filled with evenings like this, out amongst friends, grabbing life by the horns, feeling invincible. The wildness that once possessed me flits through my hair as the breeze picks up slightly. I look up at the open sky, unobstructed by clouds. Stars begin to speckle the vastness beyond, the sky slowly darkening, adding to the magic of the night.

Amber looks elegant yet youthful in her outfit. Her lime green halter top nicely shows off her toned, tanned shoulders and neckline. Paired with tiny white shorts and a simple pair of flip-flops, she looks all set for a bonfire party. Those were always my favourite kind of parties, out in the open air, the rules, and expectations lax. Everyone enjoyed them, it seemed, as no one was excluded because there was no way to restrict who got invited. Without walls to limit the number of people, or neighbours to complain that you keep the noise down, the party could easily get out of hand.

Yet, in my experience, they rarely ever did. If anything, the wide open space, the sound of waves crashing the shore, the glow of the fire, the warm bodies huddled together, the slosh of strong drinks in red Solo cups, and swirls of cigarette smoke in the air simply added to the charm of the night, making the atmosphere almost otherworldly. The very fact that you had to get close enough to the fire to see anything at all, created a sense of peace and calm, keeping conversations hushed, as soft laughter bounced across the fire, bringing smiles to the rest of those sitting around the circle.

There was almost always someone playing popular songs on an acoustic guitar. Chairs weren't needed as most people sat right on the sand, which had cooled slightly by then as the night began to set in. Those planning ahead might have thought to bring along a beach towel to sit on, which might come in handy later if partygoers decided on an impromptu late-night dip to stave off the heat.

I smile at the fond memories. Those were good times before the responsibilities and the expectations that now press on me. There had been none of that then—just plain good times.

I watch as Amber climbs aboard the boat. Trevor reaches out a hand to help her step on safely. I smile and wave, assuming she can see me in the light from the kitchen. Cradling a large glass of red wine to my chest, I can't help but feel a pang of sadness, one that almost resembles grief.

When did I become so old that I can have a daughter old enough to climb into a boat with a boy, heading off to a beach party? I feel a twinge of longing, thinking back to my younger days. When did my life stop being fun? When did I grow up and lose myself?

The motor starts up again, breaking my train of thought. I watch until the sound quiets as the boat gets further from the cabin.

They're not going very far. Just to an island in the middle of the lake. In fact, I might even be able to see them if I stand on the shore. Although she is relatively close by, I can't help but feel gutted by the distance growing between us, leaving me to wonder when or how it happened. Was it a gradual thing or had it been more sudden? Am I too dense to notice anything anymore?

I take a large gulp of wine and the ball of liquid lodges in my throat, putting pressure all the way down the canal as I swallow.

293

I shiver at the bitter taste. *Wine is made for sipping,* I chastise myself, *not for tipping back.*

You're not young anymore, a little mocking voice reminds me from the deep hollows of my mind. *Get a grip. If you hate your life so much, then change it. Stop being the victim in your own story. Stop feeling sorry for yourself and do something about it.*

I drink more slowly, pondering. Still looking out the patio doors, I don't see the view, but rather a warped reflection of myself in the panes of glass.

Chapter 40
Beatrice

We all watch Amber's departure with shared longings to escape the place in which we currently find ourselves. Not this cabin per say, but the bodies we inhabit and the lives we lead.

Looking at my parents as I often do, I've become quite skilled at noticing the little ways in which their bodies speak for them when they otherwise keep their thoughts to themselves. Both of them are meant to be my role models, examples and mentors to teach me how to conduct myself and what I should strive for. In essence, how I should live my life. But rather than respect them and wish to fulfill their wishes for my life, I find myself often pitying them. Their lives are nothing but lies.

They are both so obviously unsatisfied and unfulfilled with the choices they've made, assuming they even remember that they'd had a say in the course their lives took in the first place. In a way, their unhappiness is entirely their own doing. They have no one to blame but themselves. They live in a constant state of regret.

Thinking of all I've learned this past week, all I've seen, I feel bitterness growing inside of me, throbbing and putting pressure on my heart, tempting me to speak out, to spill the secrets, and free us all from the lies. The truth is eating me alive. But I won't spill yet. Amber and I discussed confronting our parents together as it will be safer that way. She's right, of course.

It's not lost on me that I've swapped following my parents' advice with following Amber's, but for now, she's all I've got. I'm still working things out, figuring out what I want out of life once everything comes out. Life as I know it will be completely obliterated. I'll have the chance to start again, and when I do, I'll be a force to reckon with.

Until then, I'll stick to what I know, being silent, observing, and complacent until the gates open wide, and I don't need to hold back anymore. I'm looking forward to speaking my mind freely, to having opinions of my own, to share my feelings instead of keeping things bottled up inside, like I do now. I'm ready to burst open, secrets oozing from every crack in my fragile shell.

The cabin is suffocating me. Both the heat and my parents' proximity make me feel claustrophobic. I don't trust either of them right now. Dad might hurt me again if Mom left the room, and if he dared to intimidate me or use force in her presence, she would probably just step aside and let him have his way.

She'd never dare stand up to him. She never has. I can't count on her to protect me. She lost her backbone years ago.

Come to think of it, I can't recall ever seeing her deny him anything. Mom has always opted to be complacent, willing, loving, and accepting of my father's many flaws. As loyal as she might be to him, I don't believe she truly loves him. Not with passion anyway. What she feels towards him is a duty to fulfill a role—like a soldier who fears her general's authority.

The heat weighs us down and without Amber's energy to liven things up, we decide to go to bed early. I'm glad to have the bed all to myself, at least for a few hours.

The sheets get tangled around my legs and I kick them right off the bed. This anger and resentment are new to me and I'm kind of relishing it. I envision acting on it—how delicious it might feel to give in to those impulses. But then, I'd be no better than Dad.

No, I won't let it go that far. I will use it but make it my own. I will indulge only as a means of making me feel stronger, and becoming more assertive—never to harm others. I will use this newfound anger to fuel me and propel me into trying things that excite me, to discover what I'm passionate about, but never to cause pain. I simply refuse to do so. I've been on the other end of pain, and I vow to never inflict it on anyone.

I lay on the mattress in a sport's bra and pyjama shorts, wiping sweat from my forehead. The stuffiness inside the room is unbearable. I want to crack open the bedroom door, but I resist. I'm embarrassed to admit I fear a stranger walking into the cabin and discovering me in this vulnerable position. I'd rather cook in this heat than risk exposing myself to potential danger.

My legs are restless from the lack of movement today. Sitting around on the couch doing nothing but feeling sorry for myself, allowing the bottom of my foot time to heal.

My thigh muscles protest, wanting to move, the sporadic spasms utterly uncomfortable. I shake my legs and pound my thighs with a closed fist, but it doesn't provide the necessary relief. Fully awake and irritable, I stand up and begin pacing around the small room, trying to stretch out my legs enough to let me sleep.

Next door, I hear my parents tossing and turning. I laugh bitterly, imagining how hot they must be sleeping in the same bed. Or perhaps, they are comfortably cool as there hasn't been any heat between them in years, only a cold, life-sucking draft.

I'm both glad and jealous when I think of how Amber must be enjoying her night away from us. While I'm here using my discarded T-shirt to dab the sweat from my neck, she's free to flirt with cute boys, flaunt her good looks, and toss back sugary drinks while singing by a fire with her toes digging in the sand.

I picture a boy's arm draped over her shoulders, swaying along beside her, whispering softly in her ear, making her giggle.

Had I been only a few years older, I might also have been invited to join the festivities, but to them, I'm still just a kid. They don't want to be responsible for taking care of me.

I can't really blame them. My very presence at the party would be enough to spoil their fun.

After pacing around the room for approximately ten minutes but finding no relief, I stretch my neck and I'm about to give up and lie back down on my bed when I hear a soft knock at the door.

Confused and dehydrated, I stumble off the bed and hastily grab a tank top to pull over my head. Once I'm decent, I open the door, cautiously at first, not quite sure who or what to expect from this late visit. It's Mom.

"Hi Mom," I say hesitantly, relief flooding through me, only to be replaced by confusion. "What's up? Are you okay?" Opening the door wider, my eyes automatically begin scanning her exposed arms, looking for any signs of fresh bruises.

Seeing none, I feel a gush of relief flow through me. My mom isn't perfect, but she is trapped, just like Amber and me—I've been too hard on her. She's not any freer than the rest of us. I need to remember that. My face softens a little and I truly look at my mom for the first time in a while.

Her eyes are sunken in, making her features look almost skeletal. Her hair is unkempt and frizzy from the heat, and the skin on her arms is droopy and thinning. Suddenly, I'm struck by how old she's gotten, practically overnight.

There are deep wrinkle lines on her cheeks and beside her eyes, some even visible on her chest. Her frail body looks like it would blow over with only a soft breeze. She wears her favourite silk pyjamas, adorned with embroidered lace and scalloped fringes, but it no longer suits her body.

She's nearly swimming in them, the fabric hanging loosely from her collarbone. I want to grab a soft, cushy bathrobe and wrap it around her to keep her warm but also as a way to add some bulk to her frame. She's fading away right before my eyes. How had I missed it?

She smiles, oblivious to my internal turmoil and affectionally tucks a strand of hair behind my ear with such tenderness, it almost makes me weep.

Mommy.

How I long to be touched, cherished, and loved by her in this moment. How selfish I've been. I've been blinded by tunnel vision. I'd let my own misery take precedence over everything else, blocking what's been right in front of me this entire time. I've been too caught up in my own hurts to see clearly.

Mom has always been there for me. To the best of her abilities, she's never failed me. I'd been wrong to expect so much from her. The resentment tastes cruel and bitter on my tongue. I willfully withdraw it from my heart. I want to throw myself in her arms, but I worry she won't be strong enough to hold me. She's weak physically as much as in spirit. She needs me to take over but would never dare ask so much from me. It's my turn to be the strong one now.

Her thin lips part as her eyes glint in the dark. "Dad and I are having a hard time getting comfortable tonight," she says, explaining her sudden appearance at my door. "The cabin is too hot to sleep," she adds. "We were thinking of going for a late-night swim to cool off," she smiles wide, grinning. I can feel the excitement radiating from within her and return the smile.

"That actually sounds perfect!" I nod enthusiastically and walk back into the room to find my swimsuit.

"We'll take the boat and swim a little off the shore so that we don't have to worry about running into any more zebra mussels," she reassures, winking at me.

"Thanks, Mom, that's a great idea," I say as she turns to head back to her room to change.

My swimsuit is still a little damp from earlier and I struggle to pull on the one piece as it appears to have shrunk with the water. After I wrestle it on, I slip on my trusty flip-flops and follow my parents out the door. Eager and excited to be out at night, I feel a thrill deep in my belly. Things are about to change. I can feel it.

Biting my lower lip, I remind myself to slow down my stride. I'm too eager. My legs propel me forward unconsciously, the anticipation of a night swim almost too much to bear. I've always dreamed of doing this. It feels wild and so unexpected. Although I'm with my parents, I feel reckless.

This must be what it feels like to be Amber. Living life to the fullest, doing what feels good, without any regrets. Spontaneous, free, and fun. I like the way that sounds.

Maybe those words will be how others describe me next year. The possibilities are endless. I don't have to stick to just one thing either. I can be fluid like the water, change like the waves, and go with the flow. Tonight is the beginning of my new life. From here on out, I am the master of my own destiny.

Chapter 41
Niall

We glide on the water, creating almost no ripples on the surface.

The motor is purring gently, surprisingly quiet for a boat this size. Gemma is uncharacteristically relaxed, seated at the front beside me. I'm the captain of the ship, in charge of our destination, and my wife is comfortable, trusting my capable hands.

I find myself glancing at her often, trying to read her expression. Usually she's dull and uninteresting, but I'm finding her quite beautiful under the light and sparkle of the stars. Beatrice is quiet, seemingly happy to sit by herself and stare up at the sky.

I watch in awe as Gemma begins pointing out various constellations, indicating first Orion's Belt, followed by the Big Dipper, and finally, Cassiopeia. All these years I'd never known of her interest in astronomy.

I feel an overwhelming pride settling over me, as if her knowledge of star names and placement has anything whatsoever to do with me.

I vaguely recall pointing out these very arrangements during our first months of dating, but I'm surprised to learn that she's remembered them all this time. Back then, the trajectory of our lives was limitless. We'd spent countless hours discussing our hopes and dreams for the future as though nothing could stop us. In those first months, nothing seemed impossible. Far-fetched ideas were encouraged, stories were shared without reserve, and every moment together was cherished. It was us against the world.

We had loved each other once—wholeheartedly. Blind to each other's faults, temperaments, and weaknesses, we had accepted each other completely. I'd married her after only six months of dating. Our love story had been exciting, impulsive, and full of surprises. I'd loved how Gemma always pushed the limits, explored things beyond what I'd ever imagined. She'd led our lives, and I'd been more than happy to oblige. I would have followed her halfway around the world, without question.

And then, almost overnight, everything had changed.

Gemma became obsessed with the idea of starting a family. Her every thought was completely consumed by it. It was like a hunger she could not satisfy. She was always striving, seeking, and longing for a child. My beautiful, charming, happy wife was beginning to crumble away. She was driving herself crazy and, by default, me as well.

The woman I'd married, the woman I'd fallen in love with dissolved before my eyes like a sandcastle washed away by a wave.

I was left with an obsessive, neurotic, stranger, whose desire to become a mother quickly created a wedge between us. Whether she'd been aware of it or not, she'd pulled away from me. Pushing away any concerns I'd dare to bring up, she'd attempted to appease me with unrealistic expectations and promises of well-raised, obedient children that would make me a proud father. She'd constructed well-crafted arguments about the benefits of procreating, even though she knew full-well my stance on it.

I'd wanted nothing to do with it. But she'd claimed it would help my image, help me become more successful—that being a family man would make me appear more relatable and approachable to clients and coworkers. The logic had made sense to me at the time. Her reasoning had been well thought-out, and she'd assured me that she would take care of anything to do with the children and that I wouldn't have to lift a finger.

Against my better judgement, I'd given in to her incessant begging. Before too long, Gemma had gotten pregnant with Amber. Of course, none of the promises she'd made had materialized, none except maybe, that becoming a father had indeed offered me credibility amongst prospective buyers looking to hire a trustworthy agent.

Still, at what cost? I'd lost the life I'd loved and my wife in the process.

Sitting a foot away from me, my knee practically grazing hers, Gemma is so close that I can almost feel the heat radiating off her skin. But our hearts might as well be residing on different planets.

Without meaning to, Gemma had inadvertently pushed me into the arms of another woman. I'd had no other choice. With Gemma dedicating every spare moment to motherhood, there'd been no room left for me. Having kids had transformed her, making her virtually unrecognizable.

Looking at the dark lake beyond, I steer the boat slightly to the right. We're close enough to see the glow of Trevor's bonfire. Dozens of teens are dancing on the sand, without a care in the world. Their energy is contagious.

I anchor the boat and the three of us hop into the water, jumping off the back of the boat. Shouts and giggles from the beach echo across the water. We can almost hear full conversations, but the words are muffled by the noise of the water sloshing against the boat. The air feels hot, but the water is deliciously refreshing.

We're calm and at ease as we tread water. The three of us all seem to be deep in thought. The past week has done little to reunite us as a family. If anything it has pushed us further apart.

The lake is ominous tonight. Such a contrast to the crystal basin of water we swam in only hours ago. I don't like to think about what creatures roam and slither just below the surface. I prefer to see a threat coming and know where a bite comes from. Being able to identify it takes away some of the fear and offers understanding as well as the opportunity to spring into action or create a plan. But having my vision compromised by the lack of light frightens me a little. It makes me feel vulnerable and I don't care for it.

"Mom, are you alright?" Beatrice says with concern, her voice carrying above the waves lapping against the boat.

I look over and see that Gemma is struggling to swim. One of her hands is pressed hard against her head, as though she's hit it against something.

"She's fine, Bea," I say quickly, trying to make light of it. "Right, dear?" I ask.

"Yes, I think so, sweetheart," she grimaces as she begins to swim towards the boat. "I've just got a splitting headache again, that's all." She climbs aboard and wraps herself in a towel. "It must be from all this heat."

Tilting her head back, she remarks, "Look at that. All the stars have disappeared." She pauses. "How strange. It's even darker now."

Yes, how strange indeed.

Lowering my gaze, I'm startled. Bea's eyes are filled with hate, lightning bolts aimed directly at me. She's looking right at me with a look I've never seen on her face before. The stare is so unfaltering that it sends shivers down my spine.

If looks could kill, I think, *then she's not only threatening me but making a promise.* That much is clear. My daughter wants me dead.

Chapter 42
Amber

The beach is crowded with bodies, hopping and grinding to a hip

hop song I've got downloaded on my iPod. I know all the lyrics and hum along with the beat as we dock the boat. Once the boat is secured to the dock, Trevor and Renee show me around, introducing me to people whose names I won't pretend to remember.

Everyone is so welcoming and kind. Cheers are offered as I pass by, a pink vodka cooler is thrust into my hand, and I gladly accept it. *That's what I'm talking about.* Free booze and, if I'm lucky, I might even be able to bum a smoke off someone later. I've been craving one all week.

The smells of sweat, sugary drinks, cheap beer, musty lake water, fire, and smoke fill the air. I remove my sandals and enjoy the sensation of the cool sand beneath my feet.

It's surprisingly dark in the outer circle of the fire. Silhouettes blend together in the most shadowed parts of the beach, away from prying eyes.

A couple is making out by the fire in full view of everyone, as though they are providing the entertainment for the evening, while several others gawk, unashamed of their staring. They nod along as though they approve of this public display of affection. Frankly, it grosses me out.

Renee takes me by the hand and flashes me a pearly white smile as if we're suddenly the best of friends, conspiring in a great scheme.

I don't know anything about her or any of the others for that matter. Only that Renee is friends with Trevor, and Trevor works at the caves. We didn't have a lot of time to talk on the boat. My new companion stops mid-stride on the edge of the shadows, and turns me towards her so suddenly, I almost spill my drink on her.

"You should try wearing your hair up. It would really show off your features." She winks, but I notice her staring unreservedly at my chest.

I can feel a blush staining my cheeks. I'm about to look away but she catches my eye, demanding my attention.

"Don't be shy, Amber. You're a gorgeous girl. You should flaunt it!" She gently runs a finger down my bare arm, causing goosebumps to appear in its path. My body is betraying me.

Stepping closer, she grabs an elastic from her wrist and reaches for my hair. Standing in front of me, she combs my wild curls expertly, fastening them to the top of my head in a secure bun, similar to the one I'd attempted earlier today.

"There," she declares, satisfied with herself.

Blinking at me, she pretends to adjust a loose strand of hair but uses it as a ploy to get even closer. Instinctively, I move back to offer space between us, but that only makes her grin as she takes a deliberate step closer, never breaking eye-contact with me, almost daring me to run away. I stand my ground as I usually do when cornered. Part of me is curious.

My heart beats quickly, and I focus on keeping the bottle tight in my grip as my fingers begin to sweat. I take a deep breath as she reaches out a hand towards my face. Her thumb grazes my bottom lip as though polishing its surface. Her other hand reaches behind my head, pulling my face to hers, and before I know it, her lips are pressed to mine.

The kiss is surprising, but not shocking. I've kissed other girls before, but usually as a dare. There was never any passion in it before. But here, kissing Renee, my mind blurs, taking me away from this place. I feel like it's just her and me. My free hand finds her hair and I pull her closer, deepening the kiss.

She pulls back, laughing. "Wow, tiger. Slow down," she winks at me. "We're just getting started."

Grabbing my hand, she leads me closer to the fire. My cheeks are burning, but not from the flame before me.

What just happened? I wonder. *That was one hell of a kiss. And why do I want to do it again?*

I distract myself by taking a swig from my bottle, the pink liquid is like fire as it runs down my throat. I struggle to hold back a cough.

I spot an iPod docked to a wireless speaker resting on a beach towel nearby. The sound it emits is shockingly loud.

The music seems to beat inside my body, resonating through it as though I'm nothing but a tin can. I feel empty inside. Like Renee's kiss opened a vault I wasn't even aware existed within me. She's opened my eyes to possibilities and feelings I never knew I had.

How freeing is that?

She's released something in me that I'd never even known I'd been trying to hide. Could this be the root cause of all my lashing out? The fuel to my anger? The only true limits we have are those we set for ourselves, after all.

Renee watches me from the corner of her eye, singing the song blasting from the speakers, still holding my hand. She hasn't released her grip and I don't want her to.

Her friend, Eve, comes to stand next to her. She eyes our hands and winks at me. Leaning towards Renee, she whispers something in her ear and scampers off to a darker part of the beach where a few shadowy figures stand waiting.

"Come," Renee beckons me in a whisper, her breath warm against my ear. She tugs gently on my hand, offering a flirtatious smile. "This way." She leads and I follow willingly, barely containing my excitement.

All I can think of is that kiss. I want more.

When we reach the spot, I see a circle of teens and Trevor amongst them. He raises a hand to welcome me. Everyone is sitting down on the sand and giggling. My brows furrow in confusion and I turn to Renee for an explanation.

"What's going on?" I press.

She has an amused look on her face and winks at me, grabbing my hand and bringing me closer to the circle to join the others. The gritty sand is rough on my skin. The sweet drink sloshes in my stomach.

What's going on? I want to ask again, but I fight the urge. No one speaks, and yet, everyone but me seems to understand why we're all here. What is this about? Is this some kind of ritual?

I look over to Renee again, hoping for clarification, but she only smiles reassuringly, encouraging me to go along with it.

"What are we doing?" I mouth silently, not wanting my voice to carry and for the others to overhear.

"We're going to play 'suck and blow'," Renee replies, her face breaking into a wide grin. Her eyes twinkle and I'm not sure I want to know what she means by this.

Before I can ask anything else, I watch, astonished as a girl places a small rectangular card to her mouth. The circle is so quiet as we all watch her, that we can all hear when she begins to suck on the card, the sound is like a vacuum against the card. Her eyes grow big as she quickly bends her torso towards the boy to her right who then purses his lips and sucks the card, taking it from her without letting it fall.

The card is then passed on to the next person in similar fashion. The circle reaching a girl who apparently didn't have a strong enough hold on the card as her sucking was interrupted by bouts of giggles. She drops the card and plants a kiss on the next girl's lips. This sends the entire circle into a laughing fit, all except for me.

Cringing, I feel my drink begin to rise in my throat and I think I might be sick.

I'm all about breaking rules and having a good time, but I'm not interested in kissing just everyone and anyone. Are they expecting me to play along? I don't even know these people! Is this what parties are like around here? If so, I want nothing to do with it. Whatever happened to truth or dare, or spin the bottle? Those look so innocent in comparison.

When the circle reaches me, I stare wide-eyed ahead, paralyzed by shock and disgust. I instantly regret coming here with a bunch of strangers. I stand abruptly, scattering some sand on the towel but not caring. I glare angrily at Renee, and bolt out of the cult-like ceremonial circle, rushing out towards the water.

Breathing heavily, I sink down to my knees, feeling grains of sand carve divots into them. I half-expect Renee to come running after me, but I'm not really surprised when I look back and find that I'm all alone.

Gathering myself, I swipe angrily at my cheeks. I feel so stupid for trusting her and Trevor. Their game was innocent enough, but there hadn't seem to be an option of playing or not. I'd felt forced to play along but I really hadn't wanted to. The only logical thing to do was to run away.

Blinking, I look out to the water, trying to stabilize my breath. Only then do I notice a boat out on the lake, anchored not too far from the beach. It's unusual, and the menacing, pitch-black hue of the sky doesn't help matters. The stars are all gone. Ominously, the wind begins to pick up as though I'd summoned it somehow with my anger.

I stand up slowly, squinting and just make out the familiar shape of Mom. She appears to be standing on the boat, illuminated slightly by a light aboard. Looking around the rest of the boat, I find the shapes of Dad's and Bea's heads bobbing in the inky water only a few feet from the boat. From here, they almost look like floating buoys.

What the hell are they doing? Did they come here to spy on me? Before I can truly process what I'm seeing, the wind suddenly picks up all around me, sending a gust so strong that it practically knocks me down with its unexpected force. The sky grows a shade darker than it seemed possible a moment ago. It becomes harder and harder to see the boat as a cloud of rising sand floats around me.

Shielding my eyes, I shut my mouth so as to not swallow any sand. I turn my face away, trying to catch my breath as rain and wind crash down on me. Turning my attention back to the boat, I catch sight of Mom hobbling on the deck of the boat, losing her footing as hard waves crash against it. She grips a nearby pole to steady herself.

Dark clouds fill the sky, coming out of nowhere. I blink hard, tears staining my cheeks as they clear away some of the sand that's landed in my eyes, irritating them. Catching glimpses through half-closed slits, I sink back down to my knees and watch in horror the scene unfolding before me. Powerless and far away, I can't do anything to help them. The weather was fine just a moment ago, but now, it feels like we're in the center of a tornado.

The boat seems like it might capsize. One strong gust of wind would send it over. The storm seems to be concentrated right over us somehow. The waves are intense and irregular.

I see Bea struggling and drifting farther away. My father reaches for her and grips her hand. Mom is frantic, screaming something at him, inching her way to the edge of the boat. I don't hear what she's saying but I hear the urgency in her tone. I watch on, desperate to help but unable to. I scream but my voice is lost in the raging wind.

Still, I watch. It's impossible to look away.

Mom is knocked back by another wave and staggers backwards, smashing her head on the very pole she'd been gripping moments earlier. Dad and Bea struggle in the water, losing momentum quickly. They're getting tired.

For a moment, everything seems to move in slow motion as Dad stops his frantic movements. What is he doing? I want to yell at him, but he's just bobbing there in the water, looking out. He looks like he's thinking. What could possibly be so important right now? It's like he's frozen in place.

I'm about to scream out at him to get it together and get on the boat when the next wave comes, slipping over Bea's head. I watch horrified as he releases his grip, letting her go.

"NO!" I cry out.

Helpless, I watch as the wave covers my little sister entirely, enveloping her like a weighted blanket. Frantic, I scan the surface, desperate to find any signs of Bea, but she's nowhere.

My sister is gone.

Chapter 43
GEMMA

I've only seen storms like this once before in my entire life. Panic spurs me forward and into action. I have to jump in and help her. Where the hell is Niall?

I spot him clutching the ladder, shaking from the cold or from shock. He's scanning the surface of the water, a blank look of concern on his face. His eyes meet mine and any colour left in his face drains away instantly.

Tim had mentioned something about these freak storms in the welcome package—how unpredictable and dangerous they could be. It would have been better to remain closer to land, especially at night with our limited visibility.

The sky had been so clear moments before that we'd been able to admire the various constellations.

There'd been no warning of the looming trouble ahead, no obvious indicators that the wind would pick up and unbalance the waves. In the same instant, large clouds had floated low and covered the stars entirely, plunging us into darkness.

For a moment, I fear that Niall will also get swallowed up by the lake and I instinctively begin scouring the boat compartments for something to throw to him. Under one of the passenger seats, I find what I'm looking for and extract a donut-shaped, bright orange lifesaving apparatus.

Working quickly, I tie one end to the bottom of a seat and throw the donut in Niall's direction, practically knocking him off the ladder with the force of it. He hesitates a moment, then resumes scanning the water, searching for signs of Bea. He must be contemplating going in after her, just as I am. But there is no sense in doing so, not while the storm is still raging.

He reluctantly grabs hold of the floating device and my throat constricts. Relief and agony mix together as I pull him up. I want to scream, but I can't find my voice. I'm completely soaked, and my headache has intensified to an almost unbearable pain, throbbing relentlessly, worsened by my earlier blow to the head. I'm having a hard time standing. My legs are unstable and my vision is slightly blurred. My eyes keep closing, trying to protect me from any more pain, but I refuse to shut them.

My daughter is still out there.

Distraught, I tug the cord affixed to the floating donut, and keep pulling as hard as I can, doing my best to bring Niall up the ladder. The wind is fierce and relentless, but I can't help but feel like he's fighting me.

The chord is rigid in my hand, giving me rope burn. It's as though he's pulling with all of his strength in the opposite direction. Like a part of him is refusing to be saved, as though he doesn't want to get back on board but would rather perish in the lake.

After what feels like an eternity, the tension gives and Niall begins to climb the ladder at the back of the boat. He struggles to stand on wobbly legs. He's shaking like a leaf.

"What happened!?" I yell to him over the noise, my tone a mix of concern and frustration.

"I have no idea," he admits, visibly perplexed. "One minute I had her and then..." He doesn't bother finishing, his head turning towards the large expanse of water.

But it doesn't matter. I already know what happened next. It plays on a loop in my throbbing head. I can't stop seeing Bea's head slipping below the water. A vice-like grip squeezes my heart. I'd been too far away to stop it. Even so, my hands had reached out instinctively, but what could I do from my position on the boat?

I feel sick to my stomach. Bea hasn't surfaced yet but I refuse to give up. Looking over at Niall, I consider my options. Usually when my migraines get this bad, it doesn't take long before I black-out or get so nauseous that I get too weak and sick to move. Yet, I can't risk not trying.

I know I won't be able to live with myself if I don't at least try to find Bea.

Without giving it another thought, I grab a rope I found while searching for the life preserver, tie one end of it to a handle on the edge of the boat and the other end around my waist, and dive headfirst into the pitch-black water.

I blindly look for any signs of Bea. Her navy-blue swimsuit seems like the worst possible colour choice right now. It will be impossible to locate her. She'll blend right into the lake.

I swim down, assuming Bea didn't get whisked away in the current but merely sank lower. I just pray there's still hope for her and that I'm not too late.

Somewhere above me, I'm vaguely aware that the noise has settled down. The water seems to brighten, allowing me to see a few feet ahead of me. The faint light must be coming from the moon.

Spotting a flash of white down below, I swim towards it without a moment to lose. My lungs protest with every stroke I take. I'm out of practice. Forcing my mind to focus on what I need to do, instead of on the lack of oxygen, I keep diving.

There, floating just above the lake floor is my little girl.

She's unconscious. Her hair is floating all around her like a mermaid. She looks almost angelic but in a terrifying way. It's a sight no parent should ever witness. Bea's body floats eerily, face down above a sort of underwater tomb. A Virgin Mary statue guards the bottom of the lake, her features serene. The sight of it makes me shiver. I swim as fast as I can, ignoring the pain in my head and how foreboding the scene appears.

Grabbing onto Bea's arm, I push myself off the bottom of the lake and propel us to the surface.

Finally, the water spills away, splashing my face and Beas as we reach the surface. I take large gulps of air, not caring how much my lungs sting. My arms feel weak, but I grab hold of the ladder and pull myself up each rung, gripping tightly onto Bea's waist until we are both safely aboard the boat.

Niall stares at me in disbelief. He can't believe I've found her. He still looks incredibly pale, but I can't worry about him right now. I have to help Bea.

I untie the rope around my waist and bend over her. I'm not surprised to see that she isn't breathing. Her skin is waxy and tinged with blue. I quickly check her wrist for a pulse but finding none, I begin chest compressions. Pushing hard and fast on the centre of her chest, I count the beats in my head to the song "Staying Alive" like they taught me in the first aid course I took years ago. I have no idea how I've remembered it just now, but I'm glad my brain retained this nugget of information.

I keep going until my back aches. Even then, I don't stop. I don't know if I'll ever be able to stop. They will have to pry me off of my daughter before I quit. I refuse to give up on her.

Tears run down my cheeks as I mouth the counts louder through gritted teeth. Ignoring everything around me, I'm only loosely aware of a flurry of movement approaching the boat. Niall is leaning over me, providing support with his presence. He watches on helplessly. I'm sure he's terrified and will blame himself forever if Bea doesn't make it. Without intending to, I probably will too.

A shudder beneath my hands makes me pause momentarily. Did I imagine movement? It was so subtle, like the soft flutter of butterfly wings, but I'm almost convinced I felt something. I stop briefly, giving my aching muscles a second of respite and a chance to confirm my suspicions.

Just then, Bea's chest convulses and water spews out of her mouth. I gasp.

Tilting her head to the side so the water can drain out of her mouth, I watch as she heaves loudly. I collapse on the deck of the boat, brushing slick, wet hair from Bea's face as she gulps for air and coughs. I'm immediately reminded of the day she was born, those horribly long, silent seconds before she'd taken her first breath.

She inhales and I weep, unashamed. It's the most beautiful sound I've ever heard.

Chapter 44
Beatrice

I cough out putrid water all over myself and the boat. Mom sits beside me, eyes wide and alert. I'm gasping for breath as she pulls me to her with steady tears streaming down her face. She's shaking and crying into my ear, but I don't really hear anything. There are people yelling all around us. My mind feels foggy and I'm freezing. My skin is so pale that it looks translucent.

Someone wraps a towel around my shoulders, immediately followed by another one on top of it. Everyone is tending to me, and I'm still confused. One of my arms is badly scraped and twisted at an odd angle. It's most definitely broken. I must be in shock because I barely feel the pain.

Mom is still here right beside me. She's out of breath and her hair is soaked. Did she dive into the water to grab me?

Looking all around me, I see the blurred shapes of people springing to action, but I'm having a hard time making out faces. I must be losing my mind because I think I've just seen Amber on the boat, but my sister is at a party, so logically, she can't be here.

"Bea, it's me. Are you okay?" Amber's shape materializes before me.

Am I dead? How is Amber here? What's going on?

I cough up more water. My breath rattles with the leftover liquid coating my lungs.

Holy shit, did I drown? I blink rapidly and my eyes start to focus.

Looking up, Mom looks just as startled to see her as I feel.

"Amber?" Mom says weakly. "How?" she asks, barely able to utter a word.

Amber sinks down to join us on the floor of the boat. I feel Mom's and Amber's hands touching my good arm. They seem to be aware of my inability to move the other one. They're careful not to touch it and cause me additional pain.

Dad is huddled in a corner of the boat, sitting on the floor in a little ball, his knees pulled up to his chest. I'm not sure, but I think he's rocking, trying to soothe himself.

Looking up past Amber, I notice two other shapes. A boy and girl about Amber's age. They look panicked and frightened, unsure of how to help. There's a little fishing boat pulled up to ours which must be how Amber and her friends joined us. But how did they know anything was going on? Everything happened so fast.

I remember being so uncomfortably hot in the cabin. Mom knocking on my door. The three of us heading out onto the water.

The stillness around us. Swimming—cooling off in the water. How Mom's face had contorted in pain and when she'd climbed back onto the boat, leaving me alone with Dad.

And then everything changed. The wind had picked up out of nowhere, and it had gotten darker. Waves had started lapping over our heads. By instinct, I'd reached out for Dad, but he'd hesitated to hold my hand.

There'd been a moment when I'd seen a menacing look cross his face. When another, bigger wave hit us, to my shock, he'd deliberately let go of my hand. Almost shaking me off like I was mud stuck to his hand.

I remember that moment in detail, along with the betrayal I'd felt and the overwhelming sense of abandonment. It's the last clear memory I have before another wave knocked me against the boat. I must have bashed my head and sunk to the bottom, dizzy and disoriented. After that, I can only recall fragments of what happened.

Reaching the lake floor, my arm had collided with something hard, a large stone with a face. I'd tried to swim using my good arm, but I'd already lost too much oxygen. Then, there was only blackness.

My heart is beating hard, my breath is ragged. All the coughing and spitting up of water has made my throat raw. But I'm alive. I'm still here. There's still time to make things right.

Dad had let go of my hand. He'd done it on purpose. I'm convinced of it.

Looking over at him now, I see his eyes full of regret and fear. He'd tried to kill me and silence me forever. He'd chosen his secret over my life.

He had been willing to sacrifice me to keep Mom in the dark. His cowardice disgusts me.

I look between him and Mom and open my mouth to speak— enough of this. But then, Amber places a hand on my shoulder. She looks directly into my eyes, a stare worth a thousand words. It seems to sink deep inside of my soul. I sense a connection with her I've rarely experienced before, like we're communicating without words.

"I saw," she says now, her voice no higher than a whisper, meant for only me, but spoken so clearly, so confidently, no one dares to move. Her reassuring gaze offers me the confidence that she will handle this.

It would be easy to feel resentful, or to see her actions as trying to silence me, but instead, I can see that she's looking at me for my approval, giving me control, and I love her for it. In my most vulnerable moment, she's given me my dignity back. She's offering me the chance to deal with it, in her look, in her pause, but also making clear that she's willing to step in should I wish for her to do so.

Not trusting my own voice to work yet, I hold her gaze and nod simply, giving her permission. I trust her entirely.

My lips form a straight line. This is not the time to stamp down my internal rage and plaster a smile on, pretending everything's fine. I won't let this go. Not ever.

It's difficult for me to comprehend the full extent of what has just taken place. My mind is still struggling to catch up. Thankfully, my sister is there, able to think clearly. Her eyes are burning with fire as she stands taller.

Dad is right to be scared. What is she planning?

Chapter 45
GEMMA

"I saw." That's what Amber whispered to Bea. Those two words holding so much weight that it silenced the rest of us. All we can do is stare as the wind settles around us. Everything is still and quiet, as if everyone is holding their breath.

My girls share a secret. I look from one to the other and see that both of their stares are fixed on Niall, who has been uselessly crouched far away, visibly afraid. I replay the scene in my head. The whole week comes into view.

Bea's towel slips slightly from her shoulder, uncovering a ghastly bruise on her arm. I take in a sharp breath. The shape of the mark makes it impossible to deny that it was caused by a firm grip, one that I'd witnessed myself but had wishfully played down as a figment of my imagination.

How naïve I'd been! I'm so angry with myself for not trusting my instincts, for putting my girls in harm's way, for believing my own lies.

I study Bea, meeting her eyes. She looks down, biting her lip, as though apologizing or ashamed. This makes me furious. She's the one who got hurt and yet she's the one feeling bad about it? Who is she protecting? Me? That's not her burden to carry.

Is that what Amber meant when she said "I saw" just now? But why mention that now? It doesn't make sense. Unless she's referring to something else.

As though reading my mind, Amber turns to me, locking eyes with me, willing me to believe her.

"He let her go. On purpose," she says with a calm, unblinking manner that rattles me to my core.

I stare back at her, too astonished to speak.

My legs go rigid, as though all the blood has left my body and been replaced with ice. My headache is a distant memory, my brain seems to be protecting itself from the pain, helping me to focus on what's happening in front of me. Something shifts inside me. A fury that I'd long ago tamed into nothing but a smouldering ember, begins to crackle back to life.

One look at Amber and I know without a shadow of doubt that she's telling the truth. She likes to stir up trouble, to get in the middle of things she shouldn't be a part of, but she never lies.

I glance over to Niall, cowering, making himself into a tight little ball, trying to hide. Whether from shame or from me, I'm not sure.

For the first time in a long while, I see what remains of the man I'd married. The pitiful leftovers and the masked weakness. All these years, he'd tried to make me feel small and ripped away my power. But now, as I stand over him, I see that I've always outshined him. He's been insecure and tried to hide it by cheating and controlling me. The power has shifted now.

Niall doesn't dare meet my gaze while I glare down at him. A snarl forms on my upper lip as rage builds up within me.

"You," I accuse him. "You did this!"

It's not a question. I know he's responsible for this.

He raises his hands above his head, in surrender or to protect himself from me. As though I would hurt him, as if violence is the solution to everything. I guess when it's your go-to emotion, you expect others to react in the same way. Disgusted, I swallow all the hate I want to spit at him. He's not worth it.

If I give in to anger, it will reside inside of me like it used to long ago. I can't let it back in. I've been doing so well, managing to keep it at a distance, constantly working hard to remain in control of my emotions, aiming for stability, often opting for predictability over joy. I've spent years maintaining this image of well-being for my family. Stashing away parts of myself—the wild parts, the fun parts, the emotional parts—everything others told me was bad.

Amber comes to stand beside me, my little shadow. Blood from my blood. Spirit from my spirit. She and I are very much the same, except Amber hasn't been tamed into submission. Her wild still resides within her. She's learning to control it, to use it by choice rather than letting it overtake her thoughts and actions. She's stronger than I ever was.

I feel her warm hand slip into mine and grip it tightly. The small action brings tears to my eyes. Relief or assurance, I'm not sure—she's offering me solidarity.

You're not alone, she seems to be saying.

Without words, we speak volumes. I peer at her and a small smile plays on my lips, easily wiping away the hate that was lingering close by, ready to be used. Amber banished it, replacing it with love.

My daughter does that. She can take something ugly and replace it with beauty. She is the embodiment of it. She sees boundaries and pushes against them. It's beautiful and inspiring to watch, although difficult to parent.

I laugh silently to myself. She is wonderful and perfect just the way she is. While everyone has been trying to lock up parts of her, to contain or extinguish her spirit, Amber has been determined to fight back every step of the way. Never caring about conforming or fitting in, she's her own person and set on doing what she wants. I can learn so much from her.

Looking down at Niall, I have to fight back the urge to throw him overboard. I hate him for what he did to Bea, tonight and before. The expectations set upon her were ridiculous, practically unattainable. She must have been cracking at the seams trying to please us.

I'm aware of my part in this, too. Niall is not the only one to blame for the breakdown of our seemingly perfect family. Losing myself to the idea of leading by example and living the perfect life, I'd expected too much of my girls, more than I could even expect of myself.

I look over to Trevor and ask him to drive our boat back to the cabin. The girl with him, Renee, tails behind us in the fishing boat. The two of them, understandably shell-shocked, take off immediately after we dock, barely offering any goodbyes. Amber stands on the wet grass, looking at them speed away. She doesn't appear bothered.

Standing beside her, I wrap an arm over her shoulders to offer some comfort. I can tell something's bothering her, but I'll wait until she comes to me. I won't pry it out of her, and I definitely won't force her to confide in me, but I hope she will.

I have some bonds to mend and trust to regain with my girls. Owning up to my part in this will be the first thing I do. I'd willingly turned a blind eye, choosing to pretend I didn't know more than I did, for the sake of my sanity and in a weak attempt at keeping our family happy. Little did I know that keeping silent had broken what was left of our perfect little lives.

We don't bother staying at the cabin any longer. Gathering our things, we leave it behind, along with the memory of who we used to be, or rather, who we thought we were.

Stepping over the shattered tree limbs, I'm struck by how similarly I feel. Both torn apart and exposed, but also raw and bursting open—free. I can breathe. Climbing into the driver's seat, I watch as Niall hesitantly settles into the passenger seat before I steer us out of this place for good.

Returning home, the first call I make is to a divorce lawyer. I don't hesitate or bother to hide away in a room behind closed doors. I stand firmly and confidently in full view, right in the middle of my kitchen for all to see.

Niall's face is grim and grey. He hasn't spoken a word since I accused him on the boat. Glancing around the house, he hasn't moved from the entrance, debating with himself. He seems to breathe in the air and the view, his girls standing in the kitchen, lit up by the overhead lights glowing down on us, him semi-obscured in the darkness of the entryway.

Our eyes meet.

His are searching for forgiveness or the opportunity for reconciliation. Mine stare back with cold, hard, unbudging stillness. I lift my chin. What's done is done. We're over. He screwed up, and this time, I'm not taking him back. He seems to understand this and steps back out the door and out of our lives.

Surprising myself, I don't shed a single tear.

I was partly to blame after all. In some ways, I should have anticipated such an outcome, known to some degree that it would all eventually fall apart. All the little cracks beneath the surface, the exterior thinning under pressure, exploding from within. I hadn't expected how bad the breaking would be, but it was clear to me now that it would be impossible to put the pieces back together. There was no going back.

Collecting the remaining pieces of my family, I hold my girls close to me. Bea's hair has dried and a single strand curls over her shoulder.

I wonder if she's noticed it, how quickly she's changing, morphing into the woman she's becoming. My baby girl, no longer a baby—still mine to protect, to lift up, to love, and eventually, mine to let go.

Glancing around the house we'd made our home, I spot the dried-up English Ivy from the entrance, the one I'd noticed the day I slipped in the staircase. Its dehydrated vines, gnarled and twisted, seem to be reaching out to me. I can do better. This is a new beginning—a new chance. I will take better care of myself, the girls, and this plant. I will not give up on any of these but will do my very best to ensure we're all living our best lives, whatever that might look like.

Gathering my girls close, I sigh, relieved and exhausted at the thought of what's to come. Change isn't always easy, but sometimes it's exactly what we need.

Someday we'll talk about the cages we'd built for ourselves. Placing constraints and limits around ourselves because we feel safe within them, because we were taught to prefer it that way. Along the way, we've been taught to believe that being free is scary or dangerous, and must be avoided at all costs.

We build houses to keep bad things out, and yet, sometimes we unknowingly invite them to move in. We build fences and towers to keep ourselves safe, only letting down the drawbridge for those we trust. But how well do we truly know anyone if we, ourselves, lie about who we are?

If everyone is pretending, how can we know who to let in and who to shut out?

We keep our guard up to protect ourselves, but then we never show anyone who we really are. Scared to be outcast, to be different, we attach labels to ourselves—bullet points of responsibilities and expectations associated with each—how to behave, how to dress, how to blend in, and how to fit in. All in the hope that we will be left in peace and find happiness being like everyone else.

Offering titles to those around us and to ourselves; wild, smart, wife, mother, and rejecting anyone who doesn't meet our expectations of what those roles entail. We try to fit people inside boxes designed for others, containing warped ideals we've made up over time about them, never considering for even a moment that a person doesn't always fit inside molds. We're reluctant to accept that some people will defy the norms and dare to be themselves, no matter the cost, no matter how lonely they might be.

The brave few would rather be alone than pretend to be something they aren't. They would rather live authentically, live their truth, than be confined to a cage of other expectations.

We're all free to choose but we must remember that all of our choices have consequences.

If the door to our cage is open, we can decide the path we take. We have the option to either remain in the makeshift safety of it or to fly away to discovery. Along the way, we've forgotten that we are not following a script, that we are more than just actors in a play.

We are the writers of our own lives, and we decide the direction our story takes. We don't need to create limits for ourselves as there are plenty already built all around us.

We don't have to worry ourselves into a corner by being overly careful, timid, or quiet, and we shouldn't fear our emotions, but rather let them wash over us and rage within us. We should embrace everything, feel it out loud.

We can scream, feel angry, and flap our wings right out of that cage, as is our right to do. We are given wings, not for others to admire, but to fly.

It's time to realize that the cages we find ourselves in, those same ones where we built our homes and our lives, are not always safe or the right place for us to be. We have to start trusting our wings to carry us out of our cages and lead us to where we're meant to go.

ACKNOWLEDGMENTS

I wanted to write a story about family, about sisters, but mostly, about how each of us have a role to play in our lives. We don't necessarily all fit the same molds. In fact, I honestly believe that we were never meant to. Each one of us is unique and beautiful in our own way. We have so much to offer each other, so much we can learn from one another, without needing the pressures and constraints to 'fit in'.

A friend of mine shared her story about a sudden storm occurring while she was out for a late swim at night with her family. Needless to say, it sparked my interest for a story.

A storm is the result of a cold and warm front colliding. Mix that with strong winds and the effects can be devastating and intense. Even if the storm dissipates later, carnage will most likely be left in its path, leaving signs of its destruction everywhere, hence, making it difficult to deny it ever happened. As it usually demands all of our attention, these kinds of events are almost impossible to ignore.

For me, my emotions sometimes manifest like some kind of storm. I cannot suppress them into submission, as hard as I've tried. I feel everything. For years, I was told I was too emotional, that I should grow a thicker skin—use achievements, make-up, or fancy clothes as scales to cover my body and to protect it from getting hurt. But emotions begin within us, not on the outside. I can't harden my heart because it may very well stop it from beating.

I wrote *Cages* because I was curious to explore family dynamics and pry open the ideal that we need to fit into certain boxes and hold specific titles to feel accepted by others.

I thoroughly enjoyed writing about these characters and diving into the dark parts of each one. I wish to offer sincere thanks to Chris Hinsperger, owner of the Bonnechere Caves, for providing his helpful insight, and letting me pick his brain with all my questions. If you ever get the opportunity to speak with Chris, he's got a wealth of knowledge to share, and is a pleasure to talk to! As usual, I strive to write the non-fictional aspects of my stories in the most accurate manner that I'm able to, and speaking with experts like Chris, is one of the ways I ensure that. If there are any mistakes, they are entirely of my own doing.

I'd like to thank Sherry Torchinsky, my editor, for her keen eyes, talent, and dedication to my work. My stories wouldn't be the same without her. Thank you also to Roxana Coumans for proofreading the final copy!

Special thanks to my parents, Danielle and André Landry, my extremely supportive husband, John, my incredible daughters, as well as my first & forever best friend and sister, Karine Landry. A huge shout out to Melanie MacKay, Heather Budd, Stephen McClellan, Arti Manani, and CL Walters for your support, for your time reading these pages, for your friendships, and for your faith in me. I am forever grateful to have you in my corner. I owe a great deal of thanks to the ladies of Carpe Diem writing group—you ladies kept me going! I'm so honoured to be a part of this incredibly supportive group.

Writing a book is like opening parts of your soul for others to read. Sometimes, it can feel like a trust exercise, like falling backwards, trusting others to catch you. Like most writers, I leave little gems of myself in everything I write, so I sincerely hope you enjoyed reading this story as much as I loved writing it.

ABOUT THE AUTHOR

Michelle Young is a Canadian author of multiple books. She has been featured in The Globe and Mail, appeared on television and podcasts, and is passionately seeking new ways to bring invisible battles into the light through her stories. Young lives in the country on the outskirts of Ottawa with her family.

If you enjoyed this book, please make sure to leave a review and follow Michelle Young on Facebook, Instagram and Goodreads.

Facebook.com/michelleyoungauthor

Instagram @michelleyoungauthor

www.michelleyoungauthor.com

www.ingramcontent.com/pod-product-compliance
Lightning Source LLC
Chambersburg PA
CBHW031331020726
47499CB00005B/1219